THE HATCHERY

A Walt Pitowski Novel

By
Kevin J Garrity

THE HATCHERY

Copyright 2013 by Kevin J Garrity
Revised

Cover design and layout by Teemu J Garrity

Hammer Handle Press
6197 Quaker Hill Drive
West Bloomfield, Michigan 48322
(248) 757-2751
www.kevinjgarrity.com

Published by Hammer Handle Press

ISBN 978-0-9853310-2-3
ISBN 978-0-9853310-3-0   (eBook)

ACKNOWLEDGEMENT

To Teemu and Deanna, spinners of straw into gold, to Charles, for tolerating his father's eccentricities, and to my brother George, who inflicted upon me the passion for reading too damn much.

ONE

The Hatchery

The man stood quietly in the shadows, hidden by the backsides of two clapboard-sided shacks. The outbuildings had been standing since the forties, storage sheds set atop the steep rise in the riverbank, built to accommodate the overflow of equipment from the main facility below. They had long ago fallen into disrepair, roofs leaking and walls leaning into one another for support. Rot had worked its way up from the bottom of the vertical siding, leaving gaps where the boards should have met the surfaces of twin fractured cement slabs. The northern faces of the two shacks, those places where the sun refused to shine, flaunted rising plumes of blackish mold until about knee level, followed by a foot or so of fresh green algae, before finally giving way to the unvarnished gray and ragged fibers of rough-hewn cedar.

An old privy lay on its side before him, partially submerged in a shallow depression. The privy had come from parts elsewhere, back when the State Conservation Department had closed some campground or another. It was eventually dumped behind the northernmost shed for use at a later date. To a casual observer, it would appear as if the battered outhouse had always belonged, been part of the original plan and used for years before having finally sunk into its own reservoir. In addition to the shitter, an assortment of tangled metal scraps, discarded auto parts, and empty beer and wine bottles were in the process of gradually being swallowed whole by the uncut meadow. It was but one more instance of nature reclaiming what it can.

The setting sun was almost below the horizon, the tall pines and gnarled oaks which lined the hillside casting long fingers of darkness in their wake. The man slipped through a gap in the cyclone fence. He began making his way down the incline and through a small chase of scrub oak and pine trees that stood between him and the big white building. He was well hidden, moving cautiously on the edge of darkness. The fish hatchery had been closed since Labor Day, all the fish slurped out of the raceways with a giant vacuum truck and hauled off to market or wherever they were headed. It was a seasonal thing nowadays, not like in the old days.

In the old days, the hatchery was a year-round attraction operated by the State of Michigan. They produced trout - lots of trout - which were used to stock the rivers and lakes for miles around. Fifty million trout in all, as a matter of fact. That was up until about 1990, when budgets got tight and the Conservation Department got wise to the idea that having a dilapidated, uninsulated, twenty-thousand square-foot building smack in the middle of a far northern climate might not be the best use of taxpayers' dollars. They had other, more efficient places where they could do the same work, so they pawned it off on the county for a dollar.

The county did a pretty good job of running it, at least for a while. They brokered a deal with a trout farm over Alpena way, managing to keep the hatchery open in a different sort of way. The trout farmer wasn't in the business of raising fish for the streams and lakes of the area, but rather for the private ponds and dinner tables of the North. The large white building itself was shuttered and deemed unsafe. Yet the raceways, those long cement channels perpetually fed by the glistening cool waters of the Grand Limoneaux River's East Branch, the raceways still twinkled and bubbled with the stuff of fishermen's dreams.

Shortly before Memorial Day each year, the Alpena trout farmer would bring in a large tanker truck, filled with thousands of brook trout and brown trout and rainbow trout fingerlings. They would all be released into their respective channels for what amounted to Summer Camp for Fish. A few brood stock - ten and twelve pound monsters from the deep - prowled one chamber, providing eye candy for little boys and fly casters alike. There was even a separate pond and a cleaning station where you could pay to catch your dinner. Over the course of a summer the trout would get bigger and fatter. Some would get eaten. More than a few would get picked off by an eagle that set up shop in the towering pines across the road. People passing through Rasmus would pay to see the trout, pay to feed the trout, and pay to let their kid catch the trout that would then be cleaned and bagged and dropped in a cooler and driven three hours south to the big city, where a tired and beleaguered mom would unload her minivan or SUV at ten on a Sunday night and have no idea how to cook the trout. Those fish that survived Summer Camp would be recaptured shortly after Labor Day, sucked back into the vacuum attached to the tanker truck and sent to a pond or a supermarket near you. In the meantime, the County had itself a nice little tourist attraction instead of a vacant building and a crumbling network of holes in the ground.

At first there had been talk of restoring the old white building, turning it into a museum or office space or some combination of the two, but the financing had never come together. In the small and economically battered town of Rasmus, a fancy museum is a rich man's folly. The project had stalled years ago, having gathered just enough steam to throw a new roof and a coat of white paint on the behemoth. The building looked better, at least from the road. Though the inside was a disaster, the outside was passable and the new roof halted the water damage to the hardwood floors and the pre-war timber framing. It probably wasn't enough to save the structure, but it might buy her a respite for another twenty years. It was what some might call "putting lipstick on a hog."

In the meantime, this was an autumn of uncertainty: tourism was down, property values were down, everything was down. The town was struggling, the county was struggling, and families were struggling. That trout farmer from Alpena was thinking about getting out of the fish business altogether. He said it might be time to retire, and no one knew if the hatchery would be open next year, not even as a summer whistle-stop for sightseers. Hard times were getting harder.

The man at the base of the hillside paused near the edge of the tree line. There really oughtn't to be anyone around to see him. He looked across the river and the raceways to the tiny admission booth on the main path that bisected the raceways, and then to the green storage barn that housed the Kubota tractor and other equipment necessary to the operations of a summer concession. Some vagrant had been caught living in the back of the storage barn last winter, betrayed by his own tracks in the snow come January. No movement, not a soul in sight. He kept an eye out for cars passing on the road to the north. All was quiet. He was vigilant. You had to be, in this line of work: one slip up, and you were out of business for good. He thought he heard rustling leaves atop the bluff, just beyond the fence, and paused once again. More silence. Probably a squirrel returning to his nest. He watched over his shoulder through the trees and the shadows, waiting another seven or eight minutes before deciding it was safe to proceed.

Spiral steps to his left led from the original floodplain, that wide flat of land upon which the hatchery squatted, to the second story of the great white building. The concrete stairway was spalled and fractured, large chunks of stone having jettisoned loose by the freeze and thaw cycles of cruel northern winters.   A red oak, long-infested by carpenter ants, crowded the broken walkway while widow-makers danced perilously above. It seemed silly to be climbing back up to the top of the hill after sneaking down through the woods, but it was the only way in which he could remain invisible, remain vigilant.

At the top of the stairway the man was protected from sight by the building itself to the east and north and by more overgrown shrubs and trees to the west and south. There was a doorway directly in front of him, hidden by a makeshift foyer that ran from the edge of the gutters flush down to the ground. The false vestibule was constructed of two-by-four framing and sheeted with four-foot by eight-foot sections of treated plywood, all covered with rolls of tar paper. The sloping structure was open on one end. Its primary purpose was to keep deep winter snows from sliding off the roof and barricading the main entrance. What it did best was hide a man as he was breaking into an abandoned building.

He laughed when he saw the cardboard sign plastered to the front of the vestibule: "Warning: Property Under Video Surveilence." For one thing, there was no power supply to the great white building, there hadn't been for more than a decade. The county wasn't going to pay to keep the lights on in a facility that was no longer in use. All that would do is raise their insurance rates, increase the risk of an electrical fire. He knew that the video camera mounted under the soffit was merely a decoy. At one time the fake camera had been equipped with a tiny, blinking red light. It had been years since the little light had winked at anyone. The government gatekeepers had never replaced its nine-volt battery. What really made him laugh, made him laugh each and every time he snuck in this way, was the sign itself. If the building were actually being monitored by a reputable alarm company, they'd probably know how to spell "Surveillance."

The man opened the lock with his key, slowly reaching into his back pocket and finding a mini Maglite that he kept with him at all times. The flashlight was small enough that it wasn't readily noticed in his pocket, was less than six inches overall and three quarters of an inch in diameter. Despite its small size the Maglite cast enough light that he could navigate his way through dense woods or the decaying structure of a building without tripping or falling. He closed and locked the door behind him before twisting the bezel of the little lamp to illuminate the hallway before him.

The drop ceiling had given way in multiple places, buckled by insidious rain and the additional weight of wet fiberglass insulation. Fountains of pink fiber slumped to the floor, speckled with white powder fragments from crumbling ceiling tiles. He picked his way around the first pile carefully. There were three offices lining the corridor to the left, cheap paneled rooms that had been remodeled in the early seventies. A rusted steel desk and a broken office chair occupied the first room, a broken clock dangling from the wall. The other two rooms were totally empty. Off to the right lay the doorways to a pair of larger rooms. These rooms had somehow escaped the cheap "upgrades" that marred the three rooms on the left; they still had some of their original character. Multiple layers of green, lead-based industrial paint were slathered across real plaster and lathe walls. Graffiti was scrawled across the ceiling of the first room, a memento from some earlier intruder. Hardwood trim and crown molding bore a half-century of enamel buildup, now fading to a dingy white. The man started cautiously down the corridor, warped floorboards creaking with every step.

In the last room to the right the man heard a sudden movement, temporarily freezing him in his tracks. The hair on the back of his neck stood up as adrenaline surged through his body. He twisted the head of the little flashlight, shutting off its beam. He waited for what seemed like forever, really no more than a few moments, trying to keep his breathing in check. His heart raced; his palms began to sweat. His eyes were still adjusting to the darkness. Nothing. Not a sound. He took one step, a board creaking beneath his right foot, and then another quick step. He waited some more. He was almost to the doorway, one stride to go. Trying to ease weight onto his left foot, a step closer, and thankfully no boards creaked with this subtle movement.

He could see into one half of the room but there was nothing there, just a broom and dust pan leaning against the far wall. Wait some more. Still no sound. Whoever made the noise must be hiding right around the corner. What to do? Wait him out or try to surprise him? The man was too far along to sneak back out the way he'd come in. Those damn noisy floors would give him away for sure. He wasn't armed, unless he could figure a way to use a four-ounce Maglite as a weapon, and he didn't have much working in his favor other than the element of surprise. Of course surprise could cut both ways. Who was inside the room? Hopefully no one other than some high-school kid looking for a place to hang out and get high. More movement and quiet scratching on the other side of the wall. What to do? He decided it was time to take the offensive. *Pounce and yell*, he decided, *pounce and yell.* Maybe he could scare the little bastard into jumping right out a window.

Silently he counted to five before leaping across the threshold and around the corner. He didn't quite get to the yelling part. What waited for him inside the room made enough noise for both parties, for hell hath no fury like a raccoon startled. The masked scavenger had been pawing his way through a pile of papers and other garbage in the corner when the man, flashlight in hand, had jumped at him from the hallway. The raccoon hissed, shrieked, tried to turn tail and ran face first into the corner before turning back once more and lunging straight toward his nemesis. The man dropped his flashlight to the floor.

"Holy crap." He finally found that yell he'd been planning, followed quickly by his own deep-seated laugh. Scared by a little animal. He must be losing it in his old age. He backed off a step, allowing the critter room to scurry through the doorway and across the hall into the darkness. He bent down and retrieved the runaway flashlight, all the while laughing at himself. It was downright comical now that it was over.

At the end of the corridor was another large room with a narrow stairway to the right. He followed that back down to the lower level. This was a convoluted way to get to where he was going, but necessary. A raccoon, of all things. He was still chuckling. At the bottom of the stairs the man passed a tiny shower to his left, a skinny stall lined with white sanitary tiles, just big enough for one person. What remained of a half bath was next to that, the toilet and sink long ago broken and removed, pipes dangling from the wall. Then a small string of six gunmetal lockers crowded the left side of the skinny passageway with six coat hooks and a small bench directly across from them. A turn to the right and finally he set foot in the big lab, a forty foot by forty foot room where millions of fingerlings and fry were once reared. It still smelled of fish.

He skipped past the crude wooden benches that lined the near wall of the room, covered in beakers and pots from when the building was more than just a hangout for delinquents and vermin. The far wall was where his goods were, stuffed inside one of the floor-to-ceiling cabinets that stood warped and twisted in the damp climate. A window separated these twin towers, but had long ago been broken out and covered with plywood. There was little worry of anyone spotting the light inside the big laboratory. He reached inside the first cabinet, retrieving the big black duffel that weighed nearly thirty pounds.   Scurrying could be heard again at the top of the stairs, the raccoon comfortable now that the intruder was no longer in sight.

"Damn animal," he whispered, as he turned with duffel in hand to retrace his path. He made it only one more step before staring into the muzzle flash of a nine millimeter pistol and the bullet which brought his sorry life to an end.

TWO

Walt Pitowski

Walt steered the little Samurai across North Down River Road, skittering and hopping above the craters and bumps in the surface like a water bug on the glassy dome of a pond. "Water skimmers" or "Jesus bugs" they used to call them, those multi-legged insects that appear to walk on water. He'd see them still, racing against the current in the shallows of the Grand Limoneaux River. Oh, to be a kid again.

He knew that the Samurai was not as nimble as a "Jesus bug" walking on water. Here he was gripping the steering wheel for all it was worth, just trying to make it to town for one more glorious day in paradise. The cheap tin-can vehicle didn't hold the road well, not at all. It was too light for one thing, and too top-heavy for another, prone to tipping and rolling on its short wheelbase. It didn't help that the road surface was eternally pockmarked from the snow and ice that the pavement endures each winter and spring near the 45th parallel. Still Walt's real problem was not with the design of the truck nor the quality of the pavement: his real problem was that the ball joints on the Suzuki's right side were about to give way and her suspension shimmied and wobbled, fighting to pull the little vehicle off the road and into the shallow ditch.

"This fucking truck is trying to commit suicide," Walt mumbled. "They should have named it the Suzuki Kamikaze."

Why wouldn't the little beater want to give up the ghost? Nearly a foot of metal was missing from the bottom of each body panel. The fenders flapped in the wind, swaying in even the gentlest breeze. Rust, that northern Michigan cancer that for generations has killed cars half as old and four times more valuable, was having its way with the little sport utility vehicle. All the road salt they used in the winter was nothing but a hidden subsidy to the auto companies, in Walt's opinion; more corporate welfare.

The more Walt thought about things, oxidation was near the bottom of his catalog of woes. The Suzuki's front end was shot, a collection of worn bones and elbows scarcely making contact with one another. The battered tendons had seen better days. It needed new tires and brakes, and the exhaust, or what was left of it, was held together by a network of coat hangers and tin cans. Even the windshield was held in place with that silver wonder of the working man - duct tape. All of that he could probably live with, but last week Walt noticed antifreeze on the oil dipstick: never a good sign. It was an indicator that the engine's head gasket was leaking, and he didn't have enough money laying around for that kind of a repair. It was time to cut his losses. She'd been a great little ride, but her time had come and gone long ago. Suicide was a logical next step. Unfortunately, Walt Pitowski didn't have money to upgrade to a better vehicle. He'd be lucky if he could come up with bus fare.

"Shit!" he screamed, as a coyote darted across the road mere inches from his front bumper. It forced him to swerve across the broken center line. He barely managed to avoid hitting the 'yote, which scurried into a copse of shrubs off the left side of the pavement. Thirty pounds of brown fur, muscle, and bone evaporated as quickly as it had first appeared. At sixty-five miles per hour the Suzuki shuddered and shook, the back end breaking loose and whipping wildly across both lanes while spitting gravel before Walt finally got it back in line. There was little traffic leaving Rasmus this time of day, so Mr. Toad's wild ride across the fractured yellow line and back went largely unnoticed; at least he could be thankful for that. Walt would have to remember to take his .22 and do a little coyote hunting as soon as he had a chance. They were everywhere, coyotes, and damn nuisances that had all but eliminated the rabbit and squirrel populations in the area at that. Their pelts weren't worth much, but at least he'd exact some revenge on the little bastards.

It was pathetic having to drive a vehicle so battered that a collision with an animal the size of a mangy dog might do it in. He deserved better than this, of that Walt was certain. He had a job, a good job. He was a federal employee, for God's sake, had been with the United States Geological Service for over a decade. He was a professional: not a doctor or a lawyer, maybe, but a professional with a career and a degree. It wasn't his fault he was dead broke, wasn't his fault his wife left town and then the economy tanked and he was stuck paying on a house that was worth at best half the mortgage balance. It wasn't his fault he often felt trapped and angry with the life that had been imposed upon him. Walt didn't know whose fault it was, not exactly. Nevertheless he had a list in his head, a list that started with fat-cat Wall Street brokers that had destroyed his retirement account, included his ex-wife Dora, and kept right on going: the tax man, the local cops, there was always room on the list for additional names, including the name of every politician in this podunk town and the whole God-forsaken state. Walt made a mental note to add "coyotes" to the register. "I need a new truck," he chirped to himself, as he eased a tiny plug of tobacco between his cheek and gum. It was the understatement of the year.

He passed the big military equipment facility to his right, a multi-acre complex where the National Guard stored and maintained the hundreds of Hummers and Jeeps and tanks necessary to a modern fighting force. They called this section M.A.T.E.S., though Walt still didn't have any idea what "M.A.T.E.S." stood for. He just knew that the surrounding six foot cyclone fence, topped with glittering concertina wire, meant "keep the hell out." On his left was a gravel pullout big enough for a handful of cars to park and a locked steel gate. Beyond the gate lay recreational trails and a vast swath of land that had been donated to the state for public use. It wasn't a bad little hike, if you took the main trail down to the river, but it wasn't premium hunting land either. He hadn't bothered to make the trek more than three or four times since he'd lived here. He made a mental note to try once more to take a look around and see what the land had to offer. Maybe there was some good rabbit territory down by the river. Walt noticed a battered Plymouth Breeze with mismatched fenders in the pullout, and felt sorry for the schlub that had to drive *that* piece of junk.

Walt eased off the throttle on the little Suzuki, knowing he was approaching two big curves in the road and, not far beyond, the town of Rasmus. The last thing he needed was a particular employee of the county sheriff's department, one Deputy Matt Amberson (The Jawless Wonder), nailing him for doing sixty-five in a thirty-five zone. Amberson and Pitowski had had their share of run-ins, and Walt didn't feel like adding fuel to the fire. He sure as hell couldn't afford another ticket. Amberson had given him one earlier in the year for driving with a cracked windshield, of all things (and thus the ad hoc glass replacement and duct tape gasket).

The deputy loved to set up shop just past the big s-curve, where people drove into town hot off twenty-plus miles of two lane road, interrupted by a single stop sign at Shambarger Bridge Road and very little else. Amberson would lie in wait and pull them over just past the sign where the speed limit dropped from fifty-five to thirty-five. A little further up, closer to town, the limit dropped to twenty-five, but by then the damage was usually done. Speeding tickets were an especially important revenue stream for the largely impoverished county, at least in the gospel according to Walt. He passed the grove of jack pines where the deputy usually sat in ambush, the patrol car's hood facing the road. Today there was no sheriff's car in sight.

"The Jawless Wonder must have bigger things on his mind this morning." Walt opined. "Probably a big box of donuts and his big frickin' gut." The two men had reached a truce of sorts earlier this year, after Walt helped to solve a decade-old cold case involving a decomposing body found floating in the Sparrow River, a local drug dealer, and a messy chase that led to even more tragedy. Walt was the first to discover the corpse in the river, and to pursue the truth when everyone else had given truth up as a lost cause. Pitowski came out of the incident bruised and beaten. Amberson came out of the whole thing smelling like a rose, and the darling of the media to boot. They still weren't exactly what you'd call "friends," but both men knew, without saying as much, that Walt had done the heavy lifting while the sheriff's department took all the credit. "He owes me one," Walt thought aloud.

The Suzuki crossed over the short concrete bridge, four lanes of interstate highway zipping seamlessly beneath, and sidled off onto the gravel road shoulder a few hundred feet beyond. Today was Saturday, which in Rasmus could mean only one thing: Trash Day. On Saturday mornings everyone gathers round The Compactor, a way station for a majority of the county's trash and waste; everyone who doesn't live in the city proper, that is.

City residents have regularly scheduled curbside trash pickup, thanks in no small part to the additional income tax that comes with living in a booming metropolitan city of fifteen hundred souls, give or take a few, such as Rasmus. City dwellers don't have to haul their own trash, they just wheel it out to the street once a week. Some of the businesses in town contract independently for private dumpster service. That is practically the hallmark of Rasmus royalty: if you have your own dumpster, you don't even have to leave the driveway. Everyone else in the county is on their own, which means on Tuesday or Thursday between the hours of two and seven p.m., or Saturday between the hours of nine and four p.m., you load your car up with smelly trash and whatever else you might have broken into bits and pieces or just plain quit on, and haul it to The Compactor. There is an annual fee involved, attached to all improved properties within the township.

The good folks who work at The Compactor will recycle what they can, smashing and mangling the rest into a festering stew which brews inside of a giant steel vault situated off to the side of a man-made ramp. The vault will later be transferred to a big landfill just south of Gaylord, and the tidy bales of crushed cardboard, plastic and tin get sent to a recycling center somewhere else in the state.

In theory this system should work well, with plenty of opportunity for the outlying residents to take care of their waste disposal needs in a timely and orderly fashion. In practice, most people wait until Saturday morning to do the nasty deed. If you have a job, you really don't want trash baking in your vehicle all day until after you get off work. Tuesdays and Thursdays tend to be inconvenient for the gainfully employed. This problem is compounded by non-residents, downstaters, and visitors from parts elsewhere who come up for the weekend and clean out the family cabin once every ten years or so. One guy with a utility trailer full of junk can clog the line for twenty minutes if he isn't in any hurry, and why would he be in a hurry? He's retired and on vacation, right?

Somewhere around eight-thirty-five on any given Saturday morning there is a queue of cars and trucks idling just outside the locked gate to The Compactor, stretching a quarter-mile or longer down the shoulder of the road. They are all loaded with a week's worth or more of putrid rubbish, empty laundry bottles, cardboard boxes, non-returnable glass containers, and wine bottles. Walt found himself at the back of just such a line and carefully counted the cars and trucks ahead of him: there were currently seventeen, not too bad. He looked at his watch: the gates wouldn't open for another thirteen minutes. Puffs of bluish smoke wafted from the Samurai's exhaust, a dim reminder of impending doom. Walt turned the ignition key to the "off" position and let the engine sleep.

The pickup truck directly in front of him was an older Dodge half-ton, black with white lettering on the tailgate. It was from the mid-1980's, he guessed. Its open bed was packed full with large black plastic trash bags, a deceased recliner, and the remains of what might have been a prefab bookcase or table of some kind. He couldn't see what was in the next vehicle ahead of that truck, but Walt knew that the guy in the Dodge wouldn't be unloading in any hurry. It was packing far more than a week's worth of refuse. *Probably cleaning out his cabin*, Walt guessed. Walt had a special feeling in his heart for these retirees and downstaters, guys with all the time in the world, who show up in Rasmus early on Saturday morning with the sole intent of making life hell for the working man. If they aren't at The Compactor, they're creating a traffic jam at the barbershop or the bank. Couldn't they do this crap on Tuesdays or Thursdays? Stupid old codgers and wealthy city pricks. He needed to block it out, take a mental vacation. Walt closed his eyes, just for a minute.

"Hey, buddy, you gonna move or what?"

Walt woke up startled, a hand rapping at his passenger's side front window.

"Hey, buddy!"

"Yeah, give me a minute." The rapping stopped. Walt realized he must have dozed off for a few minutes there.

The man from the passenger window walked back to a Buick LeSabre that was practically kissing the Samurai's back bumper. The line ahead of him had already moved forward. The Dodge pickup that had been parked in front of Walt was inside the gate and had made its way to the top of The Compactor's steep cement incline, where that truck's owner and his cohort were rapidly chucking black plastic bags into the crushing maw of the steel vault off to the left. A man in an orange jumpsuit, one of a handful of weekend "prisoners" from the county jail fulfilling community service requirements, was manning the controls inside the tiny wooden shack atop the rise. Most of these prisoners were working off the fines from a DUI or some lesser misdemeanor. The sheriff's office believed that a weekend or two dealing with the stench and filth of the county's garbage might prove a disincentive to reoffend. It also saved the county a lot of money on employee wages.

Walt jiggled the key in his ignition and brought life back to the beleaguered four cylinder engine. The man that had been knocking on the glass was back sitting in his own vehicle, already laying on his horn. "The same to you!" Walt hollered back through the open window of the Suzuki. A lone middle finger saluted him in the rearview mirror. Walt popped the Suzuki into gear and headed for the top of the ramp, where the Dodge was just pulling around the corner of the makeshift shack and returning back down the hill. The deceased recliner and the prefab furniture parts weren't allowed in the vault; they would have to go in one of the big dumpsters at the bottom of the run.

He set the parking brake when he reached the summit and leapt around to the back of his truck. Walt had more trash than usual, since he'd forgotten to clean out his back room for three consecutive Saturdays. There were twelve large white kitchen bags festering in the cargo area of the Samurai. He popped the hatch to the little sport ute, catching a whiff of everything he'd eaten or discarded in the last month. It did not smell good. Walt grabbed one bag in each fist, swinging his body to the left and heaving the bags over the short iron railing, deep into the mouth of the pit. He turned back to the Suzuki, grabbed two more bags, swiveling and tossing again. A third load, bags number five and six, and he was pivoting and swinging, when an arm across the chest stopped Walt in mid-movement.

"Five bag limit," the man informed him, with the overconfident voice of one who'd seized his first taste of temporary power. Walt didn't recognize the Great Pumpkin on the other end of the arm: he was a big, stocky guy, late-twenties, with an uneven buzz cut, clean shaven face, wearing an orange prison jump suit. Pumpkin Man.

"Where's Wally?" Walt shot back. "There's no five-bag limit." Wally was usually the man in charge at The Compactor and had been working there as long as Walt could remember. Wally'd put this guy in line. He didn't know who this guy was, but he sure as hell wasn't in charge of setting policy. Wally would tell him. Walt took a step to the side and resumed his throw, bags number five and six landing with a pronounced wet splatter in the vault's crushing jaws.

The big guy's arm caught Walt across the chest again, just after he'd released the twin missiles. "Wally's not working today. Five bag limit. If you don't believe me, check the county's website."

"Don't touch me again." There was anger in Walt's voice. "I'm not checking the county's website. I don't have to. You *show me* where there's a five bag limit. Since when? It's not posted anywhere. There's *never* been a five-bag limit, and besides, these are small bags. I could cram four of these little things into one big black bag." He looked at the Dodge pickup at the bottom of the hill. That guy in the Dodge had definitely brought more than five bags of trash. Walt wasn't about to put up with this bullshit, not from some guy that he'd never seen before, some guy that didn't have any authority whatsoever, some guy who probably couldn't count past ten without dropping his drawers. "Five bag limit my ass."

Why wasn't Wally here, anyway? Wally usually worked on Saturdays, the busiest day of the week. Your best guy should be working on your busiest day. Walt looked around for a familiar face, someone who knew the rules. He didn't see *anyone* he recognized, not by the dumpsters and not by the pole barn that functioned as a recycling center. They should know better than to leave the animals unsupervised. "And who are *you*, anyways?" he finally asked, looking Pumpkin Man dead in the eye.

"I work for the county," the big guy answered.

Walt knew better. "Like hell you do. You aren't a county employee. You're a *convict*, that's what you are. Some dumb-ass who beats his wife, or a drunk driver, out on a day pass. You're only here so the county doesn't have to pay some kid minimum wage to push that button in the cage." His words weren't going to soothe the tension anytime soon. Screw this guy.

Walt reached back into the Suzuki for bags seven and eight, only to be sent reeling by a stiff shove to his left shoulder. Enough was enough, as far as Walt was concerned. Getting fed a line about some imaginary "five bag limit," that was one thing. But no idiot out on work release was going to lay a hand on Walt Pitowski. He drew back and threw a sharp right cross at the big man's face. He didn't really expect to land the punch, Walt was just lashing out reflexively. Fist connected with nose cartilage, and the man in the orange jumpsuit went straight back on his tailbone. He stayed down, seated on the asphalt next to the iron railing, legs splayed and both hands cupping his face. Walt was astounded that The Great Pumpkin went down so easily.

"I think you broke my nose!" It was almost a sob, a sob muffled by the two big hands that hid his face. Walt didn't respond, he just clenched his fist in anger.

"Hey, are you alright?" a voice called. It was Delaney, the only *paid* assistant working at The Compactor this Saturday, huffing and puffing as he trotted up the ramp. He'd been hidden in the back of the recycling center, moving pallets of cubed plastic and cardboard boxes. Delaney was a good-hearted guy and was almost as well known around town as Wally - almost. His concern was aimed at Walt, not at the man seated on the pavement, blood dripping from his nose. "I just stuck my head out and saw what happened. He never should have touched you. That ain't right."

"I think he broke my nose," complained the big guy, a little calmer now, looking less likely to burst into tears but still in no rush to get back to his

15

feet. Walt suspected he was milking it, looking for any excuse to quit working in the heat and squalor.

"Since when is there a five bag limit?" asked Walt.

"What are you talking about?" responded Delaney.

"He's got no right to shove a customer," the man from the Buick chimed in. He, too, was standing at the top of the ramp, though his car was still parked at the base of the incline. It was the first Walt had noticed him standing there. Rubbernecking gawker. At least he was on Walt's side in this one.

"You wanting to press charges?" Delaney asked Walt, praying like hell the answer was "no." He was hoping against hope that Walt would think better of the idea, but Delaney had an obligation to ask. The last thing this county needed was another lawsuit. If word of this fight got out, there might be a public backlash against using cons for free Compactor labor. No free labor, and people would really start screaming: just wait until the next round of property tax bills arrived in the mail. "Charges or no charges, yes or no?"

"Not if he doesn't."

"How about you?" to the man on the ground.

"I've got enough trouble," said the big guy, cautiously rising to his feet. "We're good."

"Then head down to the barn and help move pallets. Do whatever Roger tells you to do. I'll be there in a couple of minutes." Delaney answered. He turned to Walt. "Look, I'm sorry he touched you, but we don't need this kind of trouble. It looks bad, all around. You know what I'm saying." His voice carried a tone of resignation, the resignation you find when your Saturdays are filled with cleaning up other people's spilled garbage. This morning hadn't started off well, and the day wasn't likely to get much better. The sun was beating down hard on the vault, its contents beginning to ferment.

"He shoved me first," Pitowski offered. It sounded weak, even to Walt's own ears.

"Great." There wasn't a lot of pity in his voice. "If we're done, then *please* finish unloading and let this man behind you dispose of his trash." The "please" didn't sound particularly sincere, but Walt let it slide.   Delaney and the man with the Buick started walking back to the bottom of the hill.

"He   shoved   me   first,"   Walt   lamented,   to   no   one   in   particular.

THREE

He pulled off the pavement and stopped dead in the road, contemplating the next half mile of his life. Two ruts cut deep where truck tires travelled daily, back and forth. A large hump of sand ran down the center of this earthen trail, high enough to shred the oil pan on anything that didn't have four wheel drive or a lifted suspension. A low spot in the road ahead held a good foot of water from the last rain storm. You'd need a quick head of steam and a firm grip on the wheel if you hoped to get past without burying your vehicle up to the wheel wells.

For a while things had been looking up. He'd been dating a woman, a local bartender named Pam, if 'dating' was what you wanted to call it. They were romantically involved, if nothing else; "bumping uglies," as they used to say. That counted for something. He'd managed to fulfill a dream of his: competing in and completing the Grand Limoneaux Canoe Marathon earlier this summer. Walt and his partner Jim Rivard had managed to finish in forty-sixth place, no small feat after seventeen hours and more of nonstop paddling. This year eighty-six teams had started the event, and only seventy-four had been able to finish. Forty-sixth place was good, damn good, and next year they'd do even better. Then there was the incident up on the Sparrow River, finding that decomposed body and hunting down a killer. That mess hadn't turned out exactly the way Walt had hoped, but he still took satisfaction in having pursued the truth as far as he could.

Since then his summer had turned to shit. It turned out his forty-sixth place finish in The Marathon hadn't opened secret doors to that great fraternity of paddlers, local and otherwise, that appeared to dominate the social and business culture of Rasmus. Maybe there was no secret fraternity; maybe it was all just an illusion. Either way, Walt was more than a little disappointed that having finally become one of "them," he didn't seem to garner any more respect around town than he did prior to the race. The guys that didn't like him before, and there were plenty of them, still didn't like him. Every time he bumped into Mikey Babcock (who, by the way, didn't even finish the race this year, pulling out at Kirtland's Bridge due to illness), the man looked at Walt like he was something stuck on the bottom of a freshly shined dress shoe. Babcock was an arrogant jerk. The guys that had tolerated Walt before the big race, the ones who would at least *pretend* to be cordial, well, they weren't any friendlier, either. It was as if nothing had changed. He still hadn't cracked their code.

The thing with Pam had petered out. It was as much his fault as hers, he'd be the first to admit. She'd been there for him when he was beaten and injured, and she'd stuck by him when he needed a soft place to land. After The Marathon he'd needed time to recuperate physically, and then he'd been sent to New Mexico for two weeks. A technician with the U.S. Geological Service doesn't always get the opportunity to do stream testing in New Mexico. Who even knew there *were* streams in New Mexico? Hell, it paid time-and-a-half plus a per diem. He needed the money, *had* to take the money. Anyone could see he was flat broke. He forgot to phone Pam. For two weeks, he simply forgot to call her. A week after he returned from that trip Pitowski finally got around to stopping by the Deer Track Inn, where Pam tended bar. In their one brief conversation Pam made it clear that she was already seeing someone else. Whatever relationship she and Walt shared was over, and while he knew that she had every right to be angry, it still stung. To make matters worse, Walt was no longer welcome at the Deer Track: his favorite watering hole. Life was not fair.

Now autumn was knocking at the door. It was the last week of September, with frosty mornings and warm afternoons, salmon in the rivers and a timberdoodle in every pot. Most times he loved this cooler season, hunting partridge on Sunday mornings and deer come November. The legions of fly fishermen that crowd the lakes and streams in the summertime are long gone, and you can paddle a canoe on any body of water without bumping into another person. This year seemed different. Walt had never been a particularly optimistic man; he'd long ago come to believe that people will screw you over with every chance they get. He had managed throughout most of his life, however, to stay *hopeful,* clinging to the belief that life *could* get marginally better, if only temporarily, through personal determination and sheer will. Walt felt a sense of disappointment settling in. The changing leaves only served to remind him of a long winter ahead, a winter sure to be marked by cold lonely nights and a hungry wood stove. He didn't relish either thought.

He stopped and got gas at the Speedway station, chatting up the cute clerk behind the counter. It didn't hurt to keep your options open. Walt had an early lunch at the Rasmus Diner, gorging himself on The Lumberjack

Special. He ran into Tom Dewers, one of his least favorite co-workers, on the street outside. The two spent twenty minutes chatting about a project they were working on jointly. He took a ride out to the Manistee River, doing some early scouting prior to deer season, but didn't see much that was encouraging. He picked up snacks for later at The Bridge Party Store, which was under new ownership for the third time in the last two years. You'd think someone could make a go of that location when beer, lottery tickets, and cigarettes were the three primary commodities of Rasmus.

It was already late afternoon when Walt guided the little Samurai down the rutted dirt path known as Blueberry Circle, back to the very end, where the small cul-de-sac contained a tiny A-frame that he called home. Eight houses ringed the outer edge of the oval, hidden deep in the jack pines and a mile from the nearest pavement. It wasn't much of a house. When his ex-wife, Dora, left town on the arm of another man, it was what little Walt had left to cling to. This house, his job, a golden retriever named Doofus that didn't listen to anyone (especially not to Walt), and a wheezing automobile worth less than the cost of insurance. He'd since learned not to inventory his life; it could only lead to depression.

A Shawono County sheriff's cruiser was already parked in Walt's driveway, and one of the newer deputies, Don Frederics, was playing with Doofus in the front yard. This couldn't be good. The Samurai rolled into the driveway hard, spewing gravel and sand before finally coming to a stop just short of the cruiser's rear bumper.

"The dog was in the house. You got a search warrant?" Walt could swear he'd left Doofus in the house. He also knew that he hadn't locked the sliding patio door. Hell, he never locked the patio door. What did he own that anyone would want to steal? A Zenith console television in genuine imitation wood grain?

"Don't need one." Frederics was matter of fact, throwing a tennis ball that the dog dutifully retrieved and dropped in the grass before him.

"You do if you set foot in my house."

"Evidence in plain view, animal in distress. Your dog was scratching at the door, had to take a leak. He looked pretty distressed to me, so I let him out. Look it up if you don't believe me."

"Bullshit." Walt knew better than to trust anything that came out of this guy's mouth. Maybe it wasn't entirely bullshit, but he had to believe that it was mostly bullshit. "You can't go in my house without a warrant."

"I didn't go in. I opened the door and let your dog out. You can thank me later." Doofus once again returned the tennis ball, dropping it at Frederics' feet. The officer decided it was time to ignore the dog, turning his focus to Pitowski instead. Doofus was visibly disappointed.

Walt looked him in the eye, weighing how much effort he wanted to put into this particular argument. It wasn't as if he had something to hide. Hell, the sheriff's department could rip his house apart and not find a single thing that was illegal. Walt mistrusted the government on principle. Who knew what they might try to plant on him? He also knew he wouldn't get anywhere complaining to the local court. Judge Redman was a stern woman, a woman who seriously detested gamesmanship. He'd probably just piss her off in advance of some larger problem, a problem Deputy Don was undoubtedly about to describe in detail. Why else would he be here? Walt decided to let the whole "warrant" thing go. "What can I do for you, Don?"

"Official business. You want to guess why I'm here?"

Walt had a pretty good idea why the man was there. It had to be about that jerk back at the Compactor. Walt was wondering who called the law. Was it that twerp in the Buick, or did the con finally grow a pair? Either way, Walt should be in the clear on this one. He had every right to defend himself. The guy at the Compactor, well, he'd started it, but Walt had also seen enough cop shows to know that you should never, *never*, *EVER*, offer up any information to the police that could be construed as an admission of guilt. They'd only throw it back in your face later.

"I'm not in a guessing mood. Please, Officer Frederics, tell me why you're here."

"No need to be sarcastic, Pitowski. Could you please provide your whereabouts from approximately one a.m. to three a.m. this morning?"

He'd guessed wrong: it wasn't about the Compactor after all. Now he had no idea what the deputy wanted. Walt didn't like being in the dark. It made him feel edgy and restless.

"You want to tell me what this is about?"

"Routine question. Your whereabouts last night? From one until three, as best you can account."

"In bed, alone, as best I can account. What's going on?" Real concern was beginning to creep into his voice. Maybe this wasn't just a case of the deputy being his usual stupid self.

"Anyone that can confirm that story?"

"Yeah. He's holding a tennis ball in his mouth, right in front of you. Come'on, Don, I was sleeping. What's going on?"

"You had a previous relationship with one Pamela Sharpe, an employee at the Deer Track Inn?"

"We dated for a while. We're taking a little break, exploring other options, so to speak. Why? What's she saying?"

"When was the last time you saw Ms. Sharpe?"

"Seriously, what did she say? I haven't been to the Deer Track in three or four weeks. Ask her, she'll back me up. She told me she's seeing someone else, it would be better if I didn't come around for a while. So I haven't come around for a while. What's going on, Don?"

"Someone busted the Deer Track up pretty good, just after closing last night. The place is a mess." The deputy sounded like there might be more to the story, something he was holding back.

"Shit, this is the first I've heard of it. Why are you asking me? What does Pam say happened?"

"Ms. Sharpe isn't talking. She's in the hospital with a broken jaw and a bunch of other serious injuries." He sounded more somber, if that was even possible: "Dragnet" serious.

"Is she going to be okay?" Walt was getting agitated, ready to spring into action, if only he could figure out what that action should be. Sure, he and Pam hadn't been seeing each other for a while, but he still had feelings for her. He wanted to help her, protect her. He wanted to *do something*.

"It's too early to tell. She's heavily sedated. They're trying to give her injuries time to heal."

"Jesus, Don, what kind of an asshole would do something like that?"

"Well, the sheriff thinks I might be looking straight at him."

Walt let this statement sink in. He'd been called a lot of bad things in his lifetime, some of them even true, but he had never, *never* laid a finger on any woman. God, he *loved* women, loved all *kinds* of women. As for Pam, well, he couldn't say he was *in love* with Pam, but he sure as hell liked her a lot. Even if they were no longer together, he still cared. The last thing on earth he'd ever want to do was hurt her. Yet here he was, standing in his own driveway, with the local sheriff's department as much as accusing him of being a woman beater. For the first time in a long while, Walt was rendered speechless.

"For what it's worth, Pitowski, I don't think you had anything to do with this. You might be an idiot, but you're not that particular kind of idiot. Anything else you might be able to add that could help clear this up?"

Walt couldn't decide if the deputy was being honest with him or if this was just Frederics playing "good cop" after a long stretch of playing "bad cop." Walt didn't really care either way. It hurt that anyone could think him capable of something like this. He just wanted to know that Pam would be alright, and that whoever had hurt her would pay in spades. "I don't know a thing about it, but I'm sure as hell going to find out," he finally answered, an edge of bitterness tainting his voice.

"Take my advice, Pitowski: don't stick your nose in anything. Just because I don't think you had anything to do with this doesn't mean the rest of the department agrees with me. Let us do our jobs. Stay away from Ms. Sharpe, at least until this thing is settled. Stay away from the Deer Track Inn. That should be easy, even for you. They're going to be closed for a few days while they patch it back together. If you go poking around where you don't belong, it'll only make you look guilty. We'll let you know if we have any more questions. In the meantime don't leave the state, and stay where we can get ahold of you. That means go to work on Monday and sleep in your own bed at night. Comprende?"

Walt felt as if he'd been gut shot. "Yeah, I get it," he muttered.

The radio in the squad car was squawking up a storm, electronic noise filtering through the open driver's side window. Frederics hurried over to listen in on the commotion. Walt tried to eavesdrop, but he had no idea what they were saying.

"Pitowski, I've got to go. Remember what I said about keeping your nose clean." The deputy was already sliding behind the wheel of his car. "Move that piece of crap you parked behind me."

Walt fired up the Suzuki and threw it in reverse, spitting sand and digging ruts into the driveway as he spun his way backwards into the oval. He burrowed out a pair of fresh tire tracks in the road itself as he crammed the transmission into first gear, before eventually grinding the vehicle to a halt as he pulled even with his front porch. Some moron was going to be really pissed when he came flying down Blueberry Circle and hit those twin divots.

The sheriff's car was gone in a cloud of dust, racing off to some urgent matter or another. They probably ran out of coffee at the jailhouse. Walt trudged up the three sagging steps to his front deck, whistled for Doofus to follow, and went into the house. It seemed empty. He looked around the living and kitchen area, slowly surveying the cramped space. His furniture was worn but serviceable. There were some permanent stains and burn holes in the couch, but it was still comfortable, and there were no springs poking through the fabric. A rocker sat across from the sofa, the space in between divided by a chipped coffee table. A large console television took up most of one wall. The kitchen was barely stocked, but adequate for the lifestyle of a single man who rarely entertained. Two pots and one medium-sized frying pan were squirreled away in the cabinets, along with two plates, two bowls, six coffee cups, and four glasses. There was an electric drip coffee maker on the counter and a microwave oven by the stove. The counters were dust and clutter free. For all its shabbiness the house was neat and orderly, almost military in its cleanliness. Walt had recently experienced the strong desire to put some structure back into his life. With Pam no longer around he had plenty of time on his hands. He put a small log on the fire, a fire which had died down to a small pile of embers. He opened the door and stoked the flames in the bottom of the cast iron stove. The propane tank was currently sitting empty. If he wanted to use the furnace Walt was going to have to pay for a truck to come out and fill it. A refill was going to run another six hundred dollars. He could split a lot of firewood in the time it took him to earn that kind of money.

Walt clicked on the television, giving the tubes in the analog set time to warm up. He went to the kitchen, found a clean glass, added a few ice cubes and splashing some bourbon in it. This cheap stuff tasted like possum urine, but it was the only booze he had in the house. If he ever won the lottery the first thing he'd do would be to go out and buy himself a bottle of Maker's Mark, or whatever bourbon cost more than Maker's Mark. Maybe he'd buy two bottles. Just once he'd like to drink something that went down easy. He sat down on the couch; Doofus jumped up and curled into a ball at the far end. Walt reached over and scratched between the dog's ears. "What do you know, boy? You know the truth, don't you?" For the first time in a long time Walt was feeling like a defeated man. He settled in to watch television, staying home like a good little boy.

Dog Day Afternoon was playing on the classic movie channel, with Al Pacino and his friend robbing a bank so that the Pacino character can pay for his gay lover's sex change operation. Unfortunately the bank has no real money on hand, and one thing after another goes wrong with the heist. The building is quickly surrounded by cops, and the robbers get locked inside with ten hostages. Pretty soon the whole thing becomes a media circus, a real zoo. It's amazing how a plan so simple can quickly turn on you.

Pacino's character is trying to get his wife (his real wife, not his gay lover), on the phone. He turns to his accomplice, Sal: "You know I can call anybody, they'd put it on the phone? The Pope, an astronaut, the wisest of the wise...who do *I* have to call?"

Walt could sympathize. He drank the cheap whiskey down and poured himself another. Three drinks later and he was passed out on the couch, asleep for the night.

FOUR

Doofus was scratching at the sliding door, wanting to go out. Walt got up slowly, cautiously finding his balance as he rose off the couch and rubbed the crust from the corners of his eyes. The morning sun was shining, though just barely. A thick fog blanketed the yard and everything beyond it. He opened the door and the dog bounded across the wet lawn into the mist. The air was crisp. Walt could sense that winter was just around the corner. It wasn't just the drop in temperature, the cool mornings. A slight whiff of wood smoke hung on the breeze but that wasn't it, either. Walt would swear that he could *smell* the onset of winter, he just couldn't describe it very well. It's a smell both earthy and sour, with hints of sage and wintergreen and pine needles; the clinging odor of decay, and the unmistakable, bittersweet taste of summer's end. Walt inhaled deeply and knew what was coming, like a runaway freight train bearing down from the north.

Yesterday seemed like a bad dream: not the thing at the Compactor, which was just life. Shit like that happens. There were people trying to take your rights from you every day in this country, and you had to be ready to defend yourself. If some mouthy convict gets his ass kicked once in a while for overstepping his boundaries, well so be it. That's the price he'd pay. Walt just happened to be the guy manning the toll both yesterday. Tomorrow it might be someone else's turn.

Pam being hurt, now that was really killing him. When they were together as a couple, whatever "together" truly meant, Walt was enjoying himself. When they broke up or "took a hiatus," whatever it was they were decidedly *not* doing together, Walt figured he'd get over it. Now this, well, it made him realize how much he missed and needed that woman. And she needed him, whether she knew it or not.

Walt staggered into the kitchen, put some beans in the coffee grinder, and pushed the button that would turn them to brown dust. He filled the glass pot with water, poured it into the reservoir at the back of the electric drip maker, and dumped the fresh-ground beans into the wire filter basket. He needed a shower. He left the patio door open so Doofus could let himself back in. He threw two more logs on the fire. In the bathroom, he disrobed and stepped beneath the warm spray of the shower head.

Afterwards he felt rejuvenated, alert and ready to face the world. It was Sunday morning and that presented a problem. What he'd like to do, what he'd *really* like to do, would be to find out which hospital Pam was laid up in, and go and visit her. Walt knew that wasn't a good idea, not after what Frederics said: "Stay away from Pam and keep your nose out of it," or something like that. How was he supposed to keep his nose out of it, with Pam being a woman that was so much a part of his life? She might be in Rasmus Hospital, but if she was truly busted up as badly as the deputy had said, they'd have probably sent her to Traverse City or Petoskey. He was missing her more by the minute. Too bad this wasn't Monday: he could head to the office and lose himself in his work. That wasn't an option either. This was going to be one long Sunday.

Walt decided that what he needed, *really* needed, was to get some paddling in. Go out on the water somewhere, *anywhere,* and spend a few hours in a boat, pushing his body hard. His partner from the Marathon, Jim, was out of town for the entire month of September. That took away any chance of training in the sleek C2 racing canoe. It was just as well. Hours practicing in the fragile race craft mattered for the big event, but Walt didn't need to start *serious* training until January or February. In the meantime he could stay in shape with dry land exercises: jogging, weight lifting, that sort of thing. All he really wanted on this day was to get out and spend time on the water. Whether he did or didn't spend it paddling like a madman wouldn't make or break him come next July. A little paddle therapy *might* make it easier for him to get through this day.

The coffee was good, just the way he liked it: thick as tar and nearly as bitter. Walt could never understand those guys that ordered "grande lattes" and "frappuccinos," half-caff, no fat, no foam, with a shot of vanilla and a cinnamon twist. What was that supposed to be, anyhow? Didn't they even *like* the taste of coffee? You might as well order yourself a strawberry milkshake and go back to wearing knickers. Turkish coffee, now that was something Walt could understand: stick a spoon in it and watch it stand upright. It was too bad there wasn't a Turkish coffee shop within two-hundred miles of here. He sipped the black liquid and smiled with contentment.

His mind floated back to the movie last night; what was it Pacino had said? "Who do *I* have to call?" Walt was still wondering the same thing. Who could he call that might have Sunday free to goof around and take his mind off the fact that he was now a police suspect for felony assault and more? This was not good, not good at all. The sun was already burning a hole through the fog, and he could tell it was going to be a beautiful day. He finally landed on an idea, picking up his cell phone to dial.

The two men hadn't spoken in a couple of months. Walt tried to remember why they were spending less and less time together, why they rarely spoke when once they were like brothers. Elvin had young kids and a wife, that was a good part of it. Kids suck up your time and energy, one big reason never to have any: kids that is. Wives suck up your time, your energy, and your money, although in Elvin's case the opposite was true. Elvin's wife made more money than Elvin could ever hope to earn. And in all fairness, Walt himself had been consumed with the big race and with solving "that thing up on the Sparrow." For a while he'd been spending most of his time with Pam. Both men were to blame. The nice thing about being a guy is that you can often pick up a friendship, even years later, without feeling as though you've missed a beat.

"Elvin, how are you?" He was surprised that his friend was even home to answer the phone.

"Good. What have you been up to?"

"You know, the same old stuff. Work's been hectic."

"That's what they tell me," his friend chuckled. Elvin was a stay-at-home dad and he didn't mind letting people know. He didn't have a clock to punch, no boss looking over his shoulder. He was also smart enough to realize how good he had it in life. His wife, D.J., provided well for their family and she was both good-looking and level-headed. She'd be a rare catch in any part of the world, but especially in a rural, small town like Rasmus. The only thing that ever made Elvin question her judgment was that she still stayed married to him.

"You busy today? I was thinking about taking the Bell out on one of the lakes, do a little flat water." The Bell canoe was a sturdy beast meant for recreational paddling rather than racing. It was an entirely different animal than his wafer-thin Wenonah fiberglass racer, but it was a lot more stable. Walt knew that Elvin didn't like the Wenonah. You had to be careful in that

28

thing or you'd be swimming in an instant. Honestly, the racing canoe was beginning to show its age. Too many submerged boulders and hidden stumps had punctured the Wenonah's hide over the years, the bottom of the boat beginning to look like a patchwork quilt. She'd need upgrading before the next Marathon.

"You said the Bell, right?" Elvin was making sure he'd heard correctly. He'd been duped before.

"Yeah, you up for it?"

"Sure. Where are we going? Shambarger Lake is closed for the season. Jane's Lake sound good?"

"Too round. The breeze will be blowing, and there's no place to hide. We'll end up fighting the wind the whole time. I'd rather go somewhere long and stringy. We need some water with a lot of shoreline cover. How about Pickerel Lake?" Pickerel Lake was a bit of a drive, but it was narrow and protected by tall trees all the way around, with lots of navigable back bays for shelter. At least they wouldn't be spinning in the wind, and Walt had his own reasons for liking Pickerel Lake.

"That'll work. I'll be at your house in twenty minutes."

"Great. That'll give me time to get the Bell on the roof." Walt hung up and started to load the heavy craft on top of the Suzuki. Halfway through he was beginning to wonder if this was such a good idea, wondering whether the Suzuki would even make it to the lake and back. Should they go somewhere closer? He finally decided to stick with the original plan. In for a penny, in for a pound. He finished lashing the bow and stern lines to the vehicle, running two nylon straps across the middle of the boat for good measure. Elvin was just pulling up in his Ford Ranger, parking in the weeds off to the side of Blueberry Circle, when Walt cinched the last knot.

"Hey," Walt called.

"Hey," his friend hollered back. "Walt, have you and your friends living back here on the edge of civilization ever given thought to the idea of fixing that road? I'm lucky I made it without getting stuck. I don't know how you get to work every day."

"What are you talking about? We just graded it three weeks ago."

"With what? A teaspoon?"

"Seriously, three weeks ago."

"You're making that up. Who did the work for you?"

"My neighbor. He has a small plow truck. He spent the whole day trying to smooth out the bumps."

"I figured." That explained a lot. "You might want to use some real equipment next time. They've got these things nowadays, you might have heard of them. They're called 'road graders.' Are you about ready?"

"Yeah, just let me get the cushions and paddles and put Doofus in the house." His dog was standing on the front porch. Walt whistled and the golden retriever obediently went inside. He eased the sliding door closed, grabbed his gear from the shed, and the two men got quickly underway. It was in no way Walt's fault that they had to pass the Deer Track Inn on their way to the lake.

"What's this all about?" Elvin exclaimed when he first saw the scene. He was talking about the yellow vinyl tape surrounding the front of the little roadhouse. "POLICE LINE DO NOT CROSS" was repeated endlessly in bold, black lettering. Walt eased off the gas and slid the Samurai to a halt in the gravel lot out front.

"I heard they had a little trouble. Somebody busted up the place. Let's take a quick look." It was pure coincidence that they were driving in this direction, Walt kept telling himself. Sure, he believed that, just like he believed in the Easter Bunny.

"I don't know, Walt, it's got police tape all around it. This might not be such a good idea." Elvin leaned his head to the center of the vehicle to get a better view, noticing that the window on the left side of the building had been smashed out and the door was hanging loosely from a broken frame. Nobody had gotten around to fixing either one.

"Just for a minute, Elvin, come on. You can wait out here if you want to." Walt didn't know what he was hoping to find, just that he felt a little closer to Pam by being here.

"Do what you want; I thought we were going fishing. I'll hang out in the car and hit the horn if I see anyone coming." At this point in their relationship, Elvin knew that telling Walt something was "not such a good idea" wasn't going to deter the man. It had about the same effect as waving a red flag in front of an angry bull.

"Thanks." Walt jumped out of the Samurai and ducked under the vinyl barrier, disappearing through the doorway. It was dark inside the building, and he couldn't locate a light switch. It must be somewhere behind the bar. A little daylight filtered through the broken window and the open door. His eyes slowly adjusted to the dimly lit room. Two tables were upended and a half dozen chairs lay strewn about the room. One chair was in pieces near the bar, its ladder back reduced to a pile of broken spindles. The back bar was buried in a rubble of broken liquor bottles and tiny shards of sports-themed mirrors. The door frame was cracked on the latch side from top to bottom, and the top hinge had been ripped completely free from its perch. There had either been one nasty brawl here or someone had come on a personal mission to destroy the place. In either case, Pam hadn't gone down without a fight.

Walt sat back for a minute, trying to picture the moment when things had gone awry. Some loser must have tried to rob the Deer Track, broken in the front door after closing, and Pam had battled with all her might. That's the only way Walt could explain this kind of devastation. If it had been just a fight, a couple of locals going at it with one another, Pam would have pulled her gun from behind the bar and told everyone to get the hell out. Pam never tolerated that kind of stuff.

"What did you learn?" Elvin asked as Walt slid back behind the wheel.

"The place is a mess. Somebody really did a number on it."

"Was it a robbery or some kind of a bar fight? Where'd you hear about it, anyway?"

"Don Frederics with the sheriff's department told me. They don't really know how it went down, but Pam got hurt and she's in the hospital." There was no use telling Elvin *why* the sheriff's department felt obliged to come out to his house and grill him. He didn't want to tell his friend that he himself was a *suspect* in the whole damn thing. No, Walt wasn't in the mood for that conversation.

"Is she going to be alright?"

"Don't know."

"What hospital?"

"Don't know." The two men rode in silence the rest of the way to Pickerel Lake.

Walt had a lot going through his head. He missed Pam, missed her more now knowing that he couldn't see her. That's usually how things went: you didn't really notice how badly you needed something until it was gone. It was hard to believe anyone would want to hurt her, but she was a strong-willed woman. Some punk, or more than one punk, trying to shake her down for the night's take, well that wasn't going to fly with Pam. He'd learned this summer that she was not a woman to be trifled with.

When the two friends finally arrived at the lake there was one other truck parked at what the Michigan State Conservation Department generously listed as a "boat access site." "Access" was too strong of a word. The launch at Pickerel Lake was actually no more than that place where the deeply rutted "access road," running directly beneath the high-voltage transmission lines and their sixty-foot steel towers, abruptly dumped into the water. The power lines, with their constant buzzing overhead, bisected the lake neatly in two, and the "road" picked up again on the far shore. You needed a good truck and a very small boat to get on Pickerel Lake. Four-wheel drive was advised, but not always required, to get your craft back out. God help you if it rains. Walt pulled off to the side, next to a dark green Chevy Tahoe with government plates.

It only took a few minutes to unlash the Bell canoe and get out on the water. Walt sat in the stern and his friend took the bow. The two men paddled to the north, hugging the near shoreline in silence. If there was another craft on this lake it must be tucked away in one of the back bays. The wind was blowing steadily from the west, but Walt and Elvin remained sheltered by the tall trees that grew along the edge.

"Do you want to fish here or some other spot?" Walt asked. They were on the edge of one of the deeper holes. Pickerel Lake was really no more than a flooded stream channel with a small dam located at the southern end. The original channel contained a handful of holes that went sixteen to eighteen feet deep. The rest of the lake was at most five or six feet deep, sometimes less. What resulted was some great fishing along these transition zones. Walt looked over the side. He could see where the cabbage weeds and the brown silt bottom dropped off precipitously to a murky gloom.

"Sure. Here works." Elvin was already casting his line in the water. Two minutes later he began fighting his first fish of the day. He landed a small northern pike, nineteen inches in length. Not big enough to keep, but big enough to put a smirk on Elvin's face. Sometimes this would tick Walt off to no end, that his friend was always taking that first cast while Walt was still positioning the boat. There were days when the first cast was the only cast that caught a fish and that would especially piss him off. Today it didn't seem to matter as much. Walt was hurting. He had a lot on his mind and too much time on his hands. Fishing was a distraction, but not a good enough distraction. It allowed time for contemplation. He almost looked forward to working tomorrow just to get his mind off of Pam.

The two men didn't talk much, just enjoyed the autumn day and the quiet of being on the water. Eventually Elvin broke the stalemate.

"Hey Walt, did you notice anything about that truck back at the launch?"

"What about it?"

"Notice it has government plates but no decals, no markings? Is that one of the Conservation Department trucks?" The U.S. Geological Service where Walt worked shared a building with the State Conservation Department. Walt knew the handful of guys who worked there pretty well, and he should recognize their fleet vehicles.

"Could be. They all look pretty much alike. That Tahoe doesn't have any door decals, which is a bit unusual. Unmarked isn't really their thing."

"Don't you find it strange that we've been out here half the day, but still haven't seen another boat?"

"Strange that we haven't seen another fisherman?"

"Strange that we haven't seen another boat, *period.* Where's our Conservation Officer pal? "

"Small game season opened yesterday. Maybe he's out looking for poachers."

33

"Squirrel poachers?" This would be a new category of stupid, if ever there were one. Why would you go to the trouble of coming all the way out here for illegal squirrel hunting? The trees surrounding the lake were more jack pine than hardwood, and there wasn't enough mast crop to support a good squirrel population.

"Deer poachers, genius. Hunting deer with a .22 rifle, out of season." For being such a smart guy, Elvin could say some stupid things.

"That would make some sense," Elvin agreed sheepishly. "But why the empty trailer?" The Tahoe had an empty boat trailer attached to the hitch, which would certainly suggest that there was a boat around here someplace. "I mean, you'd think if you're pulling an empty trailer there would be a boat to go with it. Besides, if you were taking a boat out to look for poachers or guys fishing without licenses, why would you go to a lake where there aren't any other boats on the water?"

"You're suggesting that the Conservation Department is somehow bound by the rules of logic," Walt answered. Both men guffawed at that.

It was well into the afternoon when they decided to head back home. They'd landed a handful of northerns, two largemouth bass, a half-dozen perch and one wayward walleye. None of the fish were big enough to keep. The two men still hadn't seen another boat on the water. By the time they got back to the launch the green Tahoe with government plates was gone. Neither Elvin nor Walt could figure out how a boat might have slipped past them unnoticed. Then again, maybe there'd never been a boat.

The drive back was quiet. Walt and Elvin didn't have much left to discuss. One other car went by headed in the opposite direction somewhere around Lovells, an older burgundy sedan of some sort. A few miles later they noticed a petite blond girl, not much more than eleven or twelve years old, walking along the road's shoulder carrying a package under her jacket. She was probably on her way to a friend's house. There weren't any houses in sight, but that's what you did for entertainment if you were a kid in these parts: walk or ride your bike. It amazed Walt that there were still places in this world where people could trust their underage daughter to trek a country road by herself.

The two men finally passed the Deer Track Inn on their way back to Walt's. Someone had affixed a piece of plywood over the broken window in the front of the bar and the door appeared to have been nailed shut from the inside. Otherwise things looked the same as they had that morning. The door frame was still fractured and one hinge was no longer attached. The temporary patches would barely keep the building secure until morning. Funny that it hadn't been repaired yesterday, but the good samaritan that did the fixing probably had bigger fish to fry. Maybe it was Pam's new boyfriend doing the work in his spare time. Whoever did it certainly wasn't a carpenter. The door would probably get repaired for real tomorrow, once the lumber yard was open for business.

Back at the house the two men unloaded the canoe into Walt's shed and Elvin scurried off to join his wife for supper. Walt let Doofus out into the yard. There wasn't much in his refrigerator, but he managed to scrounge up a can of tuna and a packet of quinoa in the pantry. One bottle of home-brewed beer from the back room washed it down. It wasn't the healthiest meal, but beggars can't be choosers. He'd have to pick up some fresh fruit next time he went to town. He turned on the radio, the hurtful blues of Sonny Boy Williamson filtering in from one of the public radio stations south of Traverse City. Walt popped the top on his porter and the dog joined him on the couch. Tomorrow would be better, he thought. Tomorrow could only be better.

FIVE

The Girl

People often mistook her for being a lot younger than she really was. Sure, she was still a kid, but she wasn't a *little* kid. She was practically an adult. It wasn't her fault that she was short. You could blame that on her mom, who wasn't quite five feet tall herself. Her dad, well, let's just say he wouldn't be playing professional basketball anytime soon. It didn't help that she had fair hair and wide eyes, which, while they might become assets later in life, right now made her look like some kind of toy doll, all innocent and everything. Say what you want, she was old enough to be out here right now, by herself, with a .22 long rifle tucked under her jacket.

The girl knew she wasn't supposed to take the gun out of the house, not without her dad. Like a lot of kids around here she'd gotten her hunter safety certificate shortly after her tenth birthday. She knew the rules. That first fall she'd spent cutting her teeth on small game, right alongside her father: rabbits, squirrel, things that were relatively easy to hit with a rifle. A lot of people around here spent a chunk of the fall shooting grouse and woodcock, but most of the time they used shotguns. A shotgun had a lot of kick, and it was hard on your shoulder, especially if you weren't all that big to begin with. Besides, grouse and woodcock were unpredictable as could be. Once they left the ground you never knew which way the birds were going to go: up, down, sideways. They were *totally* crazy. She'd been told that bird hunting was nearly impossible using a twenty-two, unless you were *really* good. The girl wasn't *really* good yet, but bit by bit she was getting there.

That second year, when she was just eleven, was more of the same. There were a few trips to the tall oak stands and a handful of bushytails for the stew pot. In December she and her dad went to the Upper Peninsula for a weekend; everybody around here just calls it "the U.P." Her cousins had a farm up there, a little place near Pickford, and they all loaded up on snowshoe hare in the wet areas behind the fields.

When she turned twelve her dad sat alongside her in a deer blind the morning of November fifteenth, watching as she took her first buck with a Marlin lever-action thirty-thirty. It wasn't a big deer, just a small fella with two spiked antlers a good five inches in length. The girl was really excited when she first pulled that trigger. When she recovered the deer it was kind of cool but kind of sad all at the same time. Being responsible for the death of a thing that big, well, it somehow seemed *different* than just killing a squirrel or a rabbit. Still, she was the first person with something hanging on the buck pole that opening day, and that counted for something: *her,* an itty-bitty twelve-year-old girl. It must have made some of those crotchety old hunters feel more than a little bit jealous. That was the best part.

This fall had been a bit of a bummer. Her dad was putting in a lot of OT at work (that means overtime, as if you didn't know!). He wasn't around much and didn't have the time to take her shooting. Here it was, more than two weeks into the season, and he *still* hadn't taken her out hunting *even one single time* yet. There wasn't much else to do for a kid her age. She'd never broken the rule about taking the gun out by herself, not before today, but she needed to do something besides the usual bumming around town. Besides, she was *a little freaked out* by what she'd seen this weekend.

Getting out in the woods seemed like a *brilliant* change of pace. "Brilliant" was on her vocab list at school this week. The girl knew she was taking a risk, sneaking the rifle out of the house on a Sunday afternoon, but sometimes you just *had to take a chance.* As long as she didn't get caught it wouldn't be such a big deal. The girl was smart about it. She wouldn't go shooting right by the house. She hiked a good five miles to the west, which might seem like a lot to a city kid, but was a drop in the bucket for a girl like her, a kid raised to roam. She went way out by the lake, where almost *nobody* went this time of year. Unfortunately there weren't many bushytails hanging around the lake either. It had been a long time and she'd forgotten how Pickerel Lake was completely surrounded by pine trees. They should have named it "Piney Lake."

There was a pair of vehicles at the boat launch. When she saw the two trucks parked at the end of the dirt path she decided to avoid the shoreline entirely. It was probably just some goofy fishermen out there, but still, they'd be wondering why a kid her age was hunting out here all by herself. She'd forgotten to grab anything blaze orange to wear so she was already breaking one law. Her dad hadn't gotten around to buying licenses yet, for himself or for her, so there was a second problem. Even if she had an orange vest and a license, she wasn't supposed to be out here with a gun unless she was accompanied by an adult age eighteen or older. Three strikes and you're out, that's what they'd say if anybody caught her, so she decided to stay clear of the lake and everything around it. Maybe it wasn't such a good idea to take *any* shots at anything. The girl wandered around the woods for a brief while, looking for varmints that she *could have shot* had she been of a shooting mind, then started down the road towards home. She slipped the twenty-two underneath her jacket, not wanting it to appear quite so obvious.

It turned out she'd made a couple of really good decisions: not shooting any squirrels while she was out there, and hiding the rifle under her coat. Around the midpoint of her hike back to the house that green truck from the boat launch passed her on the road. It was pulling an empty boat trailer, which honestly wasn't all that unusual if you were from around here. People did a lot of strange things that weren't that strange to the people doing them. The guy in the truck slowed down a little bit as he passed by, like maybe he was checking her out or something. For a minute she was afraid he was going to stop. She almost had *a freakin' heart attack,* but then he kept right on driving. That was a relief. She'd hate to have to explain herself, what she was doing out here with a gun all by herself. Besides, the driver kind of looked like he might be a cop or something. She was very glad he hadn't been drawn to her earlier by the pop-pop of gunfire. Sometimes you had to take a chance, but not *that big* of a chance, not for squirrel stew.

She'd walked another mile when that second truck from the boat launch flew past. It wasn't really a truck, more like one of those little imported things that *pretend* to be a truck. This time they had a canoe tied to their roof, and the two guys in this fake truck didn't even bother to slow down. She'd been half right about there being goofy fishermen at the lake. Again she felt a slight relief. There was way too much traffic on this road. The girl realized it would be smarter to cut through the woods, even if the walking was that much tougher. She quickly got off the highway and slipped through the forest.

SIX

Walt Pitowski

He forgot to set his alarm and was running late. Then again, it seemed he was always running late on Mondays. A cloud of blue smoke was chasing the Samurai down the road all the way into town and beyond. The cloud of smoke had been following him around for months now, and Walt knew it wasn't a good sign. There were other clouds in his life, but this one was growing all too real. He could see it and taste it. The engine had that telltale sound of metal hitting metal, like the noise you'd get if the faces of two hammers were rhythmically slapping against one other. Rod knock. Catastrophic engine failure on the way. The Suzuki's days were numbered, and this might well be day zero. He eased off the gas, knowing it wouldn't make any difference but hoping for the best anyways. When he reached the traffic signal in town his cloud had grown and was now enveloping the little vehicle as he waited for the light to change. Walt was fairly certain that people were staring at him, but then, how could they not?

"Screw it," he swore, turning right on the red light despite the street sign telling him it was forbidden. He could always claim that the warning wasn't visible through all the smoke. By the time he got to the northern edge of Rasmus, the two hammers hitting each other had turned into a pair of bulldozers going at it. "This is it," Walt cursed.

Who knew that the coming of end times would announce itself so clearly? Still the Suzuki kept on rolling. Two more miles and he'd be safely at the office. He passed the Kingdom Hall on his right, a handful of cabins scattered in the woods just beyond. A dead deer carcass lay on the left shoulder of the road. It was a fresh kill, must have happened overnight. One mile yet to go. The bulldozers under the hood had been replaced by a Farm Combine Demolition Derby. He rolled into the parking lot just as the engine seized, one small victory in an otherwise losing battle. Tom Dewers was standing outside the front door, perfectly positioned to witness the debacle.

Walt eased his way out of the Suzuki slowly, thinking that if he didn't make a big deal of it Dewers might not either. He was dead wrong.

"Hey Pitowski, your car just took a dump."

Walt turned around and bent over, staring at the ground beneath his engine, where five plus quarts of antifreeze were now seeping into the crush-and-run gravel. Steam was weeping from beneath the hood. The Samurai was toast.

"Shit!" There wasn't much else he could say.

"Hey, look at the bright side. You finally get to buy a new car."

"Yeah, with what?" Dewers should know as well as anyone that Walt didn't have any money; not "new car" money, anyhow. "I'm broke, asshole."

Dewers brushed off the insult. He'd heard worse. "You've got all that overtime coming from the Taos trip, right? Plus the per diem? I know you were too cheap to spend it while you were out there. That should get you into something that moves."

"Maybe," Walt agreed reluctantly. He was hoping to save the windfall from his trip out west, stash it away for a new canoe or something that he truly *wanted*. So much for grand ideas and chasing your dreams.

Dewers didn't have a lot of compassion for Pitowski; he'd seen this little vignette too many times before. "We're running late. Get your gear and let's get moving. You can deal with your pile of junk after lunch."

"Just give me a minute."

Dewers and Walt were supposed to work together this day, performing a ground water and stream flow analysis at the old hatchery site. Apparently the hatchery grounds contained a pair of underground fuel oil storage tanks that had been gradually leaking into the soil. The Department of Environmental Quality had been monitoring the site for over ten years, keeping track of the leakage through special monitoring wells. It would probably have been more cost efficient to dig the tanks out and backfill the soil a decade ago, but at the time there was a concern about digging too close to the stream bed. Either that or somebody had a personal financial interest in the time-consuming and costly monitoring wells. Walt wondered how many "consultants" had their fingers in the pie. The project had dragged on forever, and was just now winding down. The DEQ said everything was clean and good to go, and had even signed off that the remediation was completed.

Everything was good to go up until a few days ago, that is. Walt still couldn't figure out why the USGS was involved. It must be that somebody higher up wanted a second opinion. Hell, for a decade the contamination was the State of Michigan's problem. The State had owned the building since the nineties and it was their oil tanks that were screwing up the groundwater. It was the County's problem, too, since the County inherited the property from the State when the hatchery first closed. It was the City of Rasmus' problem because the building and grounds were inside the city limits. It was the Grand Limoneaux Anglers Association's problem because they were concerned that the leaking oil would contaminate a pristine trout stream, a stream upon which they'd spent tens of thousands of dollars trying to improve fish habitat. What it hadn't been, up until today, was Walt Pitowski's problem, and he still wasn't sure why he was getting dragged into it. "Because my boss said so," was the best he could come up with.

"Walt, you coming or what?" The sound of Dewers' voice snapped him back to the present.

"Let me run in and grab my briefcase off my desk."

In a way Walt was grateful for the hatchery project. For starters it was only a few miles from his office, which might give him a chance to sneak back to his desk and figure out what to do about his dead car. It was far preferable to having to drive a government truck to Flint or Saginaw, or to any of the more remote locations to which he was often dispatched. Secondly, and this was no small perk, working in town meant that Walt was likely to bump into people. With people, especially small town people, came gossip, and with gossip came knowledge. Walt was betting that by the end of this day he'd have a lot more information about Pam's condition and location.

He got to his desk and there was a yellow Post-It note affixed to the computer monitor. "Call Amberson," was scrawled in black ink, but no phone number. "To hell with that," Walt decided, reaching to crumple the note up and pitch it in his wastebasket, before changing his mind. If Sheriff's Deputy Amberson wanted Walt to call it was either to question him about that mess at the Deer Track, a subject about which Walt knew next to nothing, or to question him about the idiot at the Compactor, which he didn't feel like discussing. Either way, it would be simpler to pretend that he hadn't seen the note and deal with the consequences later. The note could stay right where it was.

Walt grabbed the phone, and made a quick call to Elvin. The phone rang seven times, but nobody picked up. After the seventh ring the answering machine finally clicked on. The grainy recording told him "You've reached Elvin and D.J. You've got thirty seconds or less to state your case as to why we should call you back."

Walt blurted out a quick message: "Hey Elvin, it's me. If you know anybody selling a cheap truck, let me know ASAP. Thanks." It was a long shot, but sometimes long shots pay off.

Dewers was waiting outside in the front seat of a white Ford F-250, engine idling. Walt snatched his briefcase and hurried out to meet him, hopping into the passenger seat.

"What took you so long?"

"I had to make a quick call."

"Did you see that note on your desk?"

"What note?" Lying was easier than he'd thought it would be. And a little practice never hurt.

"Never mind. You'll find out soon enough."

Five minutes later they were in the parking lot of the hatchery, Walt slipping into his Red Ball neoprene waders while his partner carried equipment down the hillside. The sun was already thawing the ground and it was promising to be a beautiful fall day.

"Pitowski, are you gonna help me carry this stuff or what?" Dewers had already lugged two loads of equipment down the hill and was coming back for his third.

"Give me a second, I'm trying to put my waders on." It was bad enough Walt had to be the one getting wet while Dewers stayed on dry land. The river was gentle here, not much more than chest deep in the middle. The current was not that strong. It wasn't that big of a deal; he'd have a gauge set up in a matter of minutes. Still, why did *he* always get the shaft? Just once, why didn't the *other guy* have to do the crap work? Walt grabbed two heavy boxes of supplies and balanced a tripod across his shoulder, then headed down the slope. He'd never failed to carry his weight and nobody was going to say otherwise.

By noon things were going better than expected and Dewers offered to take the truck and pick up some sub sandwiches for lunch. It wasn't exactly the same as winning a new truck, but Walt wasn't one to turn down a free meal. He could hear the F-250 start at the top of the rise and then the spatter of wheels on gravel as his partner left for the store. Walt stepped behind a patch of bushes along the southern side of the building, just beyond the spiral stairway at the base of the slope. He needed to take a leak and the public restrooms at the far side of the property were locked. Nobody would see him in the thick foliage. He finished his business and returned to the stairs, taking a seat on the second-from-last step.

Ten minutes later he was still waiting for Dewers, waiting for his lunch. Walt paced around at the base of the stairs, stretching his legs and his sore back. The Hatchery looked better than it did five years ago, but not by much. Walt had never really looked closely at the building, for as often as he'd driven past it. Somebody had gotten around to scraping off the old lead paint and put on a fresh coat of white. It still wasn't pretty, but the new layer might save the original wood siding.

Looking at it from where Walt stood, this wing of the building was two stories high and at least twenty-five feet wide. The wall in front of him contained a giant service door, almost like you'd find on a barn, and a smaller entryway. Both were sealed shut. Three evenly spaced windows looked out from the second story. The one nearest him, just to the right of the stairway's summit, no longer contained any glass. If you got to the peak of the stairs and tried, *really tried,* you might be able to reach across to the opening and sneak into the building that way. There was also about a fifty-percent chance that you would slip and bust your ass, falling eighteen feet to the ground below. Walt didn't feel like testing his hypothesis. Either way, somebody should board up that opening; keep the animals out.

He climbed the crumbling steps. At the top of the stairs he began walking away from the hill and along the narrow ell which comprised much of the building's second level. There were more bushes and weeds here, and a makeshift lean-to covered with tar paper extending from the gutter to the ground. It looked like a giant skateboard ramp with "KEEP OUT!" spray painted in white. It might as well have said "HEY KIDS, LOOK HERE!" Walt took a peek around the corner of the structure at the outstretched ell and saw a locked and closed door. There were five more windows along the building's side, none of which were busted. That in itself was surprising. In a bigger town, say Flint or Saginaw or Detroit, hell, even in Traverse City (which didn't usually have the scale of problems associated with large urban areas), these panes of glass would have been the first to get smashed. Maybe the kids in Rasmus weren't so bad after all.

Walt had a hard time getting around the western edge of the building, where the honeysuckle and tree of heaven had really taken over. This hadn't been weeded in twenty years. Funny that on this high side of the building, the side closest to the original parking lot (they'd long ago created a nicely paved lot on the far side of the river, down on the bottom where the land was flat and wide) and furthest from the road, nobody gave a damn about appearances. If it didn't show to the tourists it didn't matter. "Typical government," he thought. An ancient rose bush tugged and pulled at his shirt as he fought past. He worked his way around the northern face of the old barn, passing five windows that mirrored the five on the opposite side. He tried peering through their dirty glass, but the blinds were drawn and he couldn't see a thing.

A cement stairway straddled this side of the hill, too, a straight run of thirty or so steps to the bottom. Walt's path to the stairs was blocked on both ends by a locked gate, so he began cautiously creeping down the eastern slope, cutting through its thick trees and brush. At the base of the hill he found meadow once more. This side of the building, the original "front," was defined by two sets of tall columns accenting what had once been the grand entrance to the old girl. Large windows on either side of the entrance were too filthy to see inside. At the northeast corner of this wall was one last boarded-up door, an unassuming opening that had most likely been the employees' entrance. Around the corner the eastern facade presented two more windows (still intact) for each level, a recess of about twenty feet, and then two more sets of windows, one high and one low. Of these windows, the one on the ground floor closest to the southeast corner had indeed been shattered and replaced with plywood. His faith in the town's youth was fully restored. That concluded Walt's tour of the building's perimeter, and, outside of a few good places to urinate, he'd discovered nothing. Where was Dewers with those damn sandwiches, anyway?

He strolled back to the bottom of the stairs. He sat down. He waited a few minutes and then stood back up. He walked to the river and back again. Walt sat down on the steps and couldn't get comfortable, got up and leaned against the stairway's railing. He checked his watch. It had been thirty-five minutes since Dewers went to get lunch and the sub shop was less than two miles away. This was getting ridiculous.

Walt walked over to the corner of the building, the one where the window was broken and its plywood patch was just beginning to warp. Two corners of the wood had worked themselves free from the window frame. Somebody had done a hasty repair job. Somebody had probably used nails instead of screws. Everybody knows that nails will pop loose sooner or later.

Walt pushed gently on the plywood and nails in the wet wood bent and groaned. The gap widened just a bit. He pushed some more, slightly harder this time, and heard a short crack as the top left corner of the board broke off, falling to the floor inside. A single beam of light reached into the cavernous room beyond. Walt pressed his face to the tiny, triangular opening. He didn't have a full view of the room, he was just trying to get a glimpse of what lay inside.

To his left Walt could make out floor-to-ceiling cabinets, their cupboard doors mildewed and twisting. He could see drab industrial green paint on the walls and the surface of a workbench covered with dusty glass jars and rusting instruments lay to his right. How could they have left all that stuff behind? It was hard to see much else. What looked to be a metal desk was pushed against the far wall. Dust mites floated on the beam of light. Had the person looking in the window been anyone other than Walt Pitowski, he might have stopped to reflect on the eerie beauty of this scene; at least until he looked down, and saw the dead man lying on the floor.

SEVEN

The Girl

There were lots of things annoying about being "only" thirteen. One of the big ones, and older people rarely understood this when you tried to explain it to them, was the word "only" being used as a qualifier whenever someone brought up your age. Do all adults go around dismissing everything that others have to say because they are "only" twenty-four years old? Probably, but it still doesn't make it right. What *is* the magic number, she wondered? At what point are you no longer a kid? At what age do your opinions and desires start to matter to the world at large? "Only" thirty? "Only" forty? "Only" just now eligible for social security? It didn't make any sense. The word itself should be banned from use.

Some of those markers were easy, identifiable ages where you were no longer considered "only" such-and-such. The problem was that they were all so *arbitrary*. A person could get a part-time job at fourteen, but not in certain industries, and you couldn't work after certain hours during the school year. Those hours happened to coincide with when a business might actually *need* you. You could drive a car once you turned sixteen, but not before, and only if you jumped through a bunch of hoops to get your license. At eighteen you could vote. When you turned twenty-one you could legally drink alcohol, but that one was a joke, and everybody around here knew it. Most of her friends had taken their first drink, taken *many* first drinks, and they were a long ways away from being "only twenty-one." She was just now starting the eighth grade, but she knew kids that had been drinking and smoking for over a year now. Don't even get her started on the topic of sex. She hadn't done it, not yet, but she knew plenty of classmates that claimed they did.

One of the other big annoyances that came with being "only" thirteen was that there was nothing to do around here. She'd lived on the outskirts of Rasmus her entire life and she knew practically everybody in this whole town. Her mom and dad had both told her about a zillion times how lucky she was to get to grow up in a place like this, where you didn't have to lock your doors and there was fresh air and woods and streams and all that blah-blah-blah about the great outdoors, and that this was *way* better than the place where they grew up. It was more than annoying, their little speech, and she tried to think of an appropriate word for it. She was having trouble coining something that really summed it up: the best she had so far was "mega-annoying," but that sounded *so* twenty years ago. She'd have to keep working at it.

When you were "only" thirteen you didn't have a lot of options. You couldn't work and you couldn't drive a car. You couldn't smoke, at least not in front of people, and even if you did smoke it was practically a full-time job just getting the cigarettes. Plus, where was she going to get the money in the first place? Smoking was expensive. Swiping a few cigarettes from your mom or dad and bumming them off older friends was about your only chance. There were no amusement parks or arcades nearby, and besides, those things were expensive, too. You could hunt, but only with an adult. She was one of the few girls around here that was *really into* hunting, but she rarely got the chance. The movie theater was alright, but it "only" had one screen, which meant you only got to see a new movie once a week. Sometimes *that* movie sucked, and then you didn't go to the show for *two whole weeks!* No wonder some of her friends were already "doing it." At least it kept them busy.

So far she'd avoided boys, at least as anything other than friends. Not that she was frightened or anything, because she wasn't, not one little bit. Her sister was two years older than her and her sister had a boyfriend. For a while her sister had told her (in *way too much detail*) about the things she did with her boyfriend, and for a while the idea of "getting busy" sounded intriguing. Doing things with boys sounded both exciting and phenomenally gross. There were risks involved, because what happened if you accidentally got knocked up or got a disease or something?

The more she listened, however, the more she realized that her sister's boyfriend was a Totally Immature Idiot. Having watched her classmates, she was pretty certain that Immature Idiot Syndrome had infected every boy in this Whole Entire County. It was a pandemic, and there was nothing some guy could do for *her* that would make putting up with all of that Immature Idiot behavior worthwhile. Her sister made it sound like the risk was half the fun, which made the girl wonder if it was really that much fun to begin with. If the fun of "doing it" was all about the danger of something going wrong, weren't there easier and better ways to tempt fate? No boyfriends for this girl, at least not for a while.

All of this meant she had too much time on her hands and not enough to do. There were ways to fill the gaps, hanging out with friends after school and stuff like that. Hanging out only went so far and then your friends had to go home because they had an appointment or a music lesson or something, or sometimes just because their parents were Total Control Freaks. The girl wasn't burdened with any of those particular problems because both her mom and her dad worked full time, and sometimes they worked more than full time. They said it was what they had to do in order to "provide a better life" for her, which apparently included making her live in the middle of the freaking wilderness like they were all part of some survivalist TV show where there was never anything fun going on. On the plus side, they weren't around most of the day to bug her. They certainly couldn't afford music lessons or any of that stuff and, even if they could, what kind of a dork did they think she was? She wasn't about to start playing the piano or the banjo or accordion like some of the other hillbillies around here. Her sister wasn't any help, because her sister was too old to be seen hanging out with a kid that was "only" thirteen. Besides, her sister had that loser boyfriend to get all slobbery over.

Lately she'd gotten into the habit of watching people. Everybody watches people when you get right down to it. At school, at church, just walking down the street, it really didn't matter where. People were always checking out other people for one reason or another. Sometimes she'd catch folks staring at her, or staring at someone else, right up until the point where they got caught looking. Then they'd glance away, pretending like they weren't really looking at you or staring at the fat lady's butt or whatever, but you knew darn well they were. They'd get this guilty look on their face and look away real quickly, like maybe you hadn't noticed them doing it even when it was obvious what they'd been doing. They'd all of a sudden feign interest in some street sign, or a newspaper, or anything that was handy at the moment. Why couldn't they just admit it? They were *Gawking*, that's what they were doing! People are Such Freaks.

More than a few times she'd caught older guys staring at her and that creeped her out. This was different than the general category of "People Watching" that regular people like her enjoyed. She was talking about people *really staring* that creeped her out. What was their problem, anyway? She knew she was getting older herself, wasn't that far from "being a woman," as her mother liked to call it, but really, come on, you know? She was thirteen and her breasts weren't even that big yet, not like her friend Angie's. Her friends all told her she was really pretty, she had great hair and stuff like that, but what were they supposed to say? Would they really tell you if they thought you were butt-ugly? Probably not, even if you begged them for the truth. This was further proof of her "People are Such Freaks" theory of the universe.

Most of the guys, the ones creeping her out, were just older teenagers. A couple of them were guys in their twenties and thirties, you know, *really old guys* checking her out. It was downright *skeevy* is what it was. She learned pretty quickly that the thing to do, when she caught some old dude staring at her in *that way*, was to stare right back. Stare hard and show them you're not intimidated. Almost every time she'd done that it had worked. They'd backed down, slinking away like the nasty little dogs that they were: nasty, skeevy little dogs.

Right now, she was hanging out by those dilapidated old buildings behind the hatchery, smoking a cigarette. "Dilapidated," what a great word. She'd learned it this past week in vocab practice at school. It was late Friday afternoon. The girl had a great view of the back side to one of the office buildings on the main drag. People kept sneaking out the back door of that building to catch a quick smoke of their own. It was her favorite spot for People Watching. She was careful to stick close around the corner of the old shack whenever those other smokers came out of their offices, because everybody pretty much knows *everybody* in this town, and for sure someone was bound to tell one of her parents if they saw her puffing away. She was in enough shit with the folks already. Her grades had slipped a bit towards the end of last year. She didn't understand what the problem was: her grades weren't really *that* bad. All of a sudden her parents were griping about "C's," when everyone knows that a "C" is average. Heck, didn't *somebody* get to be average? We couldn't all be *above* average, could we? She'd tried to make this statistical argument with her mom one night, but it only made her mom angrier. Mothers just didn't get it.

She was standing in this spot Friday night, an hour or so after dinner. Usually the girl didn't come over here in the evenings, not unless she was hanging out with friends. This was more of a "right after school" kind of location. Sometimes it was a "cutting classes" location, but you had to be careful. It wasn't just the people coming out of the back of the building for smokes that might catch you: if you didn't watch exactly where you were

49

standing, people on the hatchery grounds could see you as well. Everybody in this town knew everybody else. But she'd made an exception, hanging around here Friday in this exact spot where she didn't often hang out. And when she made that exception, came to this place at a time when she usually wouldn't have, a strange thing happened. It happened *right here*, near these *dilapidated* buildings. At first she was frightened, more than a little, but now she was curious.

She'd been standing here behind the hatchery largely because this week's feature film sucked. Her mom hated it when she used that word, "sucked," but in this case it was One-Hundred Percent True. The movie was one of those animated things, with a bunch of big-shot actors doing the voiceovers. Once in a while she actually liked that sort of thing, especially if it had Johnny Depp in it. He was incredibly hot, and if there were any guys in this town the least bit like Johnny Depp, she'd have to rethink that whole "no boyfriend" thing. But Friday night's early show, well, a movie like that was guaranteed to be a Screamfest, with an audience full of bratty kindergartners and first graders and all other sorts of whiney, snot-nosed kids. No thank you sir, not for this girl. Her friend Angie insisted that she was going to the show, she didn't care if the theater was full of Screaming Monkeys from Hell. The girl still didn't want to go. Angie swore this was a great movie, and besides, what else were they going to do tonight? The girl told Angie that was fine then, Angie could just go by herself. She couldn't believe it when Angie actually took her up on the offer, so she was on her own until the show let out.

With nothing better to do the girl migrated to this very spot. She thought she'd have a quick cigarette and then maybe walk over to the Seven-Eleven and see if anybody else had skipped the movie. She couldn't be the *only one* who thought the movie was going to suck. It was almost dark out, and normally the girl wouldn't want to be standing around here this late, not by herself. It might not be entirely safe. Sure, she'd been here after dark on other occasions, but it was always with friends. Her plan was to have a quick one and then get going.

She was about to light the cigarette when she noticed a man sneaking down the hillside. It was unusual for anybody to be here at any time of day, let alone at dusk, when the hatchery was closed for the season. This was a spot for reckless teenagers, not for full-grown men to be prowling around at night. Any adult should know better. She didn't light the cigarette. Instead she

50

stuck tight behind the far corner of the dilapidated building and watched the man sneaking down the bluff.

It looked like he was stalking something, maybe a deer or some other animal? It took her a little while to figure out that there was another, older man already at the bottom of the hill. The older man was walking back up the exterior stairs, going into the hatchery building itself. Angie was going to be *so jealous* because this was *way more interesting* than some crappy animated film that didn't even have the voice of Johnny Depp in it. The girl knew something about watching people, and she was pretty good at it. She stayed in the shadows, waiting to spy movement from the younger man watching the older man.

The younger man eventually moved down through the trees then back up those old crumbly stairs on the outside of the building. He was following the old guy. She followed them both. She kept far enough behind that she wouldn't be spotted. The girl knew just where to hide, deep in a thicket of trees near the top of the stairwell, if she wanted to watch without being seen. She'd had lots of practice. The old guy let himself into the building. The younger guy was waiting around outside, but sneaky-like. It seemed pretty clear that the younger guy was trying to surprise the old guy. Maybe the old guy was about to get punked. After a few minutes there was a yell from the old guy inside, and then silence for a minute or two, and eventually the younger guy went inside, too.

Ten minutes later she'd heard a muffled bang, like one of the two guys in that giant white building tripped and crashed into a metal file cabinet or desk. Maybe the old guy got punked really good. Then the younger guy came back out carrying a bag, still crawling around all cat-burglar style along the outside wall of the building before disappearing into the trees on the far side of the hill. The girl lost sight of him at this point. She was more than a little worried he might double back this way. Should she stay put, or would he discover her hiding in the thicket on his way past? He might be mad that she'd been watching him. For twenty minutes she watched the hatchery door and still there was no sign of the old guy. It didn't look like the younger guy would be returning, either. He must have taken off in the other direction. The girl got an odd feeling something might be *seriously* wrong: the hairs on the back of her neck were standing on end. The old guy wasn't coming out and it was getting *really dark* outside. Ten more minutes passed before she slowly crawled out of the thicket, slinking through the trees until she was *way far away* from the hatchery building. Once she reached the parking lot the girl ran without stopping, as fast as she could, all the way to Seven-Eleven.

EIGHT

Walt Pitowski

"Pitowski, what part of 'keep your nose clean' is so overwhelmingly difficult for you to understand?" It was his new friend Deputy Frederics stepping out of the police cruiser in the parking lot atop the hill. He was noticeably unhappy. Amberson had just parked next to Frederics' vehicle with a matching county-issued Police Interceptor of his own. Sheriff Brimley himself had seen fit to leave the cozy confines of his office and was seated at the wheel of a gleaming white Ford Excursion, marked, of course, with a push bar protecting the front grill and all the extras. Here was a great use of tax dollars. Brimley didn't appear to be in any hurry to join the excitement, content to fiddle with paperwork in the front seat of the massive SUV. All three had light bars flashing red, white, and blue on the roofs of their vehicles. Thankfully they'd managed to cover the one mile from the courthouse with their sirens off. Even the lights seemed like overkill, seeing as how the guy in the hatchery was already dead. What was the rush?

"Hey, it's Deputy Dawg!" Walt shouted to Frederics with a sarcastic wave of his hand. Walt was seated at the top of the staircase. He'd called the sheriff's office as soon as he noticed the body. The county dispatcher seemed none too pleased upon receipt of this phone call: dead bodies were relatively uncommon around here other than those brought on via natural causes, avoidable accidents, unavoidable accidents, and the rare suicide. This didn't seem to fit any of those profiles and would probably mean extra work for everybody involved. "Sit still and don't touch anything," he was told, so that's what Walt did. Dewers came back with lunch. When told about the dead guy, he decided to stay in the truck. Dewers was a smart man. Walt sat at the top of the steps and managed to choke down a few bites of his sandwich before the police arrived.

"What did you say?" Frederics hadn't fully heard Walt's comment, but could only guess that it was some sort of insult. He approached the stairs at a brisk clip, with Amberson close behind. Sheriff Brimley still hadn't budged from the front seat of the albino Excursion.

"Never mind." If you had to explain a joke, it probably wasn't that funny.

"Pitowski. Why didn't you call me this morning?" It was Amberson's turn this time. He looked only slightly less perturbed than Frederics.

"Was I *supposed* to call you? Nobody told me."

"I left a message at your office." Amberson wasn't buying Walt's malarkey, not for one blessed minute. Walt knew damn well he was supposed to call him. "This morning," he added, for emphasis.

"Didn't get it." If there was one thing Walt knew about bluffing, it was that you should try to keep things simple. Don't oversell a lie. "I haven't been at my desk all day, though." He took another bite of his sandwich.

"Like hell," was all Amberson had to say to that.

"We received a report of a 10-54?" It was Frederics again, attempting to steer the conversation back to the reason they were here.

"You received a what?" Walt didn't appreciate the goofy cop-speak. Was a 10-54 some new kind of donut? Why couldn't these guys speak English? "A 10-54, is that some kind of stick up your butt?" There was nothing wrong with taking your shots when the opportunity arose.

"A dead guy," Amberson interpreted. Sometimes this was worse than having kids.

"Yeah, inside the building." Walt answered back. He set what remained of his lunch by the top of the stair railing and stood up. They obviously didn't care that Walt was hungry. Both of these guys could be incredibly self-centered. He was hoping a squirrel wouldn't steal the rest of his sub while he was out giving the guided tour.

"What were you doing inside the building?" It was Sheriff Brimley, having finally waddled over to join the other two officers. Walt noticed the deputies straightening their spines and instinctively adjusting their hats, trying to look more professional now that the boss was on the scene. It was almost laughable.

"I wasn't inside the building. I was looking through a window," Walt declared. He was not going to let them make him out to be the bad guy here.

Hell, he'd done the right thing and called 911 right away. What more did they want?

"Why were you looking through the window?" Frederics again.

What a suck-up, Walt thought. *Butt-kisser. Acting like he's leading an interrogation.*

"I was bored," Walt smiled. None of the others seemed to think his smile was appropriate. "What?" he asked. When they didn't answer, Walt stopped smiling.

"You were bored?" from Amberson. He took everything with a grain of salt, and he'd spent enough time listening to Pitowski to know that he had to wait. Sooner or later the man would quit screwing around and tell you what you needed to know.

"Yeah, bored. Dewers went to get lunch. We've been working here all morning. I was waiting for him to get back, was just looking around. I was bored." Two more cars pulled into the lot now, gumball lights on the roof flashing: a GMC Yukon and a newer Dodge Charger. These were the custom blue rides of the Michigan State Police. The State Police actually had their own paint color, if you could believe it, a shade that the Big Three manufacturers used only for them. Walt wondered why they needed their own special shade of blue. The only answer he could come up with was "entitlement." Walt was pretty certain that whoever stepped out of those two cars would be arrogant.

If it were determined that this guy had died from foul play, these entitled, arrogant troopers more than likely would be taking the lead in any investigation. Sure, there'd be some griping on the part of the county mounties, but in the end, they'd want State help with a full-blown murder investigation. Walt flashed back to what he'd seen lying on the floor of the hatchery: one old guy, scraggly white hair and beard, with a clean round hole in the middle of his forehead. Dried blood on the floor. It was hard to imagine it being any kind of an accident. Maybe Walt was wrong. He certainly hoped so. This could turn into a real goat rodeo.

"Did you touch anything?" Frederics again.

"Maybe the window frame. I was just looking around, thought I'd see what the inside of the building looked like." They seemed to be satisfied with that, for the time being at least. The two state troopers were standing with Amberson and Frederics now, getting ready to take over the show if it was required.

"Sheriff." The older of the two troopers spoke. His nameplate said "Murphy," a fifty-something guy with short silver hair under his cap and that starched look that says "I came minted from the same assembly line as every other trooper to ever wear this uniform." He even *smelled* like a cop; a mixture of Old Spice and Aqua Velva. He was tall and lean, clean shaven like he'd just come from the barber. In sum, he looked like a guy you just didn't want to cross. His partner was younger, if only by a decade, and built like a fireplug. Squat and muscular, he could've been a shot putter in college, say, twenty years before. The younger guy's nameplate read "Johnson," which Walt found quite humorous in a juvenile way. This guy was a short Johnson. "You called for backup?" Murphy asked.

Sheriff Brimley took charge of the situation, at least for the time being. "Glad you two could make it," to the state troopers. "Mr. Pitowski here is about to show us what he *claims* to have *accidentally* found. We might need your help if this turns out to be a murder scene. I'm hoping it isn't. Either way, I'd rather have you here on the front end than risk mucking it up." The state boys nodded in agreement. "Are you ready, Pitowski?"

"As I'll ever be." Walt led them down the hill.

He showed them the window with the missing pane. He showed them where he'd originally stood in the tall grass, how his feet were positioned and where his knees might have touched the wall. He showed them how he'd leaned against the window frame, so that he might better see inside. He didn't mention pushing against the plywood or accidentally breaking the corner piece off, because they really didn't need to know that part. He told them he'd found it exactly as it appeared now. Dewers was wise enough to stay clear of this mess, keeping a good ten feet between himself and the cloud of bad news that was Walt Pitowski. So far the cops hadn't bothered to collect Dewers' statement, but he knew they'd get around to it sooner or later.

"That's it?" Brimley asked, after making Walt repeat his story three times in excruciating detail and demonstrate exactly *where* he'd touched *what* on the building's exterior. Brimley was putting on a dog and pony show for the two troopers. He needed to let these guys know that the Shawono County Sheriff's Department was both thorough and professional.

"That's it," Walt confirmed.

"He's holding something back," Frederics chimed in. "I think he's lying." The deputy was certain he smelled a rat, and he wasn't going to hide his disdain. He was practically scowling.

Walt shot him a hard stare. *What is this guy's problem? Jerkwad. Who asked you, anyhow?* He was starting to believe that Frederics had it in for him.

"Great," Matt Amberson eventually sighed. He didn't sound like he thought anything was "great." He sounded tired. He sounded exactly like the man he was: a guy who'd stumbled into a career that he hadn't planned upon, with a childless wife that hated living in this town, the town she'd grown up in, and his fortieth birthday staring him down like the barrel of a gun. On top of it all, after fifteen plus years of serving the public, he was still very much considered an outsider by the people of Rasmus. He wasn't "born" here. He'd never truly "belong." Now he was looking at a dead body lying in an abandoned building and a class "A" troublemaker, Walt Pitowski, in the middle of it, whatever "it" was. Amberson ran through the list in his head and knew that he possessed all the key ingredients for both a midlife crisis and a nervous breakdown. Maybe it was time for a change.

Finally he turned and addressed both Walt and Tom. "You guys are done for the day, probably done working at the hatchery for quite a while. Pitowski, Dewers, pack up your gear and get out of here. Don't mess with anything else between here and your truck. Keep your mouths shut until we sort things out; don't start any wildfires with your tongues. We'll be in touch." He dismissed both men with a nod of his head, turning his attention to the boys in blue.

Five minutes later Walt was carrying his second and last load of equipment back up the hill and was almost to the truck when he heard Amberson's voice from the bluff below. "Pitowski! I still need to talk to you on that other matter. Make sure you call me tomorrow."

Yeah, like hell, Walt thought, but he didn't say it. "Great!" he finally shouted back.

NINE

"What the fuck, Walt?"

"What are you trying to say, Tom?" They were back in the front seat of the Ford pickup, and Dewers was giving him an ear full.

"You know damn well what I'm trying to say. I leave you alone for twenty minutes so I can pick up lunch and you have to go snooping around where you don't belong until you stumble across a dead man. Jesus, Walt, working with you is like hanging out with Bad Luck Schleprock. Marcus is gonna be so pissed off when he finds out about this. This was a simple job. We could have been in and out and back at the office before four. We could have been sipping beers and eating nachos by five. You're a walking disaster, man. What the fuck?"

"You should really try to clean up your language. It's not very professional." Dewers shot him a menacing look: Walt was the last man on earth who ought to be chastising someone for foul language, and he knew it. "It's not like I deliberately went looking for trouble, Tom. Would you rather the old guy just lay there rotting, unnoticed, for another two years?"

"You're a piece of work, you know that? I'd rather it not have a damn thing to do with *us*. I'd rather someone *else* happen to discover the dead guy. If this guy died from some freak accident, well, la-di-da, you've got a great story to tell your buddies while you're paddling down the Grand Limoneaux next summer, but what if it's more than that? Did you even think about that, smart guy, even for a second? What if somebody killed this guy, which, according to you, looks more than likely, and our names are splattered all over the news? All of a sudden you're soaking in it, Madge. There's a killer around town somewhere, and now he's going to think you and I know a lot more than we actually do. Maybe he'll think we're feeding evidence to the cops. That's grief I can live without. Why couldn't you just sit down peacefully and wait until I got back with lunch?"

"It was over forty minutes. Why couldn't you get back with the subs sooner?" That was the last the two men had to say to one another. It was a short ride back to the field station, but long enough for Walt to consider his future. Maybe it was time to get out of Rasmus, bail on this place for good. Starting over in a new locale had its appeal. There was a job posting at the main office down in Lansing, but city life never did appeal to him. New Mexico was looking more attractive by the minute.

Back at the office, the first thing Walt did was head straight to the boss's desk to make a full report. He'd rather get there first, before Dewers had a chance to give *his* version of events. Marcus Washington wasn't in. He'd taken the rest of the day off, as a matter of fact. Walt was partially disappointed, but it did allow him to dodge one potentially ugly discussion. He knew in his heart that Washington would somehow make it out to be Walt's fault that the hatchery cleanup was stalled. His boss would accuse Walt of deliberately creating problems. He would suggest that Walt was negligent in his duties, poking around a vacant structure when he should have been hard at work. By the end of their "little talk," whenever that talk might occur, Washington would be blaming Walt for the economic and social downfall of the entire county. He was grateful for the reprieve.

Walt got back to his own desk, crumpled the note that told him to "call Amberson," and pitched it in his wastebasket. He had until tomorrow to worry about that one. He checked his voicemail, but there hadn't been any calls. Funny how few messages you received when you no longer had a wife or a girlfriend. He still hadn't learned anything more about Pam. So much for the idea that working at the hatchery would allow him to churn the rumor mill. Walt phoned Elvin again, but it went straight to the answering machine. He didn't bother to leave a message this time. For a guy who didn't have to hold down a job, Elvin sure managed to avoid being home during business hours. This day was beginning to look like a total write-off.

He went down to the break room, but nobody was hanging around. Walt got some water from the cooler and found a Gala apple on the counter for a snack. Three-thirty in the afternoon was too early to call it a day; then again, what else was he going to do? He took a sweep through the office, found two guys working at their desks, inputting data. Both seemed too occupied with their work to chat. They hadn't heard about the dead man at the hatchery or they would have at least mentioned it. Neither one of them had heard a thing about Pam or the Deer Track Inn, either.

Shortly after four he took another walk through the building. Dewers was gone for the day, must have slipped out while the slipping was good. Walt decided he should do the same. He'd made it past the front door and was almost to his car before remembering that his mini-SUV wasn't going anywhere. The Suzuki sat right where he'd left it that morning, an abandoned vehicle in the making. Here was yet another kick in the head. How was he going to get home? How was he going to get to work tomorrow?

Back inside the building he searched for Marcus Washington one last time. No luck. That was now a disappointment, because Walt really needed to talk to the boss this time. Maybe he'd be allowed to borrow one of the work trucks for a few days, just long enough to tide him over. It was tempting to take a vehicle home now and ask permission later; then again (who knows), that might turn out to be a terminable offense. He wasn't going to risk getting fired over the use of a truck. He flirted with the idea of sleeping under his desk, but that thought alone was depressing. He needed to get back home. He had a couch and a dog waiting for him.

Walt started working the phones. Elvin still wasn't answering. He tried Dewers' cell, but his work partner wasn't picking up, either. That was probably deliberate, with caller ID and all. Dewers wasn't going to take any calls from Walt unless he was forced to. He tried Jim Rivard's number and struck out once more. It was almost four-thirty and Pitowski wasn't any closer to solving his problems than he'd been when the day begun. He rang the hospital asking for Pam's room, but either she hadn't been admitted to Rasmus Hospital or they'd been told to lie. She might be holed up over in Petoskey, or Gaylord, or Traverse City. Hell, if her injuries were serious enough she might be in one of the big medical centers downstate. He didn't have time to canvass all of Michigan looking for a woman who may or may not be willing to speak to him.

Again he stormed down to the break room, only to find it empty. It was now four-forty. There was one coworker remaining in the office, and that was Charlie Patterson, who lived twelve miles in the opposite direction. No way was he going to drive to Walt's house and back: the two men couldn't stand each other. Where was everybody, anyway? Didn't anybody put in a full day's work anymore? Pitowski was beginning to think the situation was hopeless, that he'd have to either walk or hitchhike home. He paced back to his desk and tried Elvin's number one last time, still to no avail.

Finally Walt landed on the idea of dialing Red Blondin. "Red" wasn't his real name. His real name was Clarence, which pretty much explained why, for as long as anyone could remember, he'd gone by "Red." His hair was brown, so the nickname didn't make a lot of sense, but it still beat the hell out of going by Clarence. Blondin ran an automotive repair shop out of a pole barn behind his house. While Walt did most of his own auto repairs, he'd come to rely on the other man when a job was beyond his realm of expertise or when he just didn't have the time to screw around with something. Blondin was a fair and knowledgeable mechanic. In fact, he was the only guy Walt trusted other than himself to perform surgery on his precious vehicles, even if they *were* junk. The two men had even hunted together on occasion. Walt knew that his Suzuki was beyond hope, but maybe Red would take pity on him and offer up some kind of a short-term solution.

It turned out to be the right call. Blondin came within the hour to examine the Samurai. It took less than five minutes for a diagnosis, and the pronouncement of Last Rites over the little machine.

"Requiescat in pace," Blondin intoned, while making the sign of the cross with his right hand.

"She's dead?" Walt double-checked. His Latin was non-existent. He was hoping there might still be a fix.

"As a doornail," his friend answered. "I'll give you a number for the junkyard: you might get two-fifty out of her." Two hundred and fifty dollars wasn't much, but there wasn't much left to be salvaged, either. It wasn't as if people would be lining up to restore *their* Suzuki Samurais with parts from this donor. He'd take what he could get.

"I don't suppose you've got something you want to sell me for around two-fifty?" Walt already knew the answer to that question.

"For *two-fifty*? I could sell you a brake job, but you'd have to supply the vehicle and your own rotors. I *do* have something you can borrow for a couple of days."

"Thanks." At least it would allow him a little time to figure things out. "What is it?"

"Pontiac Montana."

"A minivan?" Walt had to think about that. He hemmed and hawed. God, as if everyone wasn't laughing at him already. Now he'd be driving around town in a mom-mobile. Life was going from bad to worse.

"Take it or leave it, it's what I've got. It's yours until the weekend, then I need it back. I've got someone coming to buy it on Sunday."

"I'll take it." Beggars can't be choosers, and Walt was definitely feeling like a beggar.

Blondin gave him a ride back to the repair barn, where Walt was further thrilled to discover that the minivan in question was painted entirely in hot pink: "In Your Face Pink," actually. There was probably a fancy name for this exact hue, but Walt had never seen it in a dealership. Maybe it was whipped up by the same guy that ran the State Police motor pool.

"You are effin' kidding me," was all he could utter. "It looks like a giant bottle of Pepto-Bismol."

"An Earl Scheib special, aftermarket paint job. Somebody paid good money to make a car this ugly. Like I said, it's what I've got, take it or leave it," Blondin offered. If it wasn't good enough for Pitowski, then let him find his own damn ride.

It took Walt a minute to find the words. "I'll take it," he reluctantly agreed. For a few days he could endure anything, even ridicule. "You don't have anything else you're looking to sell? Something a little more....normal?"

"Not at the moment, but I'll let you know if I hear about anything."

"I'd appreciate it." That was that.

The first order of business, once he was back at home, would be to work on getting some new wheels. Payday was only four days away and Walt was expecting extra money from the Taos trip to appear on this check. That would help, but it still wasn't enough to get him into reliable transportation. If he pooled all of his assets he might have three grand, total, plus enough left over to pay outstanding bills. It would probably take five thousand to get a car worth driving. He was going to have to borrow money somewhere, and it wasn't likely to be from a bank, not with Walt's screwed up credit. Maybe his parents could help him. Walt was still weighing his choices when he pulled the pink Pontiac alongside his house.

Doofus was waiting patiently, tail wagging, at the sliding door. The dog leapt up to greet his master as soon as Walt opened the glass. He barked once, licking Walt's face before bounding off behind the house to do his business. Walt stepped inside, finding things just as he'd left them that morning, only colder. In a sense, it was disappointing. Nothing had changed. There would be some comfort in knowing that he had a partner in life, even a partner that messed up his house. Even a partner he didn't understand. Walt looked around the living room. There was a slight depression in the cushion at one end of the couch, a long clump of reddish dog hair stuck on the fabric. Other than that there were no signs of life, no indicator that a single soul other than Walt so much as breathed this stagnant air. Hell, even the dog barely made his presence felt.

He put a pot of coffee on to brew, carelessly gazing out the kitchen window. The pink abomination was blocking his view of the woodpile. He needed to split some more wood, sooner rather than later. He needed to get some propane in the tank before the *really* cold weather arrived. The most pressing issue was that he needed to find a vehicle. Sunday couldn't come soon enough in his estimation. He wanted to get that eyesore of a minivan out of his yard. On the other hand, he was going to have to move quickly to find a viable alternative before then. Maybe something would fall into his lap. He still needed to locate Pam, see if he could help her in any way, and maybe win her back. He needed to call Amberson in the morning. It probably had something to do with that idiot at the Compactor. He also wanted to know why there was a dead guy lying on the floor of the hatchery. Otherwise, life was just peachy.

The dog returned, scratching at the glass, and Walt let him in. Doofus had a quick drink of water from his bowl and resumed napping on the far end of the couch. Lazy mutt. Doofus was getting less active by the day. Walt poured himself a mug of coffee and took a seat on the other end of the sofa. He should go out and split some firewood before it got dark, but it was hard to feel motivated. There were too many things going through his mind, and the way his day had gone thus far, maybe he shouldn't leave the house. Maybe he should stay away from sharp objects, too.

He clicked on the television, scrolling quickly through the handful of channels. Over-the-air broadcast television was spotty in rural areas at best. Local news. More local news. National League baseball. Why in the hell were they showing the National League in northern Michigan? Didn't they know that the nearest club was the Tigers, an American League team nearly two-hundred miles to the south? He kept clicking. Public broadcasting (national news). More public broadcasting (the never-ending fundraiser). Alpena local news (even less relevant, if that was remotely possible). Finally he landed on the old movie channel.

"Fargo" was just starting, one of Walt's favorite films of all time. William H. Macy's character was driving an Oldsmobile, maybe a Ciera, towing another Olds on a trailer across the snow-drifted plains of northern Minnesota. Wasteland Minnesota looks an awful lot like Rasmus, Walt decided. In the opening scene Macy is driving from the middle of nowhere to the outskirts of nowhere, intent on arranging a fake kidnapping of his wife. He needs money. He shows up at a dive bar where he's supposed to meet Steve Buscemi and some other guy. Buscemi always gave Walt the creeps, no matter what movie he was in. Mostly, at least for Pitowski, "Fargo" summed up how pointless and stupid life could really be. The film was about halfway through when his phone rang. Walt looked at the clock: nearly seven-thirty and it was getting dark outside.

"Yeah?"

"Walt, it's Elvin."

"What's new?"

"Nothing much. You called me earlier and I missed it. What's going on?"

"You're not home much for a guy with no job, you know that? Hey, the Suzuki died. I was wondering if you know anybody with a decent truck for sale. Cheap."

"Is it *dead dead*, or just *kind of dead*?"

"As dead as they get, unless I want to spend four grand fixing up a vehicle that might be worth two when all's said and done." There was a momentary silence on both ends of the line.

"Yep, that's pretty dead." Another pause. "How much *do* you want to spend? What's your budget?"

"I don't *want* to spend anything, but I don't really have a choice. I'm willing to go five."

"I'm praying you mean five thousand and not five hundred."

"Of course I mean five thousand. Where in the hell does anybody get a decent truck for five hundred dollars?" Walt could feel his blood pressure rising. Jesus, did Elvin think he was an idiot or something?

"I'm just asking. I know money's tight. You're saying you've got five grand?"

"Well, not exactly, but I will by this weekend." Walt wasn't sure *where* he was going to find the money, but he should be able to put it together by Saturday. "Why, do you know somebody that's selling?"

"Does it have to be a truck?"

"I'd *like it* to be a truck, but I'd consider an SUV or something else if the price is right."

"Does it have to be four wheel drive?"

"I'd *like* four wheel drive, but I'd consider two wheel drive if the price is right." Sometimes Elvin required you to spell everything out in detail. Walt half expected another question about whether it "had to have" a cigarette lighter or if the floor mats "have to be" rubber.

"Let me ask around, I'll get back with you."

"The sooner the better."

"I'll make some calls. So how are you getting around in the meantime? I'm assuming you've got to get to work and back."

"I'm doing a public service announcement for Breast Cancer Awareness Month. Don't ask."

"Alright. Well, I'll call you as soon as I learn anything."

"Great. Talk to you later." Elvin could occasionally be a pain in the ass, but at least he was a well-connected pain in the ass. Walt was keeping his fingers crossed.

Doofus still hadn't moved from "his" end of the couch. The dog was snoring up a storm. Walt topped off his coffee and went back to the living room.

"Fargo" was still on, though it was getting towards the end of the film. Buscemi's partner in crime, what was his name? Walt couldn't remember, but he'd seen this guy in another Coen film, "The Big Lebowski," and a bunch of other stuff. The pregnant lady cop is creeping down the slippery hillside, preparing to make an arrest. When she gets around to the back of the cabin, she finds the big guy that plays Buscemi's partner. He's stuffing a victim's leg into a wood chipper, blood shooting all across the freshly fallen snow. It always amazed Walt, the sick things people managed to do to one another.

TEN

The Watcher

The Watcher could see the old man slinking his way down the hillside. Dusk was just announcing its presence in and around Rasmus, long shadows reaching the nooks and crannies of the woods and gradually settling in for the night. He'd been watching the man for a while, anxiously awaiting this early evening visitor. It was hard to predict exactly when he'd come, whether it would be Sunday or Monday or Tuesday, but he'd come. Right as rain, he'd come. The old man's stash was here, and he wasn't likely to go more than three or four days without replenishing his supply. He'd probably sold everything he had over the weekend, when the young party crowd and the aging fly fishermen and the health-conscious folks from the yoga camp all came through Rasmus. Not all of them, but some of them, just enough to keep a man in business, would need a little taste of what the old man had to offer. He never carried too much on his person, the old man, because the penalties for getting caught with large amounts of dope were tremendous. He carried just enough that he could pawn it off as for "personal use" should he get in trouble. The penalty for "personal use," or whatever you chose to call it, was generally a misdemeanor. Even if you *were* over the limit, over but not over by a whole lot, you could usually plead any charges *down* to a misdemeanor. Pay the fine, don't get caught again for six months to a year. The courts didn't have a lot of energy to expend on petty offenses. So far, the old man had managed to avoid even that problem.

The old man was out of sight once he reached the bottom of the slope. His observer crept closer to the rim of the shallow valley below, craning his neck in search of the slightest movement. For a minute he thought the old man might have detected him, when The Watcher tripped and stumbled on a stick hidden beneath the leaves. He caught himself just in time, hugging his body tight to the back side of a large oak and merging with the darkness. He knew that the old man had ceased walking, for even the slight sound of footfalls had temporarily stopped. He waited patiently for movement, for breathing, for shifting shadows. The old man waited, too, before eventually resuming his mission.

KEVIN J GARRITY

The Watcher did not want to kill the old man here at the hatchery, not particularly. A death in Rasmus would never go unnoticed. Well, it might go unnoticed for a while, especially if the death was that of an ancient dirtbag who hadn't held a real job in over forty years. Nobody was going to call the cops and report that he "hadn't shown up for work as expected," but sooner or later someone would notice. The old man must have *some* friends, even if they were worthless friends: friends who would make a stink when they couldn't find the man they called "Wood Tick" for a little weekend action.

Other options had occurred to him. It would be better and far more convenient, in fact, if he bumped off the old man somewhere in the forest, far from town. There was an awful lot of wilderness north of here, most notably the Sparrow River Forest. There were vast tracts of state land to the east and the west, places where no soul but the occasional grouse hunter bothered to tread. He could kill this Wood Tick then and there, bury his body in a shallow grave or leave it for the coyotes to ravage. Either way, the chances that the old man would be found were minimal at best. Even if his remains were discovered, what would be left to reclaim? His demise would probably be chalked up to death by "natural causes."

Unfortunately, the old man had begun to spend all of his time running in the company of two dirtbag friends. Everywhere the old man went, Dirtbag One and Dirtbag Two were with him. They were inseparable. The Watcher was beginning to wonder if the old man even went to the bathroom by himself. The chance of catching Wood Tick in the forest, by himself, was not looking so hot these days. Time was of the essence. Sooner or later Wood Tick was going to talk. When he talked, The Watcher would have a new set of problems. He did not need a new set of problems. The Watcher did not want this to turn into a triple homicide, either. *That* would attract some *serious* attention: news media, state cops, the whole shebang. This was the first time since last Tuesday that he'd managed to track the old buzzard without the company of his dirtbag friends.

The old man was on the move again, creeping up the spiral concrete stairs to the hidden doorway on the side of the hatchery. The Watcher had to hand it to him, the old guy was good. Lots of people *think* they are quiet or stealthy, but actually sound and appear like a herd of buffalo on the move. Even the good ones generally give themselves away. Military men, now they are often better than good. He had been given much opportunity to observe and stalk, and ex-military personnel were the ones that gave him the most trouble. Their professional training was part of it, but it might just be that when your

68

life is on the line, you get a whole lot better at what you're doing. Wood Tick wasn't *Special Ops* good, but he was better than most, especially for an old guy.

Five minutes, he estimated. The Watcher would give the old man a five minute head start, let him get inside and get settled. He guessed it would take less than one minute for the old man to let himself into the building once he slipped behind the plywood sheathing that shielded the door from view. Two minutes at the most. The old man must either have his own key or be particularly adept at picking locks. He'd watched Wood Tick before and knew how easily he could let himself inside. He'd allow an additional four minutes for the old man to walk down the hallway and to the basement, just to be safe. The Watcher *could* kill the old man in the upstairs hallway, if he had to, but it would be better to do it in the basement. If he did it in the basement, the sloping hills of the river valley would help muffle the sound of a gunshot.

He checked the time. Three minutes had passed. He counted slowly to sixty, then to sixty again. Once the five minutes were up, The Watcher began to move. He too had his own key and could let himself into the building in less than a minute. He slipped out of view behind the plywood lean-to that covered the entryway. He had his key in the cylinder, was about to turn the deadbolt when he heard an unexpected scuffling on the other side of the door. The Watcher froze. Wood Tick was still somewhere on the upper level of the building. He heard the old man curse, then laugh. He waited some more and could just make out the shuffling of feet followed by the creaking of boards as the old man eventually made his way down the hallway. This was slightly unexpected, but catching the old man in the upstairs portion wouldn't have been the end of the world, at least not *his* world. If he had to kill the old man on the main floor, he'd kill the old man on the main floor. What mattered most was that Wood Tick's ticker stopped ticking.

The Watcher knew that the old man's drugs were hidden somewhere on that lower level, but he didn't know exactly *where* on the lower level. He'd observed the old man before from outside the building. He'd seen a light moving past the occasional gaps in the boarded windows. The old man was a creature of habit. The Watcher almost gave himself away one last time, when he himself reached the top of the basement stairs. Even the best make mistakes. He thought he heard the old man pause briefly, down in the basement. Was it possible that his presence had been detected? The old man did in fact pause, waiting on a sound, but then he resumed doing whatever he was doing on the lower level. It didn't much matter. The old man was already down there somewhere, and *that's* what mattered. There was no way he'd be leaving this building alive.

"Jesus, it's you. You scared the hell out of me." Those were the only words Wood Tick managed to blurt out before his assassin placed a nine millimeter bullet through his skull.

The assassin carefully lifted the bulky duffel bag from his victim's shoulder. At thirty or so pounds it was cumbersome but not unmanageable. He couldn't afford to leave it behind. It would be harder to sneak around carrying this much weight, but who would be out there to watch The Watcher? He silently retraced his steps out of the building, locking the door behind him as he went. The man slid around the western face of the hatchery, crouching low behind the untended brush. He snaked his way north through the trees hugging the hillside. It was dark out; the chances of him being spotted were slim. Still, it never hurt to be cautious. He made his way to the base of the slope, clinging to shadows. A short sprint across forty feet of open ground got him to a viaduct, that wide tunnel which brought the east branch of the Grand Limoneaux River beneath the road bed twenty feet above. Once he'd passed through the cylinder, he crept into the woods on the far side of the highway. From there it was clear sailing. Half a mile to the north and one hundred yards to the west he found the car, parked along a little-used dirt lane. He placed the duffel in his trunk and drove off into the night.

ELEVEN

Walt Pitowski

Walt could use a drink. He thought about checking the refrigerator, but he knew that there wasn't anything inside. That well had run dry a long time ago. The next best idea would have been to drive to the Deer Track Inn, but that, too, was off the table. With Pam banged up and the Deer Track a wreck, who knew when they'd be open for business again? He really didn't need to be going *there* anyhow, dredging up old feelings while the woman that used to be his woman was still lying in a hospital somewhere. The smart thing to do would be to stay right where he was, catch another movie on the Zenith console, and get to bed early. Maybe he would fall asleep on the couch, even. That would be the smart course of action. On the other hand, he'd gotten this far in life without always doing "the smart thing," so why start now?

He slipped outside, uncharacteristically locking the house behind him. The way the last few days had gone, Walt didn't want to invite trouble. He couldn't say in what form grief might be crawling across his rotten threshold, but he knew grief was thinking about it just the same. For years Pitowski had doubted the existence of God, had thought that any belief in a superior being was just a crutch for the weak and the fallen. He joked about it often, ridiculing the "church people" that frittered away their Sundays lamenting their pathetic little lives while Walt himself was out enjoying the beauty and bounty of nature. Lately he wasn't so sure: maybe there was a big eye in the sky, and maybe God was just fucking with him.

In either event, God or no god, he could still use that drink. It didn't take him long to find the pink minivan at the side of the house. It was practically luminous. Once underway he decided this wasn't such a bad car if you could manage to get past its appearance. That was a pretty big "if," probably a deal-breaker in his case. It did have a ton of cargo space, though. You could probably cram a lot of gear into one of these things, and more than likely get a full sheet of plywood in the back once you flipped the rear seats down. The Montana could handle seven or eight passengers, not that it was likely to matter, but it did have the capability should he ever decide to pick up a full squad of college cheerleaders. *Good luck with that*, he thought. The Montana was built on a much longer wheelbase than the little Suzuki: one-hundred twenty-one inches versus just ninety. It would be impossible to do a U-turn in tight corners with this beast, but at least Walt didn't feel like he was getting punched in the kidneys every time he hit a bump in the road. Not a bad car, just a severely ugly one. By the time he got off the dirt road and turned left onto the paved highway, Walt was feeling pretty good about his temporary wheels. He could do worse. "What do I care what people think?" he wondered aloud.

Traffic is never heavy in or around Rasmus on a Monday night. It was a mile down the road before the first vehicle, heading in the opposite direction, blew past Walt. It was a silver Lexus SUV. The driver was blaring her horn, a series of short, sharp toots, as she waved her hand out the window at him. Pitowski didn't get a good look at the driver, but he figured she *must* be a friend that recognized him behind the wheel. While Walt couldn't remember having any friends that drove a silver Lexus SUV, it didn't mean he might not have one. He just didn't *recall* having one. This was her way of saying "hello." Either that or she was a stranger that thought Walt was cute and wanted to let him know. Six of one or a half dozen of the other, he'd take the compliment. A quarter mile further down the track a second driver, this one a middle-aged white male in a black Silverado, wailed on his horn and flipped Walt the finger. It was not his index finger, and Walt was pretty certain that the man wasn't chanting "you're number one." It was rude, it was unexpected, and it was decidedly unkind. The guy was decked out in camo and hunter orange. He was more than likely *not* someone who thought Walt Pitowski was cute and wanted to let him know of his affections. This second event Walt chalked up to coincidence: bad luck, full moon, mistaken identity, or something along those lines. Two miles later a third car, an older Trans Am, unexpectedly chucked a half-full beer can out the window as it went by. The use of a horn was not involved in the festivities, nor were any fingers waved. When the Coors Light Silver Bullet banged off the hood of his Pontiac, Walt had to admit that something more was up. He was beginning to detect a pattern. The Pepto-Montana was a magnet for the misplaced anger of lunatics and freaks of all kinds.

A few minutes later he arrived at his destination. It had been months since he'd set foot in the Red Eye Saloon, and it wasn't Walt's favorite place. Tucked on a side road at the edge of an industrial park, it was easy for him to forget the place was even there. Their food was alright, and in the daytime it did a decent trade as a bar/restaurant with the emphasis on *restaurant* rather than *bar*. Older people dined there because the daily specials were cheap and tasted no worse than the fare at other places around town. Businessmen lunched there because you could always find an open table and grab a quick burger with something cold to wash it down. Families with kids even ate there because it was roomy and relatively well lit, unlike a lot of bars that pretended to be restaurants. In the evenings all that changed.

Evenings meant the Red Eye Saloon became a *bar* in the true sense of the word, as in "my standards are slipping, lower the bar." Weekends saw the place packed with anybody and everybody: local guys, still flush with their paychecks; hunters and fishermen, cutting loose for the weekend; girls who lived on the outskirts of town, searching for a little excitement. It was often raucous. There would be music and dancing and you would have a hard time walking from one end of the place to the other. Some came for a drink. Some came for many drinks. Many came for some drinks and the hopes of a quick "hook-up" with members of the opposite sex. A few came hoping to check the box that read "all of the above." Fights were not uncommon. Mondays were quieter than weekends but there would still be a crowd, albeit a much smaller crowd. Walt found himself suddenly glad that it was only a Monday.

The exterior of the low-slung building was sided with corrugated steel panels painted a faded barn red. A handful of cars were scattered around the perimeter, parked at odd angles. The Plymouth with the mismatched fender that he'd noticed on Saturday morning was here, but he didn't recognize any other ride. There were two guys leaning against the exterior wall of the building, quietly smoking cigarettes in the dark. Things had definitely changed in the last few years. Walt could remember a time not so long ago when those two guys would be lighting up inside, seated at a table over a pitcher of Cinci Cream Ale. It was obviously for the common good, the change in the law. Smoking had been banned in all places open to the public, with only a handful of exceptions. Second-hand smoke was the bogeyman of the day. Walt knew there were worse ways to die besides cancer, but offhand he couldn't think of any. He'd be the first to admit the ban on smoking in restaurants made the food taste better. It still didn't mean he agreed with the law. He wished government would get the hell out of everybody's life. This was still America, wasn't it? Walt let himself through the screen door, the wind at his back slamming it shut behind him.

"Hey bro," the kid behind the bar acknowledged him as he walked past. "The kid" was probably in his late-twenties, and he most certainly was not Walt's "bro." He was polishing pilsner glasses with a hand towel, obviously not too busy pouring drinks. There was something fundamentally wrong with some dipshit fifteen years your junior, one you've never met, calling you "bro." Pitowski decided to let it slide this time, but it still irked him. If he ever got the chance to speak with the owners, he'd be sure and bring it up.

"Show a little respect," Walt chimed on his way past the bar.

"What?" the bartender wondered aloud.

A table on the left held two guys Walt didn't recognize: a pair of silver haired sixty-somethings sipping mixed drinks with double olives and yakking about fishing on the Manistee River. They were probably retired guys with a cabin in the area. What appeared to be a married couple sat across the room, silently picking over their wingding baskets and two bottles of Bud. Another married couple, this one actually speaking to one another, sat with their backs to the first couple. There was one vote for marital bliss and one vote against. Like the rest of the country, the odds of any relationship succeeding appeared to be about fifty-fifty.

The Tigers were playing on a large screen TV, the play-by-play muted for whatever reason. The married folks that still spoke to one another were avidly engaged in the game. Two old geezers and a lone woman held fort at the bar rail. That was where the hard-core drinkers set up shop. The woman looked like she'd been resurrected from the grave as recently as this evening. Just looking at her sent a shudder down Walt's spine. It would help if she weren't wearing clothing cut for a teenager. The geezers didn't look one bit better: their wardrobe was barely suited for a Salvation Army drop box. Not one of the three barflies would ever get loaded enough to find any of the others attractive. They were each in their own private, anesthetized world.

In the back Walt could see three younger guys and a woman hovering around the pool table. One red-headed boy and the blond girl in the group were undoubtedly under the age of twenty-one: they were sipping Cokes instead of sharing the pitcher of beer with their "legal" friends. That's what they were doing while anyone was watching, at least. "Legal" was a question of degree sometimes. "Not visibly breaking any laws" was often good enough in the north. The group was talking loudly between bouts of laughter, just horsing around and having fun. Walt could hear the familiar clatter of pool balls shaking in a rack, prepped and ready for a fresh game. The waitress waltzed past him with a quick "hi" on her way back to the bar. She was probably on her way to get another pitcher for the youngsters in the back room. Pitowski bet that she wouldn't have to refill those Coke glasses again.

He took a chair at one of the tall cocktail tables. The Tigers were leading, but they would undoubtedly find a way to blow it before the night was through. The back end of their pitching rotation had been a mess all year. He was right about the waitress: she flew past him with a foaming pitcher of amber-colored liquid in hand, headed for the pool table. After a few minutes she got around to Walt, taking his order for a bottle of Soft Parade. It was a bit of an extravagance and they'd probably ding him four bucks for one bottle, but once in a while a good beer was worth the price. There weren't too many places that carried this brew around here, and he wasn't passing up the opportunity tonight. He needed it. He deserved it. Of course he'd probably be digging through couch cushions for gas money in the morning.

Walt gazed up at the television on the wall. *How nice it would be to have cable at home*, he mused. The game was still 2-1 in the bottom of the sixth inning, and the Yankees had runners on first and second with only one out. This is where things usually went bad. The pitch count was getting up there, and the starting pitcher's arm would be losing a little zip with each and every throw. The next thing you know, there's a hanging curveball over the plate and a three-run shot goes over the right field fence. At least that's what experience had taught him: it was only a matter of time.

Three balls and a strike later, the screen door slammed and Walt looked over his shoulder in time to spot Matt Amberson and his wife, Carol, settling into a corner table. Walt quickly whipped his head around and pretended to focus on the ball game. He'd had enough of the Shawono County Sheriff's Department for one day. Maybe Amberson wouldn't notice him. Slim chance, he realized, since The Jawless Wonder noticed just about everything. The deputy was out of uniform and seemed engrossed by his wife, so at least that gave Walt hope.

Walt was watching Amberson's wife out of the corner of his eye: now there was a strange bird. He wondered why the two had never had any kids. She was certainly pretty enough, and he figured she must want kids. What woman in this part of the world didn't? Otherwise, why would anyone ever tie the knot? This wasn't California or Portland or something, where being childless was a statement of your counterculture independence. And the

Ambersons had been married long enough. Hell, half the women in this town got knocked up without even thinking about marriage: she was past due. *Tick tock*, Walt thought. He'd only spoken with her on a few occasions, but she seemed nice enough. Still, she gave the impression that something about her spirit was broken. All of that was Amberson's problem, not Walt's.

The door slammed shut a second time, and the two guys who'd been smoking outside strolled casually past. They set up station alongside a thin ledge near the pool table. Each had a bottle in hand, which meant they'd probably been in here earlier and snuck their drinks outside when they went out to smoke. You weren't supposed to take alcohol off the premises, but what was that tiny waitress supposed to do? It was hard to catch everybody that cheated the system: you'd have to have eyes in the back of your head. The young group in the back stopped talking momentarily, giving the two men what they probably *thought* were menacing looks for invading their turf, before returning to their game. The kids must think they own the place. At the very least they must think they own the back room. Walt looked the group over a second time. The youngsters should probably reconsider who they threaten: those cigarette boys looked like they could more than hold their own.

"Pitowski, how are you?" rang the voice of Matt Amberson. This was about as friendly as things ever got with him.

"Amberson, I didn't see you come in," Walt smiled lamely.

"Sure you didn't." The deputy was a lot of things, but he wasn't a fool. He knew when he was being patronized. "You got a minute?"

"Why not." Walt kicked the chair across from him from underneath the table. It slid back ten inches or so to where the deputy could easily sit down. Whatever Amberson wanted, they might as well get it over with now. It would save Walt a phone call in the morning. Besides, the invitation didn't sound optional. "Does Carol want to join us?"

"I doubt it, but thanks for asking. We're just out for a late dinner. I think she'd like to eat in peace," he answered, while taking the seat.

"Better than Rest in Peace."

"Real funny, Walt." Amberson paused for a second and gave him a stare like he was considering whether it was worth *trying* to have a discussion with Walt, before finally deciding to continue with the conversation. "In light of your earlier discovery, this might not be the best day for gallows humor."

"You're probably right, but you've got to admit, it's still funny."

"Let's agree to disagree on that one. Listen, that body you found at the hatchery? Have you discussed it with anyone?"

"You told me not to."

"That doesn't answer my question."

"Nope, didn't mention it to a soul. I was going to tell Marcus Washington, just so he didn't think we were goofing off from work, but he was gone for the day. I told my dog when I got home," he offered wryly.

"Still not funny. Well it doesn't matter, because the news is all over town anyways. Rasmus apparently no longer needs an emergency alert system, because everybody knows everybody else's business. The system has been replaced by cell phones and coffee at the diner. The guy you found took a bullet in the head, but then you already knew that, and apparently everyone else does, too."

"If it doesn't matter, then why are you telling me?"

"Just to let you know that the cone of secrecy has been lifted. You seem like a guy that might want to talk to...." he paused, searching for a polite way to put it "...somebody, sometime." Amberson had almost finished his sentence with "a therapist" but decided it would only make matters worse. Pitowski wasn't the kind of guy to spill his heart out to a shrink, no matter how much good it might do him. The mere suggestion would only rile him up.

"Did you ID him yet?"

"That's what I wanted to talk with you about. The deceased is one Rayford Jefferson Brown. Seventy-two years young."

"Don't know'em."

"I think you might."

"Don't know'em." Walt paused to think, taking a sip from his drink. "There's lots of old guys in these parts. I haven't met every single one of them."

"Think hard. A lot of people called him 'Wood Tick.' Used to ride one of those handicapped scooters up to the Deer Track Inn. He was a regular drinker there. Before he bit the bullet a few days ago, that is. You've spent your share of time at the Deer Track."

"I remember the scooter being parked up there. A Rascal or something, with an ORV flag attached to it and a reflector triangle on the back. It had some kind of a wire basket on the front with a plastic daisy, like it was stolen off a girl's bicycle. The drunkard's limo. I do remember seeing a smelly old man sitting at the bar once or twice, but I don't think I ever spoke with him. You sure it's the same guy?"

"It's the same guy. You knew his son."

"I don't think so."

"You did. Rayford Jefferson Brown Jr. Ring any bells?"

"Not to be argumentative here, Matt, but I don't know'em. Not the old man or his son. At least I don't think I do."

"I'll give you a little hint: his son went by 'Ray.' He died young, just a few months ago, up on the Sparrow River."

Walt thought for a minute. It was all becoming clearer now. Ray, the Sparrow River, a dead boy, and a lifetime's worth of misery condensed into the span of a few short months. Ray Jr. was the man Walt suspected of murder, a petty drug dealer that Walt held responsible for the loss of a young man's life. He'd never known the man's full name. Now his father had turned up dead, shot between the eyes. The old man probably wasn't any better a human being than his offspring, was probably dealing drugs himself. If you led that kind of lifestyle, bad things were bound to happen sooner or later. The business of death and destruction was not very forgiving. Walt took another sip from the bottle.

"Ah, the asshole doesn't fall very far from the tree," he finally answered.

"I think you mean 'apple,' Walt."

"Nope. I had it right the first time."

Amberson grunted. "Well here's the problem. We're looking at this *murder*, because it was a murder. No way the old man shot himself in the center of the forehead. There's no powder residue on his hands and there's no gun on the premises, at least not that we can find. He's been dead for at least a few days, probably a bit longer, because rigor mortis has come and gone. We're guessing under a week. So far we don't have a lot to go on. There are two commonalities between this case and that crap with his son. Want to guess what they are? I'll give you another hint: the first commonality, and I know that's a big word for you, 'commonality,' is drugs. They were both drug dealers: meth, heroin, prescription meds and pot, that we know of. More than likely more shit that we don't know of. We were never able to pin anything firm on the old man. Ray Jr., on the other hand, had a long history of petty arrests, and he was obviously growing dope up by the Sparrow when you crossed paths with him. Want to guess what the second commonality is?"

"You tell me. What's the second one?" Walt didn't feel like playing guessing games.

Amberson leaned across the table and got real close like he was about to impart some great secret. "The second commonality is *Walt Frickin' Pitowski*," he whispered.

It felt like all the air was suddenly sucked from the room.

TWELVE

The good Deputy Amberson had returned to his own table and was busy enjoying dinner with his wife. Walt felt as if he'd been kicked in the stomach, or even a bit lower. First that prick Don Frederics had implied that he might somehow be involved in hurting Pam and busting up the Deer Track. Walt knew that was a load of shit, and hadn't worried about it much up until this point. He figured the truth would win out sooner or later. Maybe not in politics or religion, but in personal justice as it related to Walt Pitowski, the truth would win out.

Now Amberson was practically accusing him of bumping off some old codger he'd never met. There wasn't much truth in that theory, either, but Pitowski knew better than to trust the local sheriff's department. He had to admit one could connect the dots and start seeing things even if they weren't there. It seemed as if they were piling on, and they hadn't yet brought up the one thing he *did* do, which was coldcock a convict back at the Compactor on Saturday morning. That was small potatoes, but he could imagine the prosecuting attorney describing it as "indicative of a pattern of behavior" or some such legalese. If the cops thought they could pin *everything* on him, they would. One trial, one jail cell: it could be considered a cost-saving measure. Conjuring up some false evidence might prove easier than finding the real culprits, and the one thing in this mess of which Pitowski was certain was that they'd take the easiest route to a conviction. It was the way of the north. Justice wasn't blind, it was just plumb lazy. Walt sipped the last of his beer slowly, trying to decide what his next move should be.

He was almost ready to leave when he saw the state troopers walk through the door, still in uniform. What were their names again? He had to think for a second before it finally came to him: Murphy and Johnson. It sounded like the name of a household cleaning supply company. Floor soap? Medical tape? Why did it sound so familiar? Walt would bet that they were partnered up solely because their names *sounded* like they belonged together. It was unusual to see state boys running around Rasmus at this time of night. The nearest state police post was forty miles up the track, and they had an awfully large territory to cover. You didn't often see state troopers in

Rasmus unless they were needed. There was usually a *reason* for them to be around: a fight, a shooting, something. These two must be staying the night in town, sticking close to the investigation at the hatchery.

The two troopers took a quick gaze around as soon as they came into the bar, and Walt nodded in their direction. They didn't appear to recognize him or even acknowledge his nod. That was fine by him. He didn't need to attract any more love from the police than he already had. They quickly spied Amberson at his table in the corner and went over to speak with the deputy. What was this about? He knew it was none of his business, whatever the topic, but he still wished he could listen in. The three men were engrossed in conversation, Amberson's wife silently eating her salad as they spoke. She didn't look particularly pleased to have her date spoiled by more police business. Walt figured now was as good a time as any to get the hell out of there.

The Montana was right where he'd parked it, which he realized should come as no surprise. He could probably leave it unlocked with the engine running, doors wide open in the middle of downtown Detroit at midnight, and still no one would take it. "Pinky" was almost painful to look at. He got in and it started right up. *Well, at least it runs.* Now where to? He let the engine idle as he sat in the dark corner of the lot, waiting for inspiration to strike. He rolled down the driver's side window and the warm southern wind brought in the fading remnants of summer. The weather would be changing all too soon. A few more days of this and they'd be forecasting snow by week's end.

Walt needed a plan. He couldn't just sit back and wait for the world to come down upon him. A mercury-vapor lamp was attached high atop a telephone pole, glowing over the far corner of the lot. It cast a blue-green aura over a small section of sand and gravel below. The light softened at the edges before being swallowed by the night. It was hard to imagine a lonelier place in this world. He watched the two guys that had been smoking cigarettes earlier exit the Red Eye. They headed straight to a dark Crown Vic parked at the edge of the bluish glow. Funny, Walt didn't picture them as Crown Victoria kind of guys. They looked more like the beater pickup types: all skinny and strung out on something. Ragged flannel shirts and bad complexions. They were similar enough in build that they could be brothers. These clowns certainly weren't undercover cops: whatever experience they had with the law was likely to be on the wrong side of it.

He watched them peel out of the lot and onto the highway, heading east and away from town. Two red dots disappeared slowly into the night. Walt had an urge to follow them, for no other reason than that it would give him something, *anything*, to do. It had to be better than waiting around here doing nothing. Then he recognized this for the bad idea that it was, a distraction from making hard choices about where his life went from here. Walt knew he'd better get to work.

His first stop was the Rasmus Hospital. There wasn't anybody at the front desk, visiting hours having officially ended at eight. The front doors would be unlocked, though: one benefit of living in a small community. A bigger town would have that place secured like Fort Knox. He'd spent enough time at the hospital to know his way around. He passed the elevators and the tiny chapel, letting himself into a service stairwell and up to the second floor. Ob/Gyn was his target. While he knew that Pam wouldn't be in *that* particular ward, he *did* know a friendly face that worked the night nurse's desk in the birthing center.

Carla was a pretty blonde with whom Walt had maintained a flirtatious but otherwise superficial relationship for the last few years. She was divorced, had grown kids, and appeared to have her life together. She dated occasionally, but did not appear to have a long-term boyfriend. She owned her own home outright and she drove a newer car that was bought and paid for with cash. In a nutshell, she didn't need a Walt Pitowski to mess things up. That didn't stop them from talking to one another. They'd bump into each other at the supermarket every month or so, exchanging a little small talk and a double entendre or two, before continuing on with their separate lives. They weren't exactly what you'd call *friends;* but Carla would more than likely help him discover whether or not Pam was somewhere in Rasmus Hospital.

It turned out that Pam wasn't at Rasmus Hospital after all. Pam *had* been brought here when the beating had first taken place, but her injuries were deemed too extensive for the little hospital to handle: a broken jaw, fractured skull, fractured tibia and four broken ribs. In short, Pam was a bloody mess. She'd been immediately transported by ambulance downstate to Saginaw, a bigger city with a bigger hospital, where there were surgeons and specialists more up to the task. The fact that she'd been transported by ambulance and not air-lifted by helicopter brought some small relief to Walt. If her injuries had been life threatening, they'd have called for the chopper. Saginaw St. Mary's was an hour and forty-five minutes away by car if you were really hauling ass. Walt wouldn't be making that run tonight, not if he wanted to show up for work in the morning, but at least he now knew where to find her.

He sat in the parking lot of Rasmus Hospital overlooking the main drag. The vehicle's windows were rolled down. A sultry breeze was still blowing from the south. The flow of traffic on Michigan Avenue was practically nonexistent. There wasn't much to do in Rasmus on a Monday night, and most of its citizens had been wise enough to turn in for the evening. One police car made a lazy left off of North Down River Road onto Michigan Avenue, finding its way back to the station. Walt searched through his pockets looking for a tin of snuff but came up empty. What he could really use, more than anything right now, was a cigarette. He'd quit smoking over a year ago: he didn't want to let it affect his training for the canoe marathon. He'd switched to snuff, but the urge to light up never really seemed to go away. There was something special about that rush of nicotine when the first puff of hot air explodes in your lungs. It was times like this, when things seemed more or less hopeless, that the desire to smoke was at its strongest. Chewing tobacco was a poor substitute, and he didn't even have that on hand. An ancient pack of chewing gum rested in one of the cup holders. Walt crammed two stale sticks of sugar-free spearmint into his mouth.

Another car made its way up Michigan Avenue before turning right onto North Down River. It too looked to be a Crown Vic: probably the next shift coming on to replace the sheriff's car that had just driven in the other direction. Walt looked at the digital clock on the dashboard and the display read ten-fifty: too early to call it a night, at least when the whole world was accusing you of things you didn't do.

He started the van and turned right out of the parking lot, following in the wake of the car that had passed just moments before. Walt wasn't sure where he was going, but it felt good to be moving: moving forward, moving anywhere. At the stop sign he made another right onto North Down River, eyeing the hatchery off to the side, still surrounded by the plastic yellow and black crime scene tape that danced in the wind. There were no lights on in the windows, no ninja prowlers skulking across the grounds. There was nothing but an abandoned, behemoth white building and the tattered yellow ribbons that announced an ongoing police investigation. The tail lights of the other car were barely visible in the distance. They eventually dipped and faded in the big curves ahead.

Once he reached the curve Walt stopped and turned Pinky around at the pullout behind a small grove of jack pines, the same one where Amberson often liked to sit in ambush. He drove back toward town, making a left at Michigan Avenue. He passed the hospital. He passed the brown house and the yellow house and the pink Victorian house on the one block that reminded him of Neapolitan ice cream. He passed the old-time single reel theater, its neon marquee shut down for the evening. Not a creature was stirring, not even a mouse. Downtown Rasmus was a time capsule, a silent portrait of Americana in still life. At the light he turned left once more, aiming the van south along the business loop. He stopped at a gas station, picked up a pack of Marlboro Reds, two bottles of Mountain Dew, and sixty bucks worth of unleaded. Then he ventured south again to where the roadway bled into the southbound freeway like a big river delta, flushing Rasmus's refuse and flotsam into that vast ocean of the world below. Saginaw was one hour and forty-five minutes away if you were really hauling ass: he was pretty sure he could make it in less than one-and-a-half. He hit the freeway ramp and put the pedal to the floor, hurtling through the night.

THIRTEEN

Deputy Don Frederics

There are certain guys who have wanted to join the police force since they were wearing short pants, and Don Frederics was one of them. For his friends and family, it was something they always knew but didn't fully understand. Frederics was born and raised in St. Johns, a small town ten miles or so north of Lansing, in the south-central part of the state. St. Johns is commonly known as the "Mint Festival City," although "commonly known" is a bit of an exaggeration. That tells you all you need to know right there: if the Annual Mint Festival is your biggest calling card, you're probably not competing for attention with Paris or London. St. Johns isn't a bad little town, it's just a small city surrounded by some incredibly fertile farm land and very little else. It's situated conveniently close to the state capital and is not too far of a commute from Michigan State University, or, in the derisive terms of their worthy in-state rivals, "Moo-U." It was a good place to grow up, and Frederics had the benefit of being raised in a two-parent household where his machinist father made a modest living and his mother stayed home raising little Donny and his two younger sisters.

There was no history of law enforcement in the Frederics' lineage, at least not on the winning side. They were solid, lower-middle-class people that went about their business quietly. His father worked in one of the smaller factories in the St. Johns industrial park, and his mom managed a clean and efficient household. There wasn't any family history on the wrong side of the law, either, excepting one uncle on his mother's side that had some recurring trouble with the bottle and his false belief that he could still see well enough to drive.

Donny was a kid that, from the time he was five years old, would tell any person who asked that "someday, I'm going to be a police officer." Usually this was greeted with something along the lines of "that's great, little fella" and a pat on the head. Sure he was going to be cop, just like his sister Karen was going to be an astronaut/pony farmer and little Kathy was going to be a supermodel *and* a brain surgeon. What kid knew what the heck they really wanted at that age?

Don did alright, though not spectacularly well, in school. His teachers often described him as "attentive." Report cards often noted that he "put forth great effort," not exactly a ringing endorsement. He tried out for the eighth-grade basketball team and missed the cut. That was pretty much the extent of his athletic career. He dated a couple of childhood sweethearts, though neither relationship got what you'd call "serious." He was not a physically imposing hero, nor was he the bullied runt that wanted power so that he could strike back at the world. Donald Paul Frederics was just an average kid. At no point in his childhood was there any indication of a proclivity for the order, structure, and commitment required to become an officer of the law.

Nevertheless, in his twenty-seventh year, following four years studying criminal justice at Western Michigan University and a four-year stint in the army, here he was, the newest and youngest member of the Shawono County Sheriff's Department. It was the culmination of a lifelong dream. He'd actually been on the force for slightly better than one year and ten months. Around here, barring an unexpected retirement, Frederics was likely to be known as "the new kid" for at least another ten years, and that was fine by him. This is what he'd been hoping for all along. What else was he going to do with his life? He had to admit, though, that it wasn't nearly as exciting as he'd first imagined.

There was a whole lot of aimless road patrol, writing traffic tickets and warnings, and of course filling out reams of paperwork. You'd think by this day and age, with computers and smartphones and everything, that all of that paperwork would be obsolete. You'd be thinking wrong, according to Sheriff Brimley. The Sheriff liked to have hard copy backup on everything and was slow to go digital. Frederics personally believed that Brimley was a dinosaur, living in the past. He was also smart enough to realize that Brimley was the boss, a very popular *elected* boss, who wasn't likely to be going anywhere soon, so Deputy Don kept his mouth shut and filled out forms in triplicate.

Once in a while he'd get called to a domestic violence case or a simple burglary and that livened things up. All hell could break loose in a household dispute. Then there were the weird ones. They had a big case just last year where one guy was grading the gravel alley behind his house on a riding tractor. His neighbor expressed dissatisfaction with the noise and dust by firing a shotgun directly at the driver. The tractor got hit, and the police came running when called. This was a big deal for Shawono County. There was some talk about Attempted Murder charges, but in the end the shooter got a slap on the wrist. The man's defense was something along the lines of "had I really wanted to hurt him, I'd have used better ammo." The jury of his peers, people that thought they pretty well understood the difference between bird shot and buck shot, bought his defense. True story.

By and large, most of what the deputy ended up doing fell under the heading of "old-school community relations." Keeping the peace was a priority: talking to kids at the elementary school about drugs, breaking up fights before they got out of hand, that sort of thing. If you bust kids smoking, chew them out good, scare them, and take their smokes. Let them know that you *could* talk with their parents, but you're letting them off easy *just this once.* If you bust kids drinking, take them home, chew their parents out good, and take their Boone's Farm Strawberry Hill or whatever it was that kids were slurping nowadays. Be out where people can see you, let them know who you are. Visibility was key.

Drunk drivers were probably his biggest concern. He'd have no mercy on them, take away their keys and lock them up before they got a chance to kill somebody. Sure, they'd be back on the street in a few days, but maybe a thousand-dollar fine and a month or two of weekends "volunteering" at the trash Compactor would teach them a lesson. He'd love to see stiffer punishment for drunks, but that was entirely out of his hands. What happened after an arrest was up to the county's prosecutor and judges. The longer he was on the job, the more Frederics was beginning to think that a police officer was nothing but a glorified guidance counselor with a gun and a badge.

Those thoughts explained why this was a banner week in the history of Shawono County law enforcement. Whatever had happened out at the Deer Track Inn last Friday, well that certainly went beyond your run-of-the-mill domestic disturbance. Matt Amberson was taking the lead in that investigation, but it didn't mean that Deputy Don couldn't be involved. So far they hadn't made a lot of progress solving that one. He knew they would, sooner or later. That asshole Walt Pitowski, well, he was just the kind of guy to look ripe for this one. Sure, Frederics had *told* Pitowski that he didn't believe Walt was guilty. Why wouldn't he? Lull him into a false sense of security, Basic Policing 101. You should never admit to a person of interest what you really think of him.

All the evidence pointed to Pitowski. For starters he had a history with the woman. They'd been known to be dating for months at the very least. He'd also been known to have an explosive temper. Just last Saturday he'd assaulted some guy who was working at the Compactor, though the guy he'd hit refused to cooperate. That was one of the problems around here: guys on the wrong side of the tracks wouldn't help enforce the law, even if it was for their own benefit. They didn't want to be perceived as rats by all of their rat friends. If he could get the man from the Compactor to press charges, it would help put some heat on Pitowski. At some point that woman, Pam Sharpe, would get her memory back and start talking. He knew that it was only a matter of time before Pitowski slipped up, and Deputy Don Frederics would be there to catch him when he did.

The dead guy at the hatchery, well that was pretty much a bonus. Who knew the last time Shawono County had an honest-to-God murder investigation? Not to say that it didn't happen, but it didn't happen often, maybe once every three or five years, if that. Something like this could make or break your career. Unfortunately, the State Police seemed intent on stealing this one out from underneath them. State Troopers seemed to think they were better than everyone else. Yeah, they probably *were* on another level than your average local force. They had more money and better resources was all, it didn't necessarily make them *better*. It was offensive, the way they charged into town all high and mighty, like they were the cat's ass.

Rayford Jefferson Brown Sr., the man they called "Wood Tick," had been a blight on the face of this community. Sure, he'd never been officially convicted of anything. The old coot had managed to fly just beneath the radar, selling a little bit of this and a little bit of that, a small-time, small-town dealer with his grubby little fingers in a bunch of different pies. Ray Sr. was also suspected of breaking into summer cottages when nobody was home and selling off electronics and guns and whatever he could get his paws on to his no-good friends. He was just smart enough to not get caught. That didn't mean he was so smart that he hadn't been noticed. The young deputy was nothing if not attentive. Don Frederics knew *exactly* who Ray Sr. was, and the world was a better place without him.

The deputy was shocked when Walt Pitowski found Wood Tick's body. At first he wondered if that might somehow complicate both investigations, having a person of interest in one case wrapped up in a second, even bigger incident. On the other hand, maybe it was for the best. Pitowski was undoubtedly getting nailed for that violence at the Deer Track. That was a given. Who else was there, realistically? The "random stranger" theory wasn't believable, not even to a jury that once bought into the "I would have used better ammo" defense. Was it really that much of a stretch to connect Pitowski to this murder at the hatchery? That would kill two birds with one stone. He'd have to think about that. It might be hard to prove Pitowski had a motive, but proving means and opportunity would be easy enough. With a little quality police work, a dual conviction could be in the cards. He'd take whatever he could get.

It had been a long day and it wasn't over yet. Somebody had screwed up the schedule to begin with, and then one of the other deputies had called in sick. The end result was that Frederics found himself working from eight in the morning until two that night, not a regular shift by any means. *Who knows what regular is anymore,* he groused. He'd just gotten behind the wheel of the Interceptor and started on patrol. Another officer's shift was almost ending, and Deputy Andrew Gervais was making his way back to the county building. He waved to Gervais as he pulled out of the sheriff's office parking lot.

Frederics was cruising up Michigan Avenue when he noticed Pitowski sitting in a pink minivan in the hospital's parking lot. "Could this clown make it any easier?" the deputy wondered. The guy might as well be wearing a radio tracking collar around his neck. *What kind of a man drives a pink minivan, anyway?* Should he go question Walt? He might shake him up a little, get him to squirm and kick loose a few details on the Deer Track incident. It was tempting, but Frederics decided to wait, easing the Interceptor around the corner and onto North Down River Road. There would be plenty of time to deal with his friend from the Geological Service later.

For a brief moment, cruising toward the big s-curve and beyond, Frederics thought that Pitowski might be following him. A car turned off the main drag, well behind him, seemingly headed in this same direction. Lights twinkled in the rear-view mirror, and the deputy adjusted the little switch to night time vision. For a moment he thought he saw a flash of pink. *The man couldn't really be that stupid, could he?* After a while the lights in the mirror disappeared, so he decided he must have been mistaken. His imagination was getting the best of him. He settled in for that long drive to the county line. The night belonged to Deputy Don.

FOURTEEN

Walt Pitowski

Saginaw St. Mary's was not Rasmus Hospital. The five-story sandstone block building housed over two-hundred and fifty beds in addition to a trauma center, bariatric center, sleep center, plastic surgery department, and all of the other bells and whistles associated with a first-rate medical operation in a medium-to-large city. Walt eyed the dashboard clock: twelve thirty-one a.m. The city was asleep when he rolled into town, but not *totally* asleep. Not "Rasmus" asleep, anyhow. Saginaw, for all its warts (and there were far too many to list), still had twenty-four hour convenience stores and all-night gas stations and even a White Castle to keep you fortified in the wee hours. There wasn't a lot of traffic on the streets, but there was some. Unlike some places, the powers that be hadn't gotten around to rolling up the sidewalks and putting them away until morning.

He stared at the red stone facade of the hospital, trying to calculate the best way to find Pam without drawing attention to himself. Walt realized that he had two problems. For one thing, he needed to gain entry into the hospital. There would probably be a security guard in the lobby, if the lobby was even open. Someone in a rent-a-cop uniform with a gun on his hip would be ready to tell Walt that visiting hours ended at nine. That would be *a* problem, but not an insurmountable problem. He was fairly certain there would be a way around that one.

The second larger issue, as far as Walt could tell, was that he had no idea what floor, let alone what room his possibly unconscious ex-girlfriend might be sleeping in. He couldn't call Pam and ask for directions. He wasn't likely to find a patient directory posted on the wall. There would be no "Carla" in Ob/Gyn to point him in the right direction. He'd never even set foot in this vast labyrinth, and didn't have the benefit of knowing every back stairway and janitor's closet the way he did in Rasmus. Not only didn't he know exactly *where* he was going, but he'd have no idea how to *get there* even if the room number were written on his arm in permanent marker. Walt lit his third cigarette of the night and sipped the last of a Mountain Dew Code Red. He'd need a plan.

Half an hour later he was still waiting on that plan to arrive. It was after one a.m. In that time he'd watched two ambulances pull up to the emergency room entrance. Both times the emergency vehicles backed up to the dual automatic doors. Both times they wheeled a person on a stretcher through the E.R. foyer and past the admitting desk. Most of the hospital remained cloaked in darkness. A few lights winked at him from hallways and nurses stations on the higher levels. People were still sick, doctors and nurses were still attending to the sick. A lone nurse in blue scrubs let herself out a smaller door in the front of the building, adjacent to the large revolving doors at the hospital's main entrance. Her shift must have just ended. She walked briskly to her car, keys in hand and eyes searching for potential assailants at the far edges of the lot. She arrived at her car intact, and quickly drove off to wherever she was headed.

One thirty a.m. and still waiting. A third ambulance was making the turn into the hospital drive, red lights flashing but sirens off. This must be a busy night in Saginaw. An emergency, but not enough of an emergency that they felt the need to wake the entire neighborhood. The other two ambulances had just departed, in no particular hurry to get to the next crisis. Walt still didn't have a plan, but he did detect an opportunity. He locked Pinky and hustled across the parking lot to the E.R. bay, where the white cube van with "EMS" lettering on its side was just backing up to the double glass doors. Walt tried to look official as the two paramedics stepped out of the van and began sliding a wheeled gurney, patient attached, from the back of the boxy vehicle.

"What have you got?" he asked, in what Walt believed to be his most professional tone. A twenty-something Latino man and a thirty-something African-American woman barely glanced at him as they prepared to spin the gurney around and through the hospital doors.

"Femoral neck fracture, Hispanic female, eighty-two years old," from the woman. "Nursing home slip and fall."

"Inside," Walt gestured toward the doors.

Both the paramedics gave him a funny look before the Latino guy mumbled "No shit, Sherlock."

Walt placed one hand on the tubular frame of the gurney as they slipped through the glass doors, pretending he was with the paramedics. They didn't seem to care or notice. He caught his first break as soon as they got inside. The security guard that had been stationed in the E.R. entry was momentarily away from his post. Maybe he went to get coffee, maybe he went to schmooze some registered nurse. Walt didn't care what the guy's reasoning was. In any event, the rent-a-cop wasn't *here*. Walt followed the gurney as it was wheeled through the steel interior doors toward triage, and then broke off unnoticed when he spied a lighted sign that read "stairway." He stepped into the stairwell. Walt was finally past the first hurdle, for what it was worth.

He poked his head into the hallway on two, but there were a lot of medical personnel milling about, and Walt figured it wasn't a good idea to walk into the middle of that pack. Three didn't look any better. He caught his second break when he stuck his head out on the fourth floor, because the nurse's station there was completely unattended. The hallway was empty. Pitowski eased his way around the desk and looked at one of the computer monitors flickering under the fluorescent lights. There were lots of windows open on the little screen, and what appeared to be a patient chart occupied most of the screen. It was the medical chart of someone named "Lateisha Smothers," definitely not the woman for whom Walt was searching. He scrolled through a list of tabs at the top of the screen and finally landed on something that said "Patient Census." Still no nurses in the hallway, but he knew he was living on borrowed time so long as he was standing behind this desk. He'd be hard pressed to come up with a likely excuse. Walt kept clicking. Less than two minutes later he had a room number: three forty-two. Walt stepped back into the stairwell, still undetected.

"Pam?" He barely recognized his former flame. White gauze encased a large portion of her skull. Her face was black and blue, her right arm in a cast. An IV drip was plugged into her left arm and she had an oxygen tube leading to her nostrils. He could tell she was going to be in for one long recovery: there were too many injuries to list. "Pam?" Still no answer. The room was dark, and Walt didn't want to turn on a light for fear of alerting the nurses. He touched her gently on the shoulder and she moaned ever so slightly. "Pam, wake up. It's me, Walt." She moaned a little louder this time. "Come on Pam, wake up, it's me." Nothing. "Shit, Pam, come on, wake up," a little too loud this time, but he was getting frustrated. Her eyes flitted open for a second before closing tight again. He didn't know what to do next.

"Walt." The first she'd spoken, at least to him. She was groggy, disoriented. Her eyes opened again. What was he doing at her bedside, anyway? Was this one more hallucination, a lingering effect from the morphine and Percocet coursing through her system? "Walt Pitowski?" If it was a hallucination or dream, it was a realistic one.

"Pam, are you okay?"

"Walt? What time is it?"

"Almost two."

"Morning or afternoon?"

"Morning."

"What are you doing here?" She rubbed her eyes with her left hand, the one that still worked properly. Unfortunately, it was beginning to look less and less to Pam like this was only a dream.

"I came to see *you*. I came as soon as I heard. You look like hell, by the way."

"And you still know how to flatter a lady," she answered. Nope, this was neither a hallucination nor a dream. Pitt or Clooney at her bedside now *that* would be a dream. A flying porpoise would be a hallucination. Walt Pitowski at her bedside could at best qualify as a flashback or a nightmare, depending upon the day. She was gradually coming around to the idea that it was none of the above. His presence was a reality. "Who let you in?" she asked warily. She was exhausted, but was gradually becoming aware of her surroundings.

"It doesn't matter. You look tired. Are you in a lot of pain?"

"Of course I look tired, it's two in the morning. And yes, it hurts. Christ, look at me, dumb-ass. I feel like I got run over by a semi. You drove all the way down here just to look at me?" her tone softened slightly. It was kind of charming in a boyish way, Walt coming to visit her in the middle of the night. It was also a little bit creepy.

"Yeah." All of a sudden he was feeling shy. Walt knew he wasn't the best at expressing emotion, at least not *tender* kinds of emotion. He had a tendency to put his foot in his mouth whenever he tried to get close to a woman. He cared for Pam, but words were failing him.

"Well that was sweet of you, honey, but I'm going to be alright. I'm a tough old broad. Now get out of here and go back home." She was exhausted from even this brief conversation, wanting nothing more than to fall back asleep.

"They think I did it." There, it was out.

"They think you did what?" She wasn't sure what he was saying. Sometimes talking with Walt was like talking to a kid. Who was "they" and what was "it"? Was this more morphine talking, or was Pitowski speaking in riddles? "You're not making sense, Walt."

"They think I did it. This, to you." He didn't know how to say it more clearly, but Pam didn't seem to be picking up on what he was trying to get across. Maybe the beating had affected her brain. "The cops think I beat you up."

"Well, did you?" At first he thought she must be kidding, but Pam looked like she might be serious.

"Come on, Pam, you know I didn't do this. You know I *couldn't* do something like this. Quit kidding, it's not funny. How'd it happen? What happened to you?"

"I have no idea. The last thing I remember I was washing glasses behind the bar at the Deer Track. Two days later here I am, lucky I'm alive. At least that's what they keep telling me. Personally, I'm not so sure."

"And you don't remember a thing?"

"I remember closing up shop and there was a knock at the door. I remember waking up in the ICU about eighteen hours ago, wondering why my head feels like an exploded melon and my arm doesn't work. That's about it. The doctors said I got beat up pretty bad. They say memories might come back to me, after a while, but I'm not banking on it. I'm not even sure I want to remember, to be honest. I just hope the other guy is feeling worse than I am."

"I'm sure you gave as good as you got." Walt knew it was unlikely, given her condition. Pam's assailant would have been found beaten half to death on the floor alongside her if that statement were true. It sure sounded like the right thing to say in the moment.

"I hope so. Now go home, let me sleep." Wincing in pain, she rolled over on her side, a signal that he was being dismissed.

Pitowski was almost to the door, inching slowly across the dark room, when something else occurred to him. He needed to tell her something. "Hey Pam?"

"Yes Walt."

"I love you." There was a silence.

"I know." She knew he was still standing just inside the doorway, waiting, waiting for a response. "Good night, Walt."

"Aren't you going to say it back?"

"Good night, Walt. Go home."

"I love you," he whispered once more, before sneaking out of the room and down the stairs.

FIFTEEN

The Watcher

Beating up the woman hadn't been part of the plan. It never was though, was it? Sometimes things *just went wrong*. This certainly fell into that category. The old man, on the other hand, the one they called Wood Tick, well, he had it coming. He should have *known* he had it coming. Anybody that knew him, anybody that had anything to do with him whatsoever, knew that you DO NOT SCREW with The Watcher. Period. Wood Tick had crossed the line. *He should have seen it coming,* he reflected. He'd made a choice. The old man had long since passed his "discard by" date.

It wasn't about the drugs, not really. There were lots of guys selling stuff throughout the county, guys selling stuff throughout every county in every state in the whole damn country. It was a universal problem and it wasn't likely to go away anytime soon. Whether you liked it or not, and apparently a large chunk of the U. S. population seemed to like it, drugs were here to stay. He'd heard arguments for legalizing some of it, taking the profit out of the system, and he had to admit that those arguments sounded pretty convincing: at least until some sixteen-year-old girl died from an overdose of some bad shit. Try looking her parents in the eye and discussing "free choice" and "the market economy" after that one. Fortunately, The Watcher had never been put in a position to have that particular conversation.

No, his bone of contention with the old man had been purely personal. The stuff in the duffel bag, that was all a sideshow to the larger issue. He couldn't rightfully leave the duffel bag of goodies sitting there in the hatchery, not after the shooting, because that might provide a trail back to the root of the whole problem. The old man had crossed him, crossed him in a big way, and he should have known better.

The killing itself had been relatively easy. This surprised him. Sure, he'd come close many times before, but until now it had never been necessary, taking a life. Most times there were more subtle ways to get your point across: implied threats, random violence, or a little anonymous intimidation.

Any of them were usually more than enough to make yourself heard, loud and clear. Wood Tick had presented a problem of a different sort. Where usually The Watcher was the one handing out messages, in this case the old man had threatened *him*, and it wasn't implied, either. The old man had explained quite explicitly how he intended to ruin The Watcher's career, unless he got what he wanted. It was amazing that a mush-mouthed old bastard like that thought he could flap his gums without incurring any consequences. That was impermissible.

When he'd looked into the old guy's face, standing in that musty, fish-smelling cavern of a room, there was a moment of recognition. Wood Tick almost looked like he believed that The Watcher was there to pay him a social call. He didn't appear *happy* about the visit, not exactly. It was more that he was somehow *relieved*. Was he relieved because he recognized a familiar face, a harmless customer rather than the long arm of the law, or was it a relief because he knew that what he eventually had coming to him had finally arrived? It was probably the first case. The old man had always been far too shallow and self-serving to admit his own mortality. Well, that misperception had certainly been erased. As he gently squeezed the trigger on the nine-millimeter semi-auto, The Watcher saw the awakening in Wood Tick's eyes. Now there was one less problem in the world.

After bumping off the old man at the hatchery, he'd made his way along the edge of the river and back to his vehicle. He was fairly certain that his presence had gone undetected, and was careful to follow the posted speed limits as he made his way out of town and beyond. There was no need to mess things up by driving like a lunatic. He'd followed the highway north to the Sparrow River Forest, finding a nice pullout that broke away from Wolverine Valley Road. Coyotes howled in the distance. He dug a hole three feet in diameter and four feet deep, dropping the duffel into the bottom of the pit. Of course he took the three-hundred Oxycodone out of the sack first, because that might come in handy, but the rest of that junk could rot in the grave. He shoveled fresh earth over the black bag, making sure to cover the freshly turned soil with leaves and twigs once he was done. This bag would not be found.

He'd gone home, taken a quick shower, and changed his clothes. He'd even bothered to shave, just to be on the safe side. You never know what residue might be clinging to a five o'clock shadow. The Watcher swallowed one of the little tablets, just to take the edge off. The Watcher was feeling crisp and refreshed when he headed out the door in search of a quick drink and a victory lap for having prevented one small problem from developing into a significantly larger one. Life was good, and it only got better when he found himself the lone customer in the company of that attractive bartender at the Deer Track Inn.

It was in no way his intention to hurt the woman at the bar. If anything, he was actually rather fond of her. She was cute, although a little past her prime. Blond and solid, somewhere in her late forties or early fifties, you could tell that she knew how to handle herself. You had to be tough, running a bar on your own, especially as a woman. She didn't talk much when he had the occasion to drink there. She often seemed to be stewing over something that was going on in her personal life. The woman seemed simultaneously distracted yet efficient. Despite her disposition, or maybe on account of it, she'd exuded a bit of that bossy sexuality that he found personally appealing.

The Watcher had found her attractive, but hadn't gotten around to acting on those feelings. So far their relationship had been limited to him sitting at the bar once or twice a week, slowly sipping a single beer before leaving an overly generous tip and fading into the night. Now he'd never get to find out if they were compatible. A crying shame is what it was.

When he'd first arrived at the door of the Deer Track, he had no idea how late the hour really was. Stalking, killing, driving, burying, driving again, going home to bathe and change, it all took much more time than he'd realized. Maybe it was the adrenaline rush, but his body was telling him it *couldn't* be any later than midnight. He was completely flabbergasted when he found that the door was locked. He knocked anyways. He only wanted one drink, a celebration of sorts. Maybe the door had been locked in error; maybe there was a bar full of morose locals drinking on the other side. He thought that there still ought to be a couple of hours before last call. *Please, he thought, let this locked door be a mistake.* It was out of character for him, knocking and all, but he badly wanted to sit down and have one single drink. He would inquire politely, and if no one answered the door he would go back home.

He was even more surprised when she *did* finally answer the door. The bar was closed, it turned out. It was nearly two-thirty, much later than he'd thought. Everyone had cleared out over half an hour ago. No, she couldn't let him in, even for one drink, because she wasn't going to risk losing her liquor license for anyone under any circumstance, it didn't matter who you

98

were. Finally he'd convinced the woman to let him sit at a table and warm up for a few minutes while she closed up shop for the night. She knew him, after all. He was a regular. The bartender gave in, and let him take a seat inside. She even brought him a Pepsi while he sat patiently.

For a few minutes things were going fine. She settled up the till and was putting a handful of things away where they belonged back behind the bar. The woman wasn't very chatty, but she asked how he was doing, what brought him out so late, things like that. Small talk. It was as pleasant a moment as he'd experienced in a very long time. Then she glanced at his boots, and everything went wrong.

"What's that on your foot?" she'd asked. It was a simple enough question. There was nothing malicious in her tone, but she'd spotted something. She didn't know *exactly* what it was, but it was something out of place.

He hadn't noticed until now. The man leaned over from his three-quarter full glass of Pepsi with ice and saw a faint red splatter on the upper portion of his left boot. He thought about this. It probably would have been wise to change his shoes while he was back at the house getting dressed. He *could* tell the woman that he'd been painting, or that he'd cut himself earlier in the day. He could say he'd hit a deer and must have gotten blood on his foot while dragging it from the roadway. He could say he'd been out hunting and had cleaned a few grouse right after dinner. Any of these would provide a convincing cover, if only he could pick a story and stick with it. He ran through the options in his head and was about to go with the grouse, because that seemed both manly and in keeping with the season. Grouse was definitely the way to go. Unfortunately, it was at just that moment that those pills slid out of his pocket and onto the floor. Two-hundred and ninety-nine Oxycodone tablets clattering across the hardwood would be a lot harder to explain away than any splash of red. Things devolved from there.

The woman put up a hell of a fight, he had to admit. The Watcher was glad she wasn't standing behind the bar when things went down: she'd have been a hell of a lot harder to get to, for one thing, and it turned out she kept a pretty big pistol hidden back there, for another. He didn't find that out until later. As it was he had the element of surprise on his side and she never quite made it to that pistol. For this he was grateful. She was standing over him, right there at the table, when the little yellow tablets hit the ground. He got in one good blow to the jaw, and for most women that would have been enough. He gave her a stiff kick to the ribs as she went down, and heard the crack of an arm with a second kick. He liked this bartender, actually found her quite attractive. It was a pity he'd have to kill her, too, but he wasn't about to leave any loose ends.

It was a complete shock to The Watcher when she grabbed one ankle and yanked his feet out from under him. The back of his head hit the planks like a ripe melon. There were stars swimming in the sky, and something warm began oozing through his hair. Before he could rise up and regroup, she'd delivered a chair to his midsection. Damn if she wasn't feisty. At this point he knew there'd be no turning back. She needed killing. The man rolled over in pain, flailing on the floor and lashing out with both feet. A boot connected with flesh, and another kick brought the familiar sound of breaking bones. He was back on his feet, but she was right there with him, still struggling. He couldn't imagine where she got her strength from. Tables were overturned, and he bull rushed her toward the bar rail. He got hit with something, maybe another chair? It shattered across his back, and his left leg was temporarily paralyzed. Grasping at straws and realizing that he was losing control of the situation, he grabbed a leg from a broken chair, swinging it over and over again.

Ten minutes later the place was in shambles. He could scarcely believe all that had taken place in that brief chaos, but the end result was that the woman was dead, or near enough, on the floor of the Deer Track Inn. The Watcher made his way painfully out the door, a door hanging precariously from a shattered wooden frame. He popped another yellow Oxy into his mouth, got in his car and sped away. In retrospect, he probably should have passed on that Pepsi, and he probably should have finished the job.

SIXTEEN

Walt Pitowski

"You look like something the cat dragged in." Marcus Washington was not a man with a highly developed sense of humor. Having spent thirty-plus years in the same job can do that to you. He often mistook wry observation and exhausted clichés for stellar wit. This was one of those instances.

"Yeah, I know." Walt was bleary-eyed. It was after four a.m. when he'd gotten back to the house. He'd let Doofus out for a few minutes, let the dog back in, and immediately passed out on the couch. He'd gotten a little under three hours sleep and was feeling drastically shortchanged by the Sand Man. "I feel more like something the cat threw up."

"Do you care to explain what happened at the job site yesterday? I've already got Dewers' version of events."

It figured. Not that there was much Walt could do about it, and not that Dewers' version of events would be all that different from his own. It was the *tone* of Dewers' story that would undoubtedly differ from Walt's, a tone that cast an aspersion of negligence, and possibly even *guilt,* his way. He'd be blamed for unnecessarily delaying what should have been the simplest of assignments. He'd be blamed for goofing off when he was actually on his lunch break. He'd probably be blamed for the impending collapse of the American economy, just for the hell of it. Walt could sense that Washington was already pissed off, and the day hadn't even begun. *The world loves a scapegoat*, he ruminated.

"There's not much to tell. I peeked in a window, saw a body lying on the ground, called 911, and now the cops want us off the hatchery site for a while. We got hit with some bad luck."

"It was a case of bad luck?" Washington sounded incredulous. He wasn't buying this theory, not in the least. Pitowski could tell some whoppers, but this was right up there with his biggest and best. There was no such thing as "bad luck," not in this world. You made your own fortune. Live by the sword, die by the sword, or something along those lines.

"Bad luck," Walt confirmed, and he meant it, meant it with all sincerity.

Washington silently looked him up and down, letting his mind consider all the logical responses to such a bald-faced excuse. "Bad Luck." He almost spat the words. This man was truly unbelievable. Pitowski brought more than his share of "bad luck" to any job. At some point, you'd think the guy would realize that what passed for "luck" or "the breaks" was self-inflicted misery. All of this ran wildly through Marcus Washington's mind as he considered the appropriate actions he could take, given the situation. (If nothing else, Washington was a measured man). There was no snap to judgment. He wasn't going to say anything that could come back to haunt him, say in a lawsuit from a disgruntled employee somewhere down the road. Neither was he a man to suffer needlessly. After a few minutes he finally settled on "Get the hell out of here. You can take the day off." Sending Pitowski home was as much for his own mental health as it was for Walt's.

Walt wasn't about to argue: he could use some time to himself. "Thanks boss," he chirped, and he was out the door.

When he got to the van, someone had taken a Sharpie marker and two pieces of card stock, made mock signs that said "Mary Kay Cosmetics," and duct taped them to both front doors. Jerks. This was getting old, *really* old. A new vehicle was near the top of his short list entitled "things that need to be found ASAP." Walt peeled the signs off and threw them in the back seat. Getting the duct tape's adhesive off the pink paint was going to be a pain in the butt. They probably made something specifically for that, and he'd have to stop by the auto parts store later and pick up a bottle. It wasn't hard for Walt to figure out who the likely culprit was: Dewers, getting him back for one of the dozens of pranks Pitowski himself had played on his coworker. He didn't find this at all funny.

Sleep would be welcomed, but Walt knew he was too wound up to lie around the house all day. He decided he'd check out that piece of recreational land, the one on the outskirts of town, across from the M.A.T.E.S. facility. Maybe he'd find a new spot for hunting deer or maybe he'd just burn a few calories and clear his head. If nothing else he'd kill some time. The sun was shining bright in the sky, though the temperature had dropped ten degrees since yesterday. Old Man Winter was on his way.

There were three vehicles in the parking lot when Walt reached the access gate. The Plymouth Breeze he'd noticed last Saturday morning was there once again, along with a newer powder-blue Chrysler Pacifica and a battered GMC Sierra painted in the day-glo orange of a retired county road commission truck. They all boasted Michigan license plates. The place seemed surprisingly busy for a Tuesday morning, but then, what did Walt know of the ways of the chronically unemployed? A thirty-ish woman pushing a baby stroller passed him by, walking in the other direction as he hiked toward the river. Walt pegged her as the driver of the Pacifica. She was too well put together to be driving the clanky Plymouth, and certainly not the type to be piloting a rusted out former plow truck, at least not with a baby on board.

He veered off the main path, following a few lightly-used deer runs. They were nothing more than beaten-down tracks that disappeared through the tall meadow and into the woods beyond. As Walt stepped into the waist-high grass, legions of grasshoppers leapt in advance of his every footfall. Each deer trail eventually led to either a fence or a leftover slash pile from logging operations. The slash piles, massive combinations of uprooted stumps, unsalable timber, and decaying brush, were gnarled messes that blocked his path. In some instances they were completely impenetrable. They provided good cover for small game, rabbit and squirrel and the like, but would only block his shooting lanes come deer season. This was not an area Walt would want to hunt. At least he'd learned something. On each occasion where he found his progress halted, he'd backtrack to the main walking path and continue toward the river.

The bridge was a steel and timber affair, slightly bowed and spanning the Grand Limoneaux River twenty-five feet below. The arch itself was about sixty feet in total length, stretching from shore to shore. Walt paused on the far edge of the span and watched a pileated woodpecker as it hammered its way to the top of a leafless tree. The skeletal tree was yet another victim of the emerald ash borer. Between those little wood-boring vampires and the plague of oak wilt disease, large swaths of the deciduous forest were rapidly dying off. It didn't give him much faith in the future of wildlife around here. What would the animals eat once all the acorns and nuts disappeared?

A brook trout repeatedly rose to the surface in a shallow eddy downstream. The tiny fish, less than six inches in length, kissed the river's surface as it slurped down minuscule Trico flies that hatched in the mid-morning sun. Walt watched this fish come up eight times with clock-like precision. There was a perfect rhythm to its feeding pattern. He could almost envy that fish, with its perfectly suited environment and totality of focus; that is, at least until he pictured a flotilla of drunken clowns in aluminum rental canoes plowing down the river every summer weekend, mucking up the water and spooking every creature for miles around.

He was reflecting on this, the balance and mystery of such a complex ecosystem, when two men stepped out of the shadows one hundred or so yards upstream of the bridge. They warily abandoned the protective shade of the tag alders and gnarled cedars along the water's edge for the grassy plains above. Walt caught their movement out of the corner of his eye, watching them from his perch amidst the shadows. Their thin builds seemed hauntingly familiar, as if Walt had met the two somewhere before. The pair scurried up the bank and through the meadow as if they had something or someone chasing them. They weren't running, but they moved like they were being deliberately evasive. Walt continued to glance over his shoulder and watched as they reached the footpath a good two hundred yards nearer the access gate. They still hadn't noticed him. The duo would still need to cover three-quarters of a mile back to where the vehicles were parked. Where had Walt seen these guys before? He searched his memory, but he continued to draw a blank. It had to have been recently. In any event, Walt Pitowski decided to see where they were going.

He shadowed them the whole way, clinging to the edge of the tree line so that his presence would remain undetected. Walt couldn't say *why* he was stalking these men; he was just following an instinct. There was something odd about their behavior, the way they carried themselves. He couldn't exactly put his finger on it, what bothered him about the pair. They weren't carrying jugs of corn mash or hauling a dead body on their shoulders or shooting rifles in the air while clamoring for revolution. It was just their *look*, the way the two seemed to be constantly checking over their shoulders, like a pair of kids with their hands stuck in the cookie jar. He'd had this instinct once before, up on the Sparrow River, and it'd turned out that he was correct. Well, more or less correct. Correct enough, as far as Walt was concerned.

Walt was betting on the Plymouth Breeze all the way. They looked like the kind of trouble that would be driving a piece of junk with a mismatched fender, but it turned out he was wrong. When they reached the lot, the two men got into the orange Sierra pickup and slowly pulled away. The Pacifica was already gone. At least he'd been right about the woman with the stroller.

At this point it occurred to Walt that the other car, the Plymouth, might just be abandoned. He hadn't seen anyone else in or around the river, no other potential driver walking along the main path, so what logical excuse for that extra car might there be? It didn't really matter. Pitowski waited two minutes, giving the men a head start, before sprinting to the Pontiac and following the brightly colored truck.

They headed east, away from town, turning right at the first paved road and crossing over the river to the South. They didn't seem to be in any rush. Walt hung back as far as he could, finding it was pretty easy to keep track of a brilliant orange pickup truck in the middle of the day. He also realized that, for the two guys driving along in that bright orange truck, a Pepto-Montana lingering in the rear-view mirror might be a tip that someone was tailing them. There was a reason cops didn't drive hot pink cars. He drifted back a little further, letting the Sierra become nothing more than a shiny metal dot, disappearing and reappearing with the dips and rises of the road ahead.

When he reached the stop sign a mile up the road, he realized he'd made a critical mistake. He hadn't seen the truck since the last dip in the road, a half mile back. There were a handful of places since then that the truck might have turned, but he didn't think they had. Walt hadn't even considered the idea that they *might* turn off. He never should have let them get so far in front of him: the Sierra was nowhere in sight.

The state highway in front of him ran east and west. The road he was on turned to dirt on the other side of the highway. There was no cloud of dust leading in *that* direction, so Walt ruled out the road less travelled. Did they go right, then, doubling back toward town, or did they go left on the highway and continue to the east? Walt guessed east. It seemed like the logical choice. He hung a hard left, putting the pedal to the floor in an attempt to gain ground. He'd like to catch sight of the orange truck before they turned off again. If they turned again soon, well, he wasn't likely to find them. The Pontiac held the road particularly well, even at eighty. Hell, the Suzuki probably would have vibrated into the ditch by now, shaking across the surface like those plastic men on the electric football set he'd had as a boy. *I could get used to this,* Walt mused, holding the wheel of the van loosely in his left hand.

He drove right by them the first time. Walt was still cruising along at eighty miles per hour, his mind set on autopilot. Any minute he expected to see a brightly colored tailgate on the road up ahead. He'd failed to take into account that the now boarded-up site of the Deer Track Inn was too appealing a novelty for anyone to ignore. A drinking establishment, with a broken front door and window? Who wouldn't stop and look around? Maybe there was loose inventory that needed to be secured. The Sierra was parked behind the bar, the pickup's front end barely visible from the highway. Walt blew past it like it wasn't even there, caught a glimmer of orange in his side view mirror, and immediately looked for a place to turn around and backtrack.

On the second swing past, the Montana now facing in the other direction, he slowed the van to a crawl. The two men were nowhere to be seen. Their truck was still tucked neatly behind the bar. Walt and the van rolled on by. He wanted to investigate, find out what they were up to, but Walt didn't want to leave Pinky where it would be obvious. Hell, how could they not notice this thing? He decided to stash the Pontiac in the tree-lined drive of an unoccupied cabin a quarter mile further up. Minutes later he was snaking through the scraggly jack pines on foot, inching his way to the back side of the Deer Track.

They weren't there. They weren't in the truck, which sat empty alongside the big blue dumpster and the cases of empty liquor bottles stacked neatly outside the rear entrance. The men weren't inside the bar, a fact Walt confirmed by peeking through the one window that hadn't been smashed to pieces in the brawl the other night. It was *possible* that they were hiding somewhere inside, ducking behind the bar or locked in the restroom, but highly *unlikely*. What would be the point? The back door of the Deer Track was locked and the front door had been boarded shut. It didn't look like they could have gotten in, even if they'd tried. They weren't walking around the outside of the bar, something Walt verified by quickly circling the little structure, then circling again in the opposite direction. His two suspicious friends had vamoosed.

Walt looked through the rear window of the orange truck hoping for some kind of clue as to their whereabouts. Both doors were locked. Walt took this to mean they weren't coming back anytime soon; either that or something valuable was stored inside the truck. Nobody locked their car doors around here. There was a small black duffel bag resting in the middle of the split-bench seat, a bag slightly larger than a toaster oven. It was partially unzipped, but Walt couldn't see what might be inside. Either way, it didn't look like a bag that would hold anything of value. It was too small, for one thing, and too beat up, for another. The passenger side floor of the truck was covered with empty soda bottles, crushed beer cans, spit-out sunflower hulls, and an assortment of miscellaneous papers. It looked like a garbage dump. Actually, he realized, it looked an awful lot like a truck Walt Pitowski would own. There wasn't much to learn here. He circled the building one more time to no avail. They had to be up to no good: there was no other explanation. Walt reluctantly returned to the minivan.

He thought about staking out the place, waiting for the two men to return. What would that tell him, though, even if they returned, and how much of his day would he waste in the meantime? What if they didn't come back until tomorrow? What if they never came back? He decided to give up and drive back into town. He'd talk to the cops when he got there.

It was just Walt's luck that Don Frederics was the officer at the front desk when he arrived at the sheriff's department. He'd rather talk to pretty much anyone, *anyone*, other than Frederics. Even Matt Amberson would be a better choice. Frederics was a smug jerk, and that little song and dance he'd done on Saturday back at the house, "For what it's worth, Pitowski, I don't think you had anything to do with this…," well, he was undoubtedly blowing smoke up Walt's nether regions. That was how he operated. You couldn't trust a word that came out of the guy's mouth.

"Let me get this straight, Pitowski. You want to report a crime, but you've got no evidence that a crime has been committed. You're not even sure what that crime *might be*, if indeed someone were *thinking* about committing a crime. You've no knowledge of the names of these suspected criminals, but you do have a description of a vehicle they were allegedly driving. You forgot to write down a license plate number, but the car was parked temporarily in, of all places, the parking lot of an establishment open to the general public. This you find highly suspicious. Does that about sum it up?"

"Yeah, that about sums it up. I'm just letting you know."

"Well thanks for 'letting us know.' I'll put out an APB right now, see if I can get Sheriff Brimley himself in here to work the case. Maybe he can pick you up a cup of coffee on the way here. Do you take cream and sugar? Can he get you some coffee cake to go with it? Do you think we'll need to get the feds involved?" He was now wearing his best and brightest "smug jerk" smile. It was tempting to belt him, just once, right in those bright, shiny teeth. Guess who'd be smiling then? After entertaining this joyful vision in his mind and considering the consequences, Walt managed to hold back.

"Fuck you, Frederics."

"Back at you, Pitowski. You might want to stop wasting my time. Aren't you supposed to be working somewhere? You do have a job, don't you?" The smile was gone, replaced with his regular sneer.

"I'm off for the day."

"How could anyone tell? I suggest you stay where we can find you, in case we have any questions later. Find something to do with your life, and try not to trip over any more dead bodies."

"Fuck you and your mother both, Frederics."

"Always happy to serve," The smirk returned. Deputy Don Frederics strutted back into his office, slamming the door behind him.

SEVENTEEN

He caught a late lunch at the Rasmus Restaurant. The mood in that little diner was beyond gloomy. Rumor had it that the place would be calling it quits soon, joining the legions of other empty store fronts that were slowly gnawing away at the core of downtown Rasmus. It would be one more hole in a business strip rapidly filling with holes. He wasn't sure why this surprised him, but it did. The restaurant had always been there, as far as he knew. While the town seemed to have been fighting a downward economic spiral ever since the sixties, there was a local belief that the restaurant was impervious to change. People still had to eat, right? Many businesses had come and gone, but the Rasmus Restaurant was always there, as it had been for over seventy-five years. Hanging on the wall were framed newspaper prints, faded yellow clippings celebrating the restaurant's opening, alongside articles on the birth of the Dionne Quints to prove it. Walt ate his Reuben sandwich in silence, sipping coffee and staring out the window at the cars rolling down Michigan Avenue.

The bells hanging on the front door jingled as a customer left, and another customer entered before the door had time to close. Walt gave her the quick once over. She was a thin, pretty woman with dark curly hair, here to pick up a carry-out order. Her food wasn't yet ready. She didn't have that photo-shopped beauty that you find on magazine covers: she was more the "girl next door that's still too good for *you*" type. For a moment Walt felt certain that he knew her, but then decided this was only wishful thinking. He'd met a lot of people in his life, but she seemed like the kind of woman that would run in different circles; either that or she would run in a straight line, away from the likes of him. The woman was still waiting at the front counter when Walt got up to pay. Louise was behind the register, ready to ring him up. Old, cheerful Louise.

"Was everything alright?" This was one of the things that Walt really liked about this place. Louise was always friendly, no matter what and no matter who came to her register.

"Great, thank you."

"That'll be ten-twenty-four, sweetie."

Walt handed her a ten and a one, and she made change.

"Here you go, darling. You have a great day."

"You too." Walt slipped three quarters and a penny into his pocket, then went back to the table and dropped three singles down for a tip. He went back to the front of the restaurant and was in the process of opening the door when the pretty woman waiting at the register spoke.

"You're Doofus's dad, aren't you?"

It caught him off guard, and he let go of his grip on the door's handle. He would greatly prefer not to be known as "Doofus's dad," for a lot of reasons, but hell, if it broke the ice with this young woman, well, damn straight he was Doofus's dad. "Yes I am," Walt proudly proclaimed.

"I thought so. How are you doing?"

"Great, thanks. And how about you?" He still had no idea who this vixen was, but he wasn't about to let *her* know that. Experience had taught him that women liked it if you could at least attempt to remember their names.

"Fine, thanks. You don't remember me, do you?"

"Of course I do." Walt figured this wouldn't qualify as a 'whopper' as it was more of the 'white lie' variety: an untruth told for the benefit of the recipient. It was also for his benefit, but that was beside the point. So what if he was stalling for time?

"What's my name?"

"How could I forget you?" Walt could sense panic setting in, but he wasn't ready to let on. He looked straight into her pretty green eyes, two pools as deep and inviting as the Caribbean Sea. God, she was beautiful. How could he forget? He was frantically searching his memory for where he'd met this woman before. It finally popped into his head. "JoAnn, right?"

"So you do remember. I'm sorry I ever doubted you."

"That's alright. I doubt me all the time." He thought his joke might come across as sounding a little stupid once it left his lips, but she laughed, so it must have been alright. He'd met this pretty woman just once before, earlier this year in the Sparrow River Forest. She was a schoolteacher from some suburb of Chicago and had been staying at that yoga camp up on the Sparrow River. JoAnn had given Walt and his dog a lift back to their truck when they'd become separated from the vehicle. "Are you still living near Chicago? Lincoln Park, wasn't it?"

"Not bad. You're close. Tinley Park, on the south side of town. Lincoln Park is up on the north side, a tad more expensive. No, I'm not living there anymore. I'm a local now. I figured I was spending all of my free time enjoying northern Michigan, I might as well live here and be closer to the things that I love. I got a job teaching kindergarten at Rasmus Primary School."

"Lucky kindergartners."

"You're too sweet. It's more like 'lucky me.' How's my friend Doofus?" Louise reappeared behind the register with a white paper take-out bag, and JoAnn paid her for the food.

"Great. Absolutely great." He was grinning. Walt had to remember to take better care of that dog. He'd have never guessed that Doofus was the equivalent of Willy Wonka's Golden Ticket for women.

"Glad to hear it. You treat him well, and tell him I'd love to see him again sometime."

"Absolutely." *Shit, that sounded lame.* "He'd love to see you again, too, I'm sure." *That was slightly better.*

Walt held the door as she exited the restaurant. The bells jingled behind them. JoAnn turned left at the pavement. He figured either her car was parked further up the street or she'd be walking the five and a half blocks to work. His van was parked at the curb, directly in front of the restaurant. This would be where they parted ways. He should probably offer the lady a ride, but that might be pushing it. There was no sense in coming on too strong.

"Well, you take care," he said, watching her walk away.

"You too," she answered, already ten strides further up the block.

Walt stepped off the curb, slowly opening the driver's side door to Pinky. He had the key in the ignition and was almost ready to shut the van door when he heard her voice.

"Nice car!" she yelled over her shoulder, and she sounded as if she meant it.

Walt drove slowly up Michigan Avenue. He passed the elementary school, failing to catch a glimpse of that pretty young schoolmarm along the way. She must have driven her own car. He passed the hospital, its parking lot full on this late afternoon. He turned right at the stop sign onto North Down River Road. He watched the hatchery slide by on his right, with Sheriff Brimley's white Ford Excursion and the proprietary blue GMC Yukon of the State Police parked high atop the bluff. A forest green Chevy Tahoe, this one clearly marked with the emblem of the State Conservation Department on both doors, had joined them. *What have they learned about the dead guy?* Walt wondered, but he knew they wouldn't tell him, even if he asked politely.

A county Police Interceptor appeared in his rear view mirror and Walt figured it must be deputy Amberson on the way to his favorite speed trap. Sip some coffee, eat a few donuts, take a nap, and ring up a couple of hundred dollars in speeding tickets: it was all in a day's work for his nemesis. The worst part of it all, at least in his eyes, was that it was Walt's tax dollars that were paying the officer's salary. The Police Interceptor was still behind him, but Pitowski wasn't going to give Amberson any free ammunition. He kept the Montana five miles per hour under the limit, something he found excruciatingly difficult to do when the posted speed was only thirty-five to begin with. Still, the last thing Walt needed was another citation.

He turned north onto the expressway, hoping he'd shake the tail when the good deputy continued down the surface road to his not-so-secret grove of pine trees. Walt figured he'd head north for a while, kill some more daylight. He was slightly surprised when he observed the Police Interceptor turn onto the freeway behind him. County cops generally didn't patrol the interstate. They usually left that to the State troopers. Maybe Amberson needed something from Wal-Mart or one of the big box stores up in Gaylord. Maybe he was asked to assist on a fellow officer's stop north of here. Maybe he was bored. Whatever the reason, Walt didn't appreciate him being back there, following him around like he was some little kid.

It didn't take long before Walt spotted his opportunity. He waited until there was a short line of cars between himself and the deputy, a rolling roadblock in both lanes comprised of people afraid to break the law, even by as little as one mile per hour. The presence of one marked police car could clog the flow of traffic like nobody's business. Pitowski punched the accelerator, and the Montana responded accordingly.

Thirty minutes later he was approaching the exit for Sturgeon. Walt debated whether to get off the freeway here or keep driving. Did he really need to relive all that crap from last summer? There were some ugly memories tied up in this town. He hemmed and hawed, but in the end he decided to get off the expressway. If he didn't, he'd end up driving clear to Mackinaw City, and what would be the point of that? Shit, he'd already wasted enough gas for no apparent reason.

The burg of Sturgeon was sleeping, even at four o'clock on a Tuesday afternoon. Walt decided that Sturgeon was *always* sleeping: it wasn't a place anybody deliberately went *to* as much as it was a town you went *through* on the way to somewhere else. It didn't benefit local commerce that Sturgeon wasn't truly a waypoint *between* anything other than the freeway and the forest. It was conceivable that if someone wasn't quite smart enough to get gas in Gaylord and they were running low they might stop in Sturgeon. It was also possible that if one were really hungry and unwilling to drive another twenty minutes north or south for the nearest McDonald's, they'd think about it. If indeed that was true, the options were limited. The town did contain an independent grocery store, small though it was, and the ever-popular Liquor Barn. You could get a shrink-wrapped torpedo sandwich from one of the two gas stations, though you'd be best advised to skip any sub that contained mayonnaise. Freshness dates are rarely provided on filling station sandwiches. Walt was suddenly glad that he wasn't hungry.

Thirty bucks worth of unleaded was all he really needed. He rolled up to the pump at the old Best Oil station. One downside to Pinky, he was quickly realizing, was that while she wasn't exactly a gas hog, it took an awful lot of cash to fill up a twenty-two gallon tank. It didn't matter that he was getting about the same miles per gallon as he did in the much smaller and significantly less comfortable Samurai. What was eating him was that he'd pretty much have to take out a home equity loan if he ever decided to fill this cavernous fuel tank. It was annoying, was what it was. He knew if he were being logical that it shouldn't matter. Thirty bucks was thirty bucks. The money still bought the same amount of fuel. If you were averaging somewhere between twenty-six and twenty-eight miles to the gallon, and the stupid minivan was, then there wasn't much to complain about. Yet it still ticked him off. He let the pump slow down considerably when it reached twenty-nine dollars and ninety cents, clicking in the last nickel's worth of fuel one squirt at a time.

He'd barely started to screw the gas cap back in place when he saw the orange Sierra rumble up the freeway exit, blow through the stop sign at the top of the ramp, and swing eastbound onto Wolverine Valley Road. He'd be damned if those bastards weren't heading into the state forest. Walt sprinted inside to pay for his gas. That's where he got stuck waiting in line behind the lone customer, a heavy-set man in his early forties. This customer couldn't make up his mind between the eight different types of scratch-off lottery tickets they had available. He seemed unable to process what should be a simple choice, even by northern Michigan standards. There was one acne-scarred kid in his teens working behind the counter, attempting to answer the portly guy's inane questions as best he could.

After thirty seconds of deliberation Walt's patience was about used up. He *had* to say something. "Just pick one buddy, they're all losers."

"How do you know? Have you ever bought one? Who do you think you are, anyhow?" The man was defensive and whiny, and Walt figured the little cretin must still be living in his mother's basement.

"Could you please just pick one?" Walt was asking nicely, or at least as nicely as he could given the circumstances. The orange truck was getting further away by the second.

"I will when I'm good and ready." The man turned his attention back to the clerk. "Which do you think is better, the Holiday Treats game, or the Pirate Treasures?"

Unbelievable. Walt wasn't giving up that easily. "Look, pal, I'm in a hurry. Can I just pay for my gas? It'll only take a second." *Where do these people come from?* he wondered. The man was still ignoring him.

"I think the odds are pretty consistent either way," the clerk answered Lottery Guy. This kid must be one of the smarter gas station jockeys in the area. At least he understood the odds. "It's kind of a matter of personal preference, sir. You know, whatever floats your boat."

Mr. Indecisive continued to ignore Walt. "Well that's a tough one, then. I'll take one of the Holiday Treats and two of the Pirate Treasures. No, hold on a second. Make that one Holiday Treats, one Pirate Treasures, and one Triple Red Bingo. Two! Make that two Triple Red Bingos. Ah, to heck with it...two Holiday Treats, one Pirate Treasures, and two Triple Red Bingos. And throw in one of those five dollar Happy Pumpkins. Hey, are there any new games coming out in the next few weeks?"

Walt was pretty sure he was only seconds away from having a stroke. *Can that happen? Can I really blow a gasket and drop dead, right here and now?* You read about things like that happening all the time. There's a perfectly healthy man in the prime of his life. Then one day, *bam*, he's dead on the floor of a crappy gas station in the middle of nowhere. The deceased's friends and family are always quoted in the local paper: "He seemed like he was in such good health." "I don't understand what he was even *doing* in that gas station, anyway. Why wasn't he at work?" "It's the Lord's will." Sometimes death didn't sound like such a bad option.

Just as Walt felt about ready to test this hypothesis, let the blood vessels blow and the chips fall where they may, the clerk stepped up and saved him. To the man with the lottery fetish, the kid politely quipped "Sir, if you don't mind, I'd like to let this gentleman pay for his gasoline. It'll only take a second." Pitowski nearly kissed the clerk on the lips.

Lottery Guy mumbled in acknowledgement, but Walt shot him an angry stare anyway. If *anybody* deserved the snide eye it was this guy. Pitowski slapped thirty bucks down on the counter and dashed out the front door. He sprinted to the middle of Wolverine Valley Road, straining to see into the distance. The orange Sierra was long gone.

EIGHTEEN

Deputy Don Frederics

There were all types of people in Rasmus that could be classified as pains in the ass. The town had its wife beaters and its chronic drunks. There were fighters, usually kids not much past high school with no grasp of the future, getting into weekend scrapes that put them on the express route to nowhere. By the time they got much older than that, they'd lose a few battles and realize that fighting was a young man's game. There were petty shoplifters who liked to blame their behavior on everyone but themselves, and B & E artists that broke into cabins and houses, depreciating property values, raising insurance rates, and ticking off homeowners. Like every other place in America, Rasmus had drug dealers and prostitutes, although the latter category was woefully underrepresented because it was so easy to get it for free. "Free" might mean a few rounds of drinks or a meal, but at least no money changed hands. The area included poachers and check kiters, speeders and run-of-the-mill vandals. There were people that would break into your home to steal the copper plumbing and the a/c unit just for scrap. There was even the occasional embezzler or tractor assassin. At the moment, however, none of these criminal types was as likely to draw the ire of Deputy Don Frederics as a man who had yet to be convicted of anything whatsoever, one Walter Pitowski.

Generally the deputy didn't let the job get under his skin. "You can't take everything home with you or it will eat you alive." That was advice he'd received from his friend and co-worker Matt Amberson the first day on the job. He'd heeded that lesson well, quickly adapting to the idea that once he was off the clock, he was off the clock. Whatever happened on the job stayed there, since you couldn't afford to carry grudges in a town this size. It's hard enough being a small town cop. You don't want everyone ducking for cover every time you enter a room. A man needs to be able to walk into a restaurant or a grocery store without it always ending in a pissing match. In *theory* it was great advice, but in *practice* it was a tough rule to follow.

There were many times the deputy ran into people he'd arrested for one crime or another, or maybe the relatives of someone he'd arrested, and the chirping would begin. For some reason the county's miscreants figured he was fair game once he took off his uniform. Obviously these folks weren't well versed in Michigan civil and criminal law. If he wanted to be a hard head about it, most of the clowns that tried to threaten him, goad him into a fight, or otherwise assault him would be in jail by now. Of course if he wanted to be a hard head about it, his boss and the county prosecutor would be tearing him a new one by now. Neither of them wanted that kind of workload, and it would make it all but impossible to ever get reelected. "You can't lock up half the damn county!" Brimley would be screaming. Frederics had learned to diffuse these situations, move on with his day, and let it go; at least until now.

It was hard for him to say why it was that Pitowski pushed his buttons. Up until recently the man wasn't even a blip on his radar screen. Sure, he'd pulled him over for speeding a couple of times, and both times he'd let Walt go with a warning. Amberson had busted the guy's balls far worse with a citation for a broken windshield and a violation for ten over within the last year. The events of the last week, that sheer violence at the Deer Track Inn, the badly beaten woman in the hospital (allegedly close to getting out soon) who just *happened* to be Walt's ex-girlfriend, and then Pitowski stumbling across the murder scene at the hatchery, well, it was all so damn *convenient*. He couldn't think of any other word that better fit the situation. The only thing missing in these two cases was for someone to wrap them up and place a shiny little bow on top. Walt Pitowski fit the package.

When Walt had come into the station earlier that day, shouting his conspiracy theories about two guys in an orange truck casing the Deer Track Inn, Frederics hardly knew what to say. At first he thought about laughing. The two men that he was describing the deputy knew all too well. They were a couple of brothers and small-time thieves from Mioe, men whose best friend in this world, up until recently, had been Rayford Jefferson Brown Sr. Now that Wood Tick was dearly departed, the two only had each other. They were punks and dopers, members of that sub-category of assholes that the officer described as "fighters." The pair were already in their early thirties: too old to keep it up and too dumb to realize that their challengers would keep getting younger and stronger. What was Frederics supposed to say, with Pitowski describing in detail a pair of criminals that the deputy knew all too intimately? He could hardly blurt out, "Yeah, I know exactly who you mean. I was at their house yesterday."

He'd blown Walt off, dismissed his complaint and sent him packing. But Deputy Don knew that wouldn't be the end of things. If nothing else, Pitowski was relentless. The man was like a dog with a bone. He wasn't going to let go until he got what he wanted, or until someone kicked him in the teeth hard enough to shake him off. Frederics mulled over the options.

Could he pin the woman's beating and the mayhem at the Deer Track on the Connelly brothers? It wouldn't be that hard, probably no more difficult than hanging it around Pitowski's neck. Sure, the Connelly boys didn't have a personal history of dating Pam Sharpe, but that shouldn't matter. Include the drug angle and he could always make it for a small-time robbery gone bad. Of course, if the woman ever regained her memory that could throw a monkey wrench into everything. So far she hadn't remembered a thing, but there was always a chance that the truth would come back to her in widescreen, high-definition technicolor.

The bigger risk, at least the bigger risk for Deputy Don Frederics and his career in the Shawono County Sheriff's Department, was that the Connelly brothers would start spouting off about some interpersonal relationships and business dealings in this county that were best kept from public consumption. Tie that into the murder of Rayford Brown Sr. and things could get even messier. God only knows what might come out in the laundry if that ever happened. It would be better to leave the brothers out of this completely, at least for now, and deal with their issues separately and definitively. That still left Pitowski as the likely fall guy in this whole mess, and what a lovely fall guy he'd make.

After dealing with Walt and his "complaint" about the two suspicious men in a truck, the deputy hunkered down in his office with the door closed. He had a lot of paperwork to catch up on, but that wasn't the real reason he was staying inside. He stayed inside because he didn't trust himself. He was worried that if he went out on patrol he might find himself sinking further into this morass of squalor that emanated from the dead man and his friends. If he sank any deeper in the muck he might just drown. He ate lunch at his desk, something Deputy Don rarely did. Sheriff Brimley popped his head in the door while he was eating, just to remind the deputy of a meeting scheduled for later that week. Frederics assured him he'd be there. Around one o'clock Brimley came back, opening the door without knocking once again. He was the boss, so there wasn't much you could do about it.

"Frederics, everything alright?"

"Yeah, boss, just getting caught up on some paperwork. Do you need something?"

"Andy Gervais is coming off the road in bit: he's not feeling well. He's going home for the day. I need you to go out and cover the rest of his patrol. Two until six."

"No problem, I'll get going in a half hour or so. But I was supposed to do the drug awareness speech at the middle school around two-thirty."

"I asked Amberson to cover for you on that one."

"That'll work. Who's got Amberson's slot?"

"Rodriguez."

"Sure. Just give me twenty minutes."

Brimley snorted and closed the office door. *So much for hunkering down,* Frederics sighed. He was almost out the front door when Amberson caught him in the lobby.

"Frederics, you've got road duty?"

"Yeah, covering for Gervais."

"Thanks. Hey, I think we're almost finished at the hatchery. Johnson and Murphy sent a photographer from the State crime lab in Lansing. Barnes, I think his name is. He and Brimley are over there right now. Lewis Carter from the Conservation Department was supposed to join them. I think they've got nearly everything they need. If you get a chance, tell Washington over at the USGS that they're good to go tomorrow morning. We'll be done before then."

"No problem, I'll get over there later today. Why is Carter at the hatchery? What does he care?"

"He said it's because the hatchery used to be a State building back in the eighties, but I think he's just curious. This is his first chance to see a real life murder scene. Life can't be all that exciting for a fish cop."

"A good reason not to become a fish cop."

119

"One of many. I've got to grab the display board and get over to the middle school." With a quick wave of his hand Amberson dashed off to the supply closet and Frederics sauntered out to his vehicle.

He hadn't gotten more than two blocks from the courthouse when the pink minivan materialized before his very eyes. A beater Chevy Colorado signaled and turned left onto one of the side streets. *Imagine that*, he thought, *someone that knows how to use a turn signal.* Immediately in front of the Colorado, sure as shinola, there was Walt Pitowski, putzing along. Not that he was breaking any laws at the moment, but Frederics had just about had his fill of Walt Pitowski for one week. Now would be as good a time as any to have that "unofficial" chat, away from prying eyes and well out of earshot of anyone that might remember their conversation later. Maybe the dog wouldn't let go of the bone, but it was still worth trying a few kicks to the teeth.

The van turned right at the stop sign, catching North Down River Road east past the hatchery. The deputy followed at a distance. He didn't want to do this in town, not with witnesses. It turned out to be a good decision because the chief's Excursion, along with a Trooper Blue Yukon and Lewis Carter's green truck were all parked in the lot at the top of the bluff. *Talk about your potential witnesses.* Three blocks later Pitowski turned onto the freeway ramp heading north. This caught the deputy by surprise, but he kept the Interceptor right behind Walt. He'd have guessed that Walt would stick to the little roads that led toward his home. If the pink van was destined for some remote corner of the woods, all the better. Once on the freeway, the deputy hung back even further. There weren't many vehicles as easy to tail as this one: that color stuck out like a lit flare. Pitowski was holding close to the legal speed limit for a change, yet another gift from above. This was going to be too easy.

Three cars slipped back into a single-file line directly between the Montana and his Crown Vic Interceptor. A few cars passed him in the left lane before those drivers realized it was a police car they were leaving in the dust and not-so-subtly tapped their brakes. A parade of red tail lights flickered before him and then everyone settled into an even pace. There was now a healthy six pack, three cars in each of the two lanes ahead, driving sixty-five miles per hour between Frederics and his prey. *You couldn't ask for better cover,* the deputy reflected. It shocked the daylights out of him when, a few miles further up the road, Pitowski suddenly floored the Pontiac, disappearing up the ribbon of concrete in the blink of an eye.

Frederics cut the Interceptor hard left through a low spot on the grassy center median, doubling back toward Rasmus. He'd catch up with Pitowski later. It was a shame to lose him like that, with unfinished business still sitting on the table. In the meantime, he set his sights on the hatchery. Maybe he could learn something from Brimley and the other two men.

NINETEEN

The Girl

First of all, what kind of town chooses as their school nickname the "Helgrammites?" I mean, seriously, you know? In the Upper Peninsula there are lots of schools with funny nicknames, and Rasmus sometimes plays them in the years when this town's football or basketball teams are talented or lucky enough to get to a district final. The Watersmeet Nimrods, everybody knows about them. How about the Kingsford Flivvers, or the Iron Mountain Nordics, or even the Houghton Gremlins? Sure, those nicknames *sound* strange, but at least there is some historical basis for their goofiness. "Helgrammites?" They are ugly little insects that live under rocks at the bottom of the river. If you've ever seen one, and you probably haven't unless you spend a lot of your time digging for bugs at the bottom of stream beds, they look a lot like centipedes: skinny, nasty little things with too many legs and a pair of pincers on the front. They aren't even a real insect species it turns out, at least not a *true* species. A helgrammite is the larval stage of the dobsonfly, as anyone who went to school in this town can tell you. They make you learn that in science class. But *sheesh*, that nickname pretty much tells you all you need to know about this place.

This town was all whipped up about the Rasmus Helgrammites football team and their 6-0 record, which is apparently a pretty good season for them. They haven't made it to the state championships in like, *practically forever,* and right now that's all anybody can talk about. *"Do you think they're going to win it all?"* That was a stupid question, at least as far as the girl was concerned. *Every* little town in northern Michigan that has a 6-0 football team is sure that they are going to win it all this year, just like they were sure they were going to win it all last year. They'll be sure they're going to win it all when they are 7-0 and 8-0, too, right up until the state high school playoffs when some other town that you'd have to dig out a magnifying glass and a map to find comes to play. Then those other teams arrive, with kids twenty pounds heavier and two degrees meaner, and they beat you up and take your lunch money. It happens all the time. There is always somebody bigger, tougher, or hungrier living in a tiny place not just three hours but *eight hours* from the nearest real city. No wonder those Upper Peninsula kids are always so pissed.

Besides, the girl knew for a fact that the Helgrammites' starting quarterback, Teddy Tidewater (his real first name was Theodore, but he would *kick your ass* if you ever called him that to his face because it reminds him of one of the singing Chipmunks) was doing it with the girl's older sister and she was already *a month late* for her period. One *major* reason not to be doing it, as far as the girl was concerned: the chance of getting knocked up by some *Hayseed Hotshot* like Teddy Tidewater. "Hayseed Hotshot." She'd heard somebody at the pizza place call him that behind his back and she liked it so much that she decided she'd steal it. Teddy might be a really good quarterback, especially since he was only a junior, but obviously he wasn't bright enough to even use a condom correctly. The girl knew the Hayseed Hotshot's mind wasn't going to be one-hundred percent in the game this Friday. She was pretty sure that East Jordan was going to clean their clocks, *but good.* That's why she wasn't at the after-school pep rally at the high school with everybody else this Tuesday afternoon. It was hard to get fired up for a hopeless cause.

Her best friend Angie wouldn't come and hang out with her because, once again, Angie insisted "there will be boys at the pep rally." Angie ought to get her head examined. Right there was your next Candidate of the Year for Getting Knocked Up, as far as the girl could see, and she wasn't even in high school yet. She was just plain *Boy Crazy,* and that wasn't a condition you'd wish on your own worst enemy.

The girl strolled down Main Street. It was *incredibly boring* because pretty much every kid in town was over at the pep rally. The sidewalks were empty except for the usual old people and a parade of moms with babies in strollers. It would be nice to go into the pizzeria or Seven-Eleven and grab a bite to eat, but that wasn't going to happen. She didn't have any money. The girl was too young to get a real job and besides, her parents were constantly Ruining Her Life because they refused to give her an allowance. Well, they did give her *some* allowance, but not nearly enough. How much fun are you really going to have for ten dollars a week? She was broke and bored, and all her friends were busy with Helgrammite Fever.

She meandered over to her usual spot, the one behind those outbuildings on the backside of the hatchery, but she couldn't stick around there, either. There were cop cars everywhere. The sheriff had his giant white Ford

Excursion parked in the lot at the top of the bluff, and there alongside it was a blue SUV from the State Police and a green one from the Conservation Department. There was another car, too, one of those Fords that the regular County Mounties got to drive. If you were a thirteen-year-old girl looking to light up from a stolen pack of Newport Lights, this was not the place to be.

When she'd run from this very place Friday night, racing through the dark as quickly as her young legs would carry her, the girl didn't tell a single person what she'd seen. What was she going to say, and who would she say it to? *"I was out smoking a cigarette,"* now there was a great conversation starter, a virtual poison pill with any adult. *"I saw a younger guy follow an older guy into the building,"* well that seemed like a ticket to Permanent Grounding and a series of long, daily lectures on Situational Awareness and Making Better Choices. No thank you. It wasn't as if the information she had to offer was all that useful or specific. It had been *dark out,* for cripes sake. She couldn't really describe that younger man even if she tried, so she'd kept her mouth shut.

By the time she finally reached the Seven-Eleven that Friday, the girl was severely out of breath and pale as a ghost. It was a long run, at least six or seven blocks. Two kids from her algebra class, Jennie and Taylor, were just coming out of the store with Big Gulps in their hands. They asked her what was wrong and she made up a fake story about some high school kids she didn't know chasing her down the street. It looked like they believed her, and it was *way easier* than trying to explain what had really happened. Jennie even gave her the Big Gulp she'd just purchased. It was the jumbo size, too.

Saturday, the day after this happened, she'd spent the whole day bumming around the house. Her mom asked her if she was sick or something, because it was "so unlike" her to lie around watching TV all day and never even go outside, *not even for a minute.* She wasn't really thinking about bringing up what she'd seen, not at that point and not with her mother. Besides, nobody knew there was a *murder* or whatever it was that had happened at the hatchery. It was just two men sneaking around, then one loud noise, and her getting creeped out and running away. Still, she was happy to stick close to home for that one day.

By Sunday she'd finally gotten over it and decided that she was being childish by staying so close to home and mommy like she was some kind of Big Baby. Good grief, she was Practically in High School Already! Well, she *would be* by next fall. When her parents took off to visit Aunt Ida in Posen that afternoon, the girl pretended she wasn't feeling well. Her parents reluctantly let her stay home alone. Not fifteen minutes after they'd left the house, the girl seized the opportunity to borrow her father's .22 rifle and head out squirrel hunting. That hadn't worked out quite the way she'd expected: the girl never even got around to firing the gun that afternoon. She did take a lengthy walk in the woods, though. The girl covered nearly a dozen miles on foot, as a matter of fact. It felt great to be out in the woods, watching and listening to the sounds around her. Carrying the gun was a bonus, even if she didn't get to use it. All of that was completely worth the risk of getting caught.

That was *before* she learned that the old dude in the hatchery was Capital "D" Dead. Now she was beginning to wonder if she ought to tell someone what she saw. What was it they always tell you, "the truth shall set you free?" The girl wasn't so sure. Sometimes the truth could get you locked up. More often than not, "you have the right to remain silent" was a better rule by which to live.

Yesterday she'd gone to school and there was nothing out of the ordinary all morning long. Around two in the afternoon whispers started circulating about the cops finding a dead body in town. That had everybody worked up. I mean, *how cool was that?* Nothing exciting like this *ever* happened in Rasmus. Most of her classmates were giddy with anticipation like they were part of something Totally Newsworthy. She was tempted to brag a little bit, let on that she'd been hanging around the hatchery when it happened. The girl knew better, though. She figured that whatever she'd seen in the dying light Friday night, well, it *might* be important. At the same time, she suspected it *could* make her a target for the younger guy that was following the older guy, if it turned out the older guy's death wasn't an accident. Unlike her classmates, she wasn't entirely sure this was a good thing, being part of something So Big It's Like Watching High-Def. A good mystery is only good if you're not the next intended victim.

By that afternoon the rumors were still swirling all over town: a dead guy was discovered on the ground floor of the hatchery. At first nobody knew if it was an accident or a murder, but everybody had their own theory. Some people were sure it was a death by drug overdose. Others could swear that they knew a source within the police department, and that source had said it was a murder. Some of the Church People believed he might have been a homeless guy who died of hypothermia, and its members were starting a fund to help with the twin problems of poverty and homelessness in rural Michigan. The girl had her own ideas, and she knew a lot more than she let on. She thought about the cops and what they might be looking for in that musty old building. She was still hoping that it had been an accident.

After school she'd walked over to the hatchery. The girl's curiosity was getting the better of her and she thought maybe if she looked around, remembered what it was like to be watching on that Friday night, it would help her decide whether or not to Spill Her Guts. That was such a funny phrase, "spill your guts," like this was some old black and white movie or something and she was the gangster's girlfriend. What did those old-time criminals call their girlfriends again, a "mole" or something like that? No, she was pretty sure it was a "moll."

She walked over to the hatchery hoping to get a feel for things and then figure out what she should do next. The police were crawling all over the place, up and down the hill like ants. It looked like hanging around there might be a Major League Bad Idea after all. The girl went home early and had dinner with her family. Her folks didn't say a word because they figured she still wasn't feeling well. That was it for Monday.

Today at school the rumor mill had quieted plenty, because by now everybody had heard that the dead guy was some old man that nobody in school actually knew, and he'd been shot in the head. Shot right between the eyes. You wouldn't think news like that would calm anybody, but it eliminated about ninety percent of the crazy ideas that people had floating through their brains. No more Terrorists from the Middle East. No more Russian Spy Invasion theories to kick around. No more Government Assassination of The Man Who Knew Too Much. The victim was just some old loser from east of town. He lived out in the sticks, way past her house, where the real huckleberries lived. He wasn't important enough to draw the attention of terrorists or spies or men in black.

Now it was down to the "why" of the whole thing, and while it was fun to come up with *potential* reasons why somebody would want the old guy dead, middle school kids don't really have that much information when you get right down to it. Why does anybody kill *anybody*? It never makes any sense. By the end of the day the frenzy of speculation had died down to a quiet hum, and a renewed preoccupation with the big rally for Helgrammite Fever Forever took over the school. "Helgrammite Fever." It even *sounds* like a disease.

It was Tuesday afternoon. The pep rally was going on right now and the girl was busy trying to decide what she should do. She couldn't just stand around the back side of the hatchery, staring at four empty cop cars. Sooner or later someone was bound to come out and ask her why she was there. "Excuse me young lady, but don't you have someplace else you ought to be?" She could hear it already. There probably wasn't *any* good answer, if the question ever got asked.

It looked as if the police had opened up a small door on the lower level of the hatchery, allowing some light into the building. It would be nice to look inside, see what they were seeing, but there was no way to get close enough. She considered heading over to that viaduct that ran beneath North Down River Road. Unfortunately, that would put her on the far side of the building, and she wasn't going to see Jack Squat from there. She could cross the river and head to the opposite side of the property, beyond the fence and way to the east. There was a patch of woods over there where it would be easy to hide, but the woods were a few hundred yards away, and that seemed like an awfully long distance for People Watching. The girl searched around for other options. Then she remembered the thicket of trees at the top of the stairwell.

She looked around cautiously. The police and whoever was with them were still inside the building. She could hear men's voices floating up from the bottom of the hillside. It was hard to tell exactly what they were saying, but she might learn something if she got close enough and listened *really carefully*. The girl checked over her shoulder: there wasn't anyone outside the office building behind her. There were no cars driving on North Down River Road and there wasn't anyone doing maintenance on the hatchery grounds, either. As long as the cops stayed inside, this was her chance. She crept over to the tangle of bushes and trees, burrowing deep inside the mess.

They were taking photos, the men in the hatchery, at least that's what it sounded like. She couldn't really see anything other than the dark rectangle of the open doorway and an occasional pair of legs walking past. The Sheriff was inside, but he was being pretty quiet, at least for him. He could be an intimidating guy, especially if you were a young girl who wasn't always a Goody Two Shoes and He Knows Exactly Who You Are and He Knows Exactly Who Your Friends Are, too. It seems like the harder you try to schmooze a guy like Sheriff Brimley, the more he sees right through you. It's like he's got x-ray vision and that pack of stolen menthols in your shirt pocket is right there in his sights, clear as day. He doesn't have to say much, *you just know* that he's on to you.

There were at least three other voices inside the hatchery. One guy's name was Barnes. It sounded like he was taking a lot of pictures, and he kept talking about where people were standing and asking Sheriff Brimley and the other men to get out of the way so they wouldn't be in the photo's background. It shouldn't really *matter*. It wasn't as if the dead guy was going to be sending these pictures out with his annual Christmas cards or anything. The third guy they kept calling "Carter," and she wasn't sure if that was his first name or his last name. He sounded as if he might be some kind of a trainee. Carter was asking a lot of questions, like he'd never been to a crime scene before and was trying too hard to learn everything all at once. He reminded the girl of those smarmy kids you get in class once in a while: they think they're impressing the teacher with all of their questions when all they're really doing is ticking off Every Single Classmate in the Whole Entire Universe. The Sheriff and this photographer Barnes sounded like they were getting annoyed with Carter, the smarmy kid, but they were too polite to tell him to Just Shut the Hell Up Already. She knew the feeling. The fourth guy's voice sounded familiar, but she couldn't picture which of the local deputies it belonged to.

It turned out that hiding in the little clump of trees and bushes, while it *seemed* like a good idea initially, wasn't all that productive. Twenty minutes passed and all she'd found out was that the lighting in that building "sucked," according to Barnes, and that this Carter guy liked to talk a lot. This was turning out to be a Ginormous Waste of Time and the girl was beginning to *seriously regret* skipping that pep rally for a chance to sit in the woods listening to a bunch of cops talking about nothing. Maybe catching Helgrammite Fever wasn't such a bad thing after all.

She was just about to call it quits, slink back out of her brushy lair and stroll on over to the high school, when the four men in the hatchery stepped into the sunshine, locking the door behind them. Now she was stuck. They were no more than seventy feet away, walking in this direction, and the men still had no idea that she was here.

She knew Sheriff Brimley well, just like every kid and every adult in Shawono County knew the portly officer. He was an icon in this town: you couldn't *not* know him. The other County Mountie, he looked familiar. He must be the "don't do drugs" guy with the local police force. If there was some stupid thing the cops felt like they had to do, like searching school lockers or directing traffic after the fireworks, he was exactly the kind of sucker they sent out. He should look familiar: she'd probably walked past him a dozen times. *That guy must be the low man on the totem pole*, the girl thought.

The other two, the state cop and the one that looked like some kind of forest ranger, well, she didn't *expect* to recognize either of those guys. Why would she? She'd never gone to prison and she'd never been caught poaching or starting any forest fires. As her parents liked to remind her, she was *only thirteen, for heaven's sake.* The girl was fairly certain she'd never seen the man in blue or the man in green before. It was hard to tell, since, as a kid, you learned not to make eye contact with adults unless you absolutely *had to.* Unless you stare closely they all start to look alike.

The girl watched as the four men continued to stride toward her. As they approached the base of the spiral staircase the girl had an epiphany. She looked them over one more time, Brimley and the three guys she didn't know. One of the men, however, she'd seen just this past Friday. She'd watched him in this same exact location, creeping up and down these very steps. Sure, the light hadn't been very good that night, but there was no doubt it was the same man. Fear set in. What if he figured out who *she* was? What if they were all in it together and the others helped him apprehend her? Springing from the underbrush, the girl ran for her life.

"What the hell was that?" Trooper Barnes asked as the girl sprinted toward town.

"Local kid, probably just curious," Brimley answered in his usual gruff tone. It wasn't anything to get too excited about.

"Do you always have kids hanging around a crime scene?" It was Barnes again.

"Can't cordon off the whole city," Brimley responded. Hell, these State guys acted like their shit didn't stink.

"You might want to try," Barnes shot back, and the sheriff decided to let it rest. What was the benefit of getting into a war of words with the Michigan State Police? It wasn't a smart move for any local official.

"Any idea who she is?" this was from Lewis Carter, the Conservation Officer.

Sheriff Brimley looked at him inquisitively. Why the hell should *he* care? The sheriff knew it was a mistake letting that fish cop hang around the hatchery. The guy was constantly asking stupid questions and running his mouth, blabbering and prying into things that were none of his damn business. "No idea," Brimley answered, and they both knew it was a lie.

By now, Don Frederics was hurriedly walking to his patrol car in silent pursuit.

TWENTY

The Watcher

That girl hiding in the bushes near the hatchery, well, that was a kick in the head. He wasn't sure why it caught him by surprise. A murder in Rasmus? That ought to bring bystanders from all over northern Michigan. You just didn't see things like this all that often, and it should be expected that every bored teen and pre-teen kid in town would want to catch a glimpse of the murder scene. The fact that you'd personally *been to the spot* where a murder had taken place would bring major bragging rights in any school.

It didn't shock him so much to discover a kid hanging around the hatchery, not in the least. But the fact that it was just *one* kid, that she wasn't with any friends her age, though, was disconcerting. A *group* of teens you would expect, but one solitary kid, especially a girl her age? That waif of a girl, a skinny little thing with shoulder length blond hair who looked not much more than eleven or twelve years old, she didn't strike The Watcher as a lone wolf type. It didn't make any sense. Kids usually got their courage from the pack.

No, what was getting to him was how well hidden the girl was in her little snarl of bushes at the top of the staircases. The four cops couldn't have been more than fifty feet away when the girl burst from her hideaway. The fact that she was so well hidden in the woods opened up a host of other questions. You didn't just stumble upon a hideout like that: you'd have to know it was there to begin with. It was better than most natural deer blinds he'd seen, blinds assembled by hunters and woodsmen with decades of outdoors experience. Obviously the girl knew her way around the grounds, and *that* was in and of itself a major concern.

If the kid was able to mask her presence so well in the middle of a Tuesday afternoon, where four trained law enforcement officers failed to notice that she was in the vicinity, well, what else had he missed? Was she there last Friday night, watching him as he followed Wood Tick into the building? Was she there when he exited the hatchery alone? Could she identify him?

Her reaction today would certainly suggest that she'd seen *something*. Why else would she be running like she'd just seen a ghost? This couldn't be good. He thought about the possibilities.

It was a good bet that Sheriff Brimley must know every kid in a town this size: God knows the Shawono County Sheriff's Department performed a lot of community education and public safety work at the local schools. Unfortunately, when Lewis Carter had asked the girl's name, Brimley hadn't offered anything up. He worried about that, too. Did that one attempt to solicit the girl's name come across as heavy-handed? It seemed like an innocent enough question given the circumstances. Was Brimley himself hiding something? He didn't think so, at least not at the time, but anything was possible. The sheriff's curt response, however, had put the Conservation Officer on the defensive, and the man had backed down. The State Trooper wasn't going to press the issue, either. Had the sheriff blurted out the kid's name, well, that would have been too damn easy. Her name would have echoed through that river valley for all the world to hear. It would have been a gift. Nothing was ever that simple. Besides, there were plenty of other ways to learn what he needed to learn.

That had been Tuesday. He'd spent a chunk of time driving around Rasmus, trying to catch a glimpse of the little imp around the schools or the shopping district. Unfortunately, there was a massive pep rally for the football team over at the high school. Practically every kid in the area was packed into the gymnasium, rooting for the Fighting Larvae, as he liked to call them. Had he known this to begin with, that everybody was at the high school, he'd have known exactly where to find the girl. But he didn't learn about the football rally until over an hour later when the cashier at the Sunoco station let it slip in casual conversation. By the time The Watcher got over to Rasmus High the rally was finished and damn near a thousand kids were pouring into the streets en masse. Good luck finding one short, towheaded girl in that crowd. He thought he might circle around some more and hope for the best, but by then a Police Interceptor containing Deputy Matt Amberson appeared in his rearview mirror. The Watcher didn't want to risk calling undue attention to himself, so he swallowed another Oxy and headed out of town.

Wednesday he'd awakened with a severe headache and the realization that there were too many loose ends for his liking. That kid, for one thing. Who knew what she'd seen last Friday night, or when she was likely to tell someone? That was one loose end, one he'd have to deal with sooner rather than later. You couldn't leave a thing like that hanging, waiting to blow up in your face.

The woman from the bar, Pam Sharpe, she was another loose end. He'd been incredibly unlucky in that she'd somehow lived through that beating, yet just as fortunate that she couldn't remember a thing. It was funny how fate could screw you with one hand and give back so generously with the other. Again he had to ask, how long was it likely to last? How long was it going to take before her memories came rushing back to her? And when her mind did clear and her past returned, how long would it be before the pendulum of justice crashed down upon his head? He should have finished her off when he had the chance. The man downed two more pills, hoping to shake the cobwebs from his mind. He hadn't been counting, but it sure looked like those three-hundred yellow tablets in a baggie had turned into something closer to two-hundred and change, all in a few short days. He'd have to monitor his intake.

There was a third loose end, as well, with those two dirtbag drug dealers, the Connellys. They'd been hovering around Wood Tick like flies on stink prior to the old man's death. The Watcher assumed he was nobody to them. While he'd bought occasional supplies from Wood Tick, substances that were not approved for consumption without a doctor's prescription, he'd always been careful to make his purchases when they were clear of any potential witnesses. The Connellys had never seen him and Wood Tick together, as far as he knew. For a man in his position, even the *perception* of impropriety could bring the house down. At the very least it would cause a lot of sleepless nights, and The Watcher didn't need additional grief.

With the passing of Rayford Jefferson Brown Sr., the Connellys had inherited much of Wood Tick's illicit trade. They weren't nearly as smart about it, though, or as sneaky. Old Wood Tick had been at it for decades and knew the ins and outs of staying off of law enforcement's radar. These two guys, they couldn't have been more obvious if they were trying to be. They were idiots. This was no skin off The Watcher's nose. He had his own little baggie of joy sitting on the coffee table right there in front of him. He didn't need what the brothers were selling, at least not today. Should he ever need more there were other, better places in which to find it.

Rayford must have kept written records. He hadn't expected this complication, but it goes to show that the world is full of revelations. Either that or he'd been flapping his toothless gums whenever he was two sheets to the wind. Last Saturday night the Connellys had approached *him, The Watcher,* asking in a not-so-subtle fashion if he needed some pharmaceutical assistance. The Watcher of course declined, threatened to run them in, but the men made it clear that he was on their customer list. Dirtbag One and Dirtbag Two were insistent that they expected his return business or they'd start talking. He couldn't afford that kind of publicity. The Connellys were not only loose ends, they were loose cannons. They didn't know it, but the brothers had just signed their own death warrants.

Currently there were three problems, or four problems if you counted the brothers separately. Either way, the thing to do was to sit down and prioritize, then deal with things as efficiently as possible. That's what he'd been trained to do. The Connellys might be trouble, but they weren't the most pressing of his issues. If those dirtbags started running their mouths, it would create just as much misery for them as it would for him. They were dumb, but they couldn't possibly be *that* dumb. At least he hoped not. He'd deal with them, but not right away.

The last he'd heard that bartender from the Deer Track Inn was still in a hospital down near Saginaw. She was the wild card in this whole thing. Did he have a week, an hour, or a lifetime before her memory returned? There was no way of knowing. If there was no way of knowing, there was no way of assessing the risk. The best he could do was hope: hope that her brains remained scrambled, at least for a while, and deal with her as soon as she was safely back in town. To try and make a move while she was lying in a hospital bed surrounded by nurses and doctors and security, that would be utter insanity. Waiting was the smart move. Wait until she was nearby and he could make it look like an accident.

That left the girl. He didn't know her name. He didn't even know what she looked like, not exactly. All he'd caught was a glimpse of her as she burst out of that clump of bushes and trees near the hatchery stairs. He could guess her approximate height and weight, could describe the color and the length of her hair. If he had to guess he'd say she was about eleven or twelve years old, though he might be off by a year or so in either direction. She was wearing blue jeans, sneakers, and a black hoodie, the official uniform of youth. He knew this described about thirty percent of the entire fifth, sixth, and seventh grade classes at Rasmus Middle School. He did the math in his head and figured she was one of about ninety to a hundred kids in town that looked and dressed exactly like her. You could narrow that down, eliminate the really tall ones and the really fat ones and the list might shrink down to forty or fifty girls. It was still hopeless. Unless she did something to tip her hand, The Watcher knew he'd never find her.

All told, this was rapidly getting out of hand. How had his plan unraveled so badly? Killing Rayford Brown Sr., that wasn't an option. It had been a necessity. He couldn't afford to have the old puke threatening him with exposure, and there was no doubt that Wood Tick was threatening. Wood Tick was under some pressure from the State Police and was threatening to leverage his purchasing history as a means of getting off the hook. Imagine that, being exploited like some kind of bargaining chip for a two-bit pusher.

The Watcher was a professional, so he'd handled it like a professional. He'd planned it so well, right down to the very last detail. He stalked the old coot like the animal that he was, mapping his movements and habits from a distance. He took him out with one clean shot between the eyes before sliding away in the darkness. The gun was a throwaway. His car had been waiting in the wings, tucked away in a place where no one would notice. The drugs he'd found in that bag were safely buried in the forest miles from here. There was nothing to tie him to Wood Tick, at least nothing of which he was aware. The hatchery? He'd thought it was a convenient venue. What had gone wrong?

From the moment he entered the Deer Track things had spun out of control. First the woman, noticing blood on his boot, then the fight. The fight was not part of the plan, and it ended badly. He was still amazed that she survived. The two brothers, knowing more than he'd ever suspected. Finally Pitowski, fool that he was, discovering the body on Monday. Hell, he'd figured the body would be there for six months or more before anybody stumbled across it. By then there'd be very little left to investigate. As it was they had a fresh crime scene, and although he didn't *think* he'd missed anything, even the best make mistakes. Lastly the girl. Who could have anticipated there'd be a witness? *If* she was a witness. He still didn't know how much she'd seen. He needed to find that girl.

TWENTY-ONE

Walt Pitowski

Hallelujah for Fridays. That's all Walt had to say on the matter. It had been a long week. He never did find that orange pickup truck in Sturgeon. The vehicle could have disappeared anywhere, and he wasn't about to expend another thirty dollars worth of gas searching in vain. He'd puttered around town a few times, checking driveways and parking lots to no avail. They'd probably made a beeline for the state forest, but Walt knew that trying to locate them there would be a lost cause. There were too many nooks and crannies, too many places to hide in that vast expanse of wilderness.

Wednesday he was back at work. He had some check stations to recalibrate, four of them over near the Jordan River Valley and beyond. It was one of the nicer days he'd seen in a long time. The warmth of the past weekend had returned, albeit temporarily. There wasn't a cloud in the sky. The Jordan River wasn't far, not much more than an hour to the north and west of Rasmus. The difference was amazing, though. Rasmus was a land of jack pine forest and high sand plateaus. In Rasmus the seasonal temperatures might be extreme, hot in the summer and thirty below come February, but the view rarely changed. There was a very long, somewhat drab "pine tree with snow" season. This was followed by a very long, very drab "pine tree with mud and black fly" season. There was also a very brief, drought-riddled "pine tree with sun" season. Often during this latter stretch, the "pine tree with sun" part that many called "summer," the sun was optional. The heat and drought, however, remained mandatory. Between "summer" and "snow" seasons, Rasmus might experience a few good weeks of bird hunting.

The Jordan River Valley, on the other hand, was a fertile land of twists and turns. Wedged against Lake Michigan in the far northwest corner of the Lower Peninsula, the area had been carved and sculpted by the retreating fingers of the last glacial era. Roads ducked and weaved over hummocky terrain, twisting and snaking around the vast ridges and rocky deposits on the way to their destinations. If you didn't know better, you might be tricked into thinking you were in the foothills of the Appalachians or the Cascade

Mountains. The Valley got a lot more snow in the winter, a byproduct of being closer to Lake Michigan. It was enough to support more than a handful of ski resorts, but the area didn't pay the same price in temperature extremes come summer and winter. The thermometer never actually made it to "stinking hot" or "subarctic freezing" in the Jordan Valley.

The forest over here was almost exclusively comprised of hardwoods, and Pitowski noted that the fall foliage was fast approaching peak color. Flaming red and burnt orange, the turning leaves made the horizon burst with pigment. Artists travelled from across the country to paint scenes such as this. Travel buses brought in loads of downstate tourists on day trips throughout late September and early October: one-hundred dollars and up, round trip, for the right to watch a better world pass by your window. Walt was soaking it all in on the government's dime.

The best part of the day, and what made this trip particularly enjoyable, was that Tom Dewers wasn't available to go with him. Dewers had been sent to Pennsylvania for the remainder of the week and Walt was working solo. Tooling along in one of the Geological Services' newer F-250 pickups, listening to Creedence Clearwater Revival and the Dave Matthews Band on compact disc, it just didn't get any better than this. Walt did what he needed to do at each of the gaging stations and there were no surprises. Four stations and four rivers, including the Jordan, the Elk, the Platte, and the Boardman, and Walt didn't take an unexpected swim in any single one of them. He even enjoyed a great lunch at a little family-run restaurant just outside of Alba. Who knew you could find homemade sauerkraut pierogies and hand-stuffed kielbasa up this way? It was a top-notch day across the board. He returned home tired but happy. He'd almost forgotten about his problems.

Thursday had been slightly less pleasant, but not horrible. This day sent him to the Manistee River Basin. Walt needed to service three gaging stations on the Manistee River near Sherman, Mesick, and Wellston, plus two stations on the smaller Pine River at Hoxeyville and Tustin. The Manistee itself was a river both bigger and more prone to flooding than all the others. The daily discharge rate on the Manistee River at Mesick averaged over one-thousand cubic feet per second, nearly ten times the amount of water rolling through those smaller streams. By the time the river reached Wellston, that rate grew to fifteen hundred cubic feet per second. Bigger water brought additional risk. It wasn't necessarily more *dangerous* water: Walt knew that any river could be dangerous, but there was less margin for error when working on the big boys.

The Manistee River cut through flat land. This area still contained a decent mix of hardwoods and pine, but it wasn't nearly as picturesque as the far northwestern corner of the state. When he arrived at Mesick he found his monitoring equipment had been badly damaged and that took longer to repair than he could have guessed. Walt was fairly certain some yokel had sabotaged the station, but that would be a hard thing to prove. The equipment was only a few hundred yards downstream from Hodenpyl Dam, a place renowned for its brown trout fishery. When the browns were spawning, the shoreline would be packed with men from all over the north trying to "land the big one." Inevitably there was more than one jerk in any crowd. It wouldn't surprise Walt in the least if some huckleberries had smashed his gage, only because they could. Walt got it fixed, though, and continued on his rounds. He arrived home late that evening, ate a quick dinner, and fell immediately to sleep.

While it hadn't been all *that* good, Thursday was still better than Friday. Despite the fact that the Manistee River Basin was not nearly as pleasant as the Jordan Valley and all her majesty, just about *anything* was better than that collection of glorified drainage ditches near Flint and Davison that helped feed the Saginaw River Basin. Friday brought a different kind of trip. Swartz Creek, Thread Creek, Kearsley Creek - it didn't much matter which one. They were all tannin-stained cesspools running from one blighted urban dump to another.

There was a lot of resentment in Rasmus over the bigger cities to her south, and much of that ill will was deserved. Hell, he'd seen an article on the web just last week that rated Flint and Detroit numbers one and two as the most dangerous cities in America. The study was based on violent crime statistics and didn't even include the risk you incurred by coming into contact with pestilent surface water. "We're number one" had an entirely different meaning around here. "We're number two" probably meant someone had crapped in the river yet again. Traffic was horrible, and you had to watch your vehicle and yourself or you'd wind up short one truck's worth of equipment and one wallet. Walt dreaded these necessary missions into the urban jungle, a place where your life was worth less than the change in your pocket.

On a positive note, he hadn't been carjacked, mugged, drowned, shot at, or otherwise accosted during his day spent in the greater Flint area. A couple of threatening looking guys tried to wave him to the curb while he was driving through one neighborhood, but Walt kept right on moving. That was as close as he came to disaster. He was on his way back to where he belonged. West Branch was coming up on his right, the town's water tower painted with a giant yellow smiley face. He was only forty miles from home and rapidly approaching the end of his work week. *Hallelujah for Fridays.* Dinner and drinks were migrating to the forefront of his mind.

Pam was on the mend, and there was a chance she'd be discharged from the hospital as early as next week. He'd learned this from a timely phone call to a friend of a friend, or more specifically, a phone call to a friend of Pam's. Walt knew he was fortunate to have found any friend of Pam's who was even willing to speak with him. They were *her* friends, not *his.* Most of them made that crystal clear. He was, to many people that knew and loved the woman, "persona non grata," or, more specifically, "on the shit list." Walt couldn't blame them. Regardless, she was getting better, or so he heard, and that was a good thing.

That wasn't the only good news of late. His parents, still living back in Providence and getting up there in years, had agreed to lend him two grand at zero interest. They'd want to be repaid, sooner rather than later, but sounded flexible on the how and when of the matter. That, combined with this week's paycheck and the retro pay from the New Mexico trip, would give him about fifty-five hundred dollars to throw at a "new" vehicle. That kind of money wasn't going to get him into a new Bugatti, but it should be enough to purchase a dependable set of wheels. He had yet to find any car or truck that interested him, at least in his price range. Everybody seemed to think their old trucks were plated with gold. On the other hand, Walt still had two days before Red Blondin needed the minivan back. In a weird way, he was going to miss Pinky.

Walt got back to the office and parked the F-250 behind the building. The Montana was right where he'd left her, and, thankfully, didn't have any "Mary Kay" signs or other bad gags affixed to her. That stuff was getting old, really old. The pranksters in the office must have moved on to harassing someone else for a while. Walt needed to file three reports and input some accumulated data before calling it quits for the week. He punched in the four-digit security code to the outside door, and stepped into the dark building. Everyone else had departed for the weekend. The place felt empty, and in a strange way Walt appreciated the solitude: he was master of the entire operation.

At his desk Pitowski hit the power button on the computer and waited as the cranky desktop slowly worked its way up to speed. He left the overhead lights off. It was a bit like being in a big, dark cave. He got to work and quickly lost track of the time. No disturbances, no annoying coworkers to bother you: this was the life. As peaceful as it was, Walt nearly jumped out of his seat when the phone rang. He glanced up at the clock on the wall. It was nearly eight, long past the point where he'd expect a call to his direct line.

"Hello, Walt Pitowski, USGS. Can I help you?" He thought it might be Marcus Washington, and he wanted to sound professional. Washington was a stickler for telephone etiquette.

"Hey Walt, it's me, Elvin. I wasn't sure if you were back in town."

"I'm back in town. What's going on?"

"Not much. I assume you're still looking for a vehicle?"

"Still looking for a vehicle," he confirmed. "Why, have you got something?"

"Maybe. My father-in-law, over in Lewiston. He runs a used car lot." This was news to Walt. It might have been helpful had Elvin mentioned this little detail before. It was just like his friend, conveniently forgetting to mention that he had a connection in the used car business until now. "How about a 2003 Ford F-150?"

"How many miles does it have?"

"One-hundred and six thousand."

Walt mulled it over before finally speaking. "That's a lot of miles."

"Not really. It's a ten-year-old truck, Walt, what do you expect?" Elvin let that one soak in for a moment. "Are you interested?"

"Maybe. Is it a regular cab or extended cab?"

"Even better. It's a crew cab, four doors. They come in handy if you ever have passengers. Smaller V-8 engine, I think it's a four point six or something. Four wheel drive."

Walt pondered that for a few more seconds. It was unlikely he was ever going to need four doors, but you never know. "Any rust?"

"A little surface bubbling at the right rear fender skirt, but that's about it. Nothing you can't clean up yourself with a grinder and a can of touch-up paint."

"How much?" This was probably where the bad news arrived. He'd looked at similar vehicles, and even without the crew cab they were well out of his price range. This sounded too good to be true.

"It books at over eighty-five hundred dollars, but he's doing me a favor. If you want it, you can have it for six, that's his last and best offer. He hasn't even put it on the lot yet, just took it in on trade today. Some old guy used it as a down payment on a dually. He says he'll hold it for you until Monday. If he puts it out on the lot it'll be gone in less than a week. Are you in or are you out?"

Walt knew he only had fifty-five hundred, but this sounded like too good of a deal to pass up. "I've got one more question." It sounded petty, but Walt still had to ask. Too many things in his life had spiraled beyond his control. He needed to draw the line somewhere. This was something that really *mattered*. "What color is the truck?"

"Metallic Silver."

"Tell him it's sold."

Now one problem in Walt's life was nearly resolved. He still had to figure out where he was going to dig up that additional five-hundred dollars within the next forty-eight hours, but hell, he'd find the money somewhere. Walt shut down the computer, locked the door behind him, fired up Pinky and began the drive home.

It was already dark outside, it had been for well near an hour. The days were growing shorter and shorter. October fifth, the calendar read, and autumn was firmly entrenched. In some parts of the country that might mean another two months of balmy days and chilly nights. In Rasmus, Walt realized, the end was near. "Pine tree with snow" season was just around the corner. The high temperature today had only gotten into the low forties, and the weathermen were calling for snow flurries before Monday. He was driving along, briefly mourning the loss of another season, when something caught his eye.

There was fire in the sky. Five glowing lights, burning bright in intensity before dimming ever so slightly, drifting in a "v" shaped pattern above the horizon. If he didn't know better he'd swear it was a UFO. It hovered high in the distance before descending slowly toward the ground in what appeared to be a perfectly controlled landing. The whole process took more than fifteen minutes. Walt pulled off to the shoulder to watch the spectacle unfold.

When the five lights finally dropped below the tree line, Walt estimated they were five or six miles to the north and east. It was state land up that way, miles and miles of nothing: no cabins, no homes, just a whole lot of trees and not much else. Walt chuckled to himself. The county dispatcher would probably get more than a handful of calls about the "alien invasion" taking place in Rasmus. There would be reports of little green men running amok, confiscating everyone's guns and taking away their liberties. Good luck with that "take me to your leader" stuff, because you'd have a hard time finding a leader in Shawono County. "Mister alien," they'd have to say, "if it's a leader you want, you've landed in the wrong place."

From a distance, you'd swear the bright lights provided the outline of a strange fixed-wing aircraft or a flying saucer. In reality, Walt knew the lights were nothing more than flares that the military used to light a battlefield during nighttime maneuvers. The National Guard must be running training exercises in the forest. A red glow momentarily crested above the tree line before fading to black. The show was officially over. The aliens would have to wait for another day.

Walt restarted the van, barely slipping it into gear and getting back on the road. He'd scarcely covered a hundred yards in total before a streak of brown fur shot through the headlights' beam. Walt slammed on the brakes, smacking his head hard on the steering wheel. He felt fortunate the airbag didn't inflate. *Damn did that hurt.* He'd probably have a knot on his forehead come morning. *Another frickin' coyote. Man, they are everywhere.* He'd almost splattered this one, too.

He let the van idle at the side of the road. Pitowski was beginning to wonder if the coyote was an omen of bad things to come. Occasionally Walt believed in signs. Then again, what was it Marcus Washington kept telling

142

him about luck? Some baloney about there being no such thing, that what happened in a man's life was all his own doing. Walt called bullshit on that. This coyote, for instance, what could Walt have done to avoid that? It was pure luck was what it was, an animal running through the woods at night. There was no rhyme or reason to its pattern, no logic behind where the coyote chose or didn't choose to go. It was all happenstance. He was on the wrong road at the wrong time and probably in the wrong car as well.

The only thing you could do in this world, the only control a man had over his own fate and destiny, was to pay attention to his surroundings, remain vigilant, and always, *always* expect that the worst is yet to come. Taking those steps didn't mean you could control what happened to you. It was more like buying insurance, a means of mitigating the inevitable damage. You might not be able to stop the train from coming, but you can learn to stay off the tracks. Pitowski was still exploring this philosophical line of thought, weighing luck and fate and the injustices of life, considering if those granola heads at the yoga camp might be onto something with their belief in "karma" and "becoming" and "inner engineering," their talk of "transcending personal limitations," when a bright orange GMC Sierra pickup roared past him on the left. Now *that* was a sign from God.

TWENTY-TWO

It wasn't hard to follow the truck, but it was hard to know if the two men in that bright orange vehicle knew he was right behind them. They'd been racing by at close to seventy miles per hour when they'd first passed, so maybe their minds were somewhere else. Maybe they wouldn't notice a neon pink van in their rear view mirror. Another group of five military flares lit up the moonless sky to their north, pasting a reddish glow across the horizon. It might not be the Northern Lights, but it was still eerily beautiful.

Walt barely had time to process that thought before the silence was shattered by the deep-throated rumble of two Mark-82, five-hundred pound bombs pounding the National Guard's practice range miles to the north. The sub-sonic tremors were enough to rattle the windows in his van and shake the walls of homes for miles around. That explosion of ordnance was a sound you tried to get used to around here, but those big bombs still managed to rattle teeth. Walt spotted four Black Hawk helicopters flying in tight formation miles off in the distance. Seconds later a pair of fighter jets streaked low over the highway in front of him, one so close that Walt thought he might be able to reach out and touch the fuselage. Someone unfamiliar with the practice habits of our military could easily be duped into believing the apocalypse was at hand.

At Shambarger Bridge Road the GMC rolled through the stop sign and made a hard left onto the highway toward the north. Walt followed doggedly, three-quarters of a mile behind. There was a series of five sharp curves in the next two miles, and Walt lost temporary sight of his quarry as they wheeled through the twists and turns. He considered closing the gap, but he also knew there were very few places for the men to turn out. Twice deer darted out in front of the minivan, freezing in the headlights, and twice Walt managed to stand on the brake pedal and swerve around them. Maybe the guys in that truck ahead wouldn't be so lucky.

Then the road settled down into a relatively straight and true path for twenty miles more or less due east, all the way to Mioe. The GMC was dead ahead of him, though the gap between the truck and Pinky had widened to nearly a mile. They must not have experienced the deer slalom course. Walt settled in for the long haul: he wasn't sure why he was chasing these men to begin with, but he knew it needed to be done. They were involved in what had happened to Pam. He couldn't say why he was so sure of this fact, he just was. He'd catch them when he caught up with them. Another set of flares exploded in the evening sky, and another throbbing pulse seeped through the body panels of the minivan.

They crossed the North Branch of the Grand Limoneaux fifteen miles outside of town. The road necked down slightly at a narrow bridge protected with an aluminum guardrail, its shiny metal blackened and bent where previous travelers had errantly misjudged the width of the span. A small convenience store stood sentry on the far side of the road, its door locked and windows shuttered for the night. He caught a reflection in the Pontiac's headlamps; more eyes flickering at the sides of the road, deer and smaller varmints grazing along the freshly mown shoulder. It amazed Walt that auto body shop owners weren't all millionaires. A small fawn bolted across the concrete in front of him and he gently tapped the brakes once again.

Two miles later the Sierra turned, angling right onto the mushy sand surface of Wafer Trail. A little ways further and it made a gentle break to the left, heading east once more on the even less-traveled Silty Creek Road. They were tracing the rim of the Grand Limoneaux River Valley, these men, deep into the cedar swamps. There was nothing out this way, no cabins, no military, and no convenience stores. The thick cedars and wetland buffered the edges of the gently rolling river before it eventually met up with the Grand Limoneaux's broader and deeper mainstream five miles to the south and east. This was as close to the middle of nowhere as you could get, at least as far as Walt was concerned. This *was* nowhere. It was swamp. It was wet. It was thick. It was bear country.

In the distance ahead Walt saw brake lights, the orange pickup slowing to a crawl before turning into some sort of driveway. He brought the minivan skidding to a halt half a mile from the shack. Through the trees he could make out a dim porch light, something he certainly didn't expect. Who knew that there was power out this far, let alone a cabin? Walt backed the van up, found a flat spot off to the side of the spongy lane, and pulled deep into the brush. He could only hope that he'd be able to get it back onto the road when the time came.

He crept through the woods noiselessly. A flashlight would have come in handy, but he'd forgotten to grab one in his haste. Picking his way through the tangles and trees was difficult, and his eyes took a while to adjust to the near-total dark and fog. The dim porch light bulb was his only beacon. Eventually he found a spot not far from the weathered dump and leaned back against a gnarled cedar.

"Now that was funny."

"Yeah, I don't know, Billy, sometimes that stuff you do stirs up more trouble than it's worth."

There were two of them inside the cabin, sitting at a small wooden table and drinking brown liquid from tall Tony the Tiger glasses. The little building couldn't be more than four-hundred square feet, maybe less: big enough for one decent room, a kitchenette table and chairs, and a half-bath with no tub. It reminded Walt of some of those older shacks up around Lewiston, little hideaways built from whole logs, assembled vertically rather than in the more traditional horizontal design. They were designed for weekenders, mostly hunters, fishermen, and snowmobilers. Never were they designed for permanent housing. This one was in horrible condition, her roof line sagging and the asphalt shingles warped and cracking with age. Clumps of moss and algae hung from the gutters, and black mold and rot was working its way up from the damp ground below. That was what he could see in *this* light. He could only imagine what it looked like in the daytime. It was what most people would refer to as a "tear down."

Walt crept closer to the shack, now only twenty feet away. The trees were thick in here and he had no trouble finding cover behind which to hide. Thankfully the two men had opened a window. It was a little late in the year for that, but Walt was betting that the little place didn't even have a furnace. He could hear every word, and he had a decent bead on them.

"Oh hell, Slip, you know it was funny. You just need to lighten up."

"Well, she didn't think so."

"Yeah, well, she don't know a lot of things." It was friendly banter, what sounded like life-long buddies swapping tales from a night on the town.

"All I'm saying, Billy, is we got a business to protect. You pissing off that tramp at the bar, stirring the shit, well, it don't do us no good. It calls attention to ourselves, is all. If you want it so bad, why don't you just bust out your wallet and pay for it next time?"

"Let me worry about protecting our business. I'll do the worrying about Tammy Lee, too. I've got her wrapped around my little finger."

"More like the other way around, and it ain't just her finger that's got you all wrapped up."

The one called Billy snorted at this remark, downing the remainder of his drink and walking over to the cabinet by the sink to pour himself another. "Shit. You ever hear anything more from our friend in law enforcement?"

"Not yet, but he'll be back. He's got to go somewhere."

This was finally getting interesting. It was the first thing either man had said that sounded remotely meaningful to Walt. He'd been sitting out here with his back to a tree, butt soaking wet from being in contact with the cold ground. Finally, something that might mean something. Who was their friend in law enforcement and why would he be coming back? The two men didn't sound frightened, more like they expected a visitor and were welcoming the occasion.

"Ol' Rayford usually had a pretty big stash somewhere. What do you think happened to it?" Billy was doing the asking.

"I think whoever bumped him off took it, that's what I think."

"I tend to agree on that."

There it was, an admission that the men were friends of old Wood Tick. Walt had known all along that these two were up to no good, and now they'd damn near admitted that the dead man was their partner. Partner in what? Out here it could only mean one thing. He shifted his weight to one side, taking a little pressure off his spine. The moisture from the ground had already wicked its way from the seat of his pants up to his thighs, and it was starting to itch. There were reasons people chose not to live out this way.

"You think the cop's got it?" It was the one called Slip asking the question this time.

"Got what?"

"All of it. The whole shebang."

"Don't know."

"How 'bout that shit went down at the Deer Track?"

"I agree, how about that?"

"Not what you'd expect."

"I agree on that, too." Billy finished his drink.

Walt had heard enough. He wasn't sure what he was going to do with this information, but he'd heard enough. No doubt these two guys, Billy and Slip, had been the men that busted up the Deer Track and put the love of his life in the hospital. They were punk drug dealers, somehow tied up with the man he'd found in the hatchery. They were involved with at least one of the local cops, too, although "local" could easily mean an officer from Mioe or even another county, once you got out this far. Still, it seemed like their tendencies leaned toward Shawono County.

His first reaction was that he should kick in the door and beat the living daylights out of both of them. Anybody that could do what had been done to Pam, well, they didn't deserve to live. On the other hand, there were two of them in there, and only one of him out here. They might have guns. They might have a friend, asleep on the couch, which he couldn't see from out here. Two men he might be able to take, but three? Probably not. There were a lot of variables here that Walt couldn't predict. The more he thought about things, the more he realized he'd be needing some support. It would be better to return to Rasmus, regroup, and set a plan in motion.

Walt stood up cautiously, silently brushing the leaves and needles from his wet pant legs. The two men were still yacking away at the kitchen table, oblivious to the greater world outside their window. They were back on the subject of Tammy Lee, whoever she was. They'd get theirs soon enough. Who was he going to enlist in this battle, who could he count on? That fat-ass Brimley? There'd be no point in that conversation. Brimley wouldn't believe him, for one thing, and would be too lazy to do anything, for another. Amberson or Frederics? Either or both of them could be that "friend in law enforcement" these two losers were talking about. Walt didn't trust either one of them, any further than he could throw them. That pretty much ruled out any cop in any department. Elvin? Elvin ran the other way at the slightest whiff of trouble.   It dawned on Walt that this was *his* problem, his and his alone.

He was back at the van, about to open the driver's side door, when he felt a tap on his shoulder. Walt's first reaction was to turn around swinging, but he tamped that impulse deep down inside. If there were two of them, or if either Slip or Billy had a gun, throwing wild punches was the worst thing he could do. He'd have to come up with another solution. How they'd found him he wasn't about to guess. He thought he'd managed to sneak away unnoticed. Walt raised his hands high in the air, the universal sign of surrender, slowly turning to face his executioners. If his pants weren't already wet from sitting on the ground, they should be now. A look of astonishment washed over his face as he stared straight into the eyes of Shawono County Sheriff's Deputy Matt Amberson.

TWENTY-THREE

They'd been sitting like this for over an hour, Amberson on one side of the desk, silently shaking his head and looking like he had no idea what to say, and Pitowski on the other side, unsure whether to be angry, frightened, or indifferent.

"Explain to me again how you ended up at that cabin on Silty Creek Road."

"I told you once, Amberson, I was following a lead. Do I need to call a lawyer?" After the initial shock of Amberson sneaking up on him like that, surrounded by darkness in the middle of the swamp, things had settled down. The deputy had "asked" him as quietly as possible to get in his "ugly-assed van," drive with his lights off until he reached Wafer Trail, and then follow the cruiser back to the police station. It beat a bullet in the forehead, which is what he'd expected, so Walt quickly agreed. Now that they were safely inside the sheriff's offices Walt was fairly certain that a bullet wouldn't be forthcoming. He still didn't trust this man, but had the deputy intended to kill Walt, his perfect chance had come and gone.

"You don't need a lawyer, Walt, you need a shrink. In case you haven't noticed you're not a policeman, Pitowski, and, at least for the time being, you're not a suspect. You aren't even a 'person of interest.' I'm sure you've heard that term at least once before. What were you doing out there, poking around in the swamp?"

"I told you, I was following those two guys that were in the cabin, Slip and Billy. Talk to Frederics. I filed a report."

"You filed a report?" This was a new detail. The revelation brought more head shaking, more disbelief. The hits just kept on coming. "When?"

"Well I tried to file a report. I was here on Tuesday. I can't guarantee Frederics actually wrote anything down, but I tried." It wasn't Walt's fault if an officer didn't do his job.

"And you reported...." He let the sentence trail off at the end, waiting for Walt to fill in the blanks.

"Suspicious behavior. And trespassing. They were trespassing at the Deer Track, but Frederics didn't want to hear about it. I was in here on Tuesday, but he blew me off like it didn't matter. They were stomping around back behind the Deer Track when it was all boarded up, and then I lost them. That's not even the thing, this is way bigger than that. I heard everything Amberson, they admitted it. Those guys out at the cabin, they admitted what they did. When it gets out, it's going to blow this town wide open." Maybe he'd said too much. He looked the officer dead in the eye. Walt still wasn't sure which side of the law this cop was walking. Was he a good cop or a bad cop? It was hard to read Amberson's expression. Maybe Walt was going to need that lawyer after all.

"Look, Pitowski, I don't know what kind of conspiracy theory du jour you're serving, but I've had those two guys under surveillance for damn near a month, and you almost fucked it up tonight. I'm about to bust them for distribution of narcotics, and there's nothing like having some technician from the Geological Service inject himself into the middle of an ongoing investigation. Great work, Colombo. What other treats do you have in store?"

Walt weighed the answer carefully. It sounded like Amberson *might* be working the right side of the street, but hell, it didn't mean everyone in the Sheriff's Department was. How can you really tell who's honest and who's not? He thought back to what the taller guy "Slip" had said. They'd been talking about the "stash," and that whoever killed the old man probably had taken Wood Tick's drugs. "You think the cop's got it?" Those were Slip's exact words. It was an officer, maybe Amberson. If it wasn't this cop, it was one of his buddies. Brimley or Frederics, or maybe even those state cops, Masters and Johnson or whatever the hell their names were. Better to trust no one than to trust the wrong one. He decided to tell Amberson as little as possible, feed him just enough information to put him on the scent of these Connelly guys. Then he could wait, see if Amberson followed through. Justice for Pam was all Walt really wanted, anyways.

"Well, what have you got? Why were you tailing them?" The deputy was still waiting on an answer.

"Nothing, Matt. They were just talking about smoking weed, and I heard them say they beat up Pam."

"What were their exact words in this confession of theirs? How did they admit to what happened at the bar last Friday night?" More disbelief danced in Amberson's eyes. He knew enough of Pitowski to fact-check every word.

"That Slip guy said, 'How about that shit went down at the Deer Track.' And the other one, Billy, said, 'I agree, how about that?' That's what I think I heard."

"*That's* their confession?" Amberson's disbelief increased, if it were even possible. Disbelief that his career had come to this: sitting in this dank room in the middle of the night, drinking vending machine coffee over a gray metal desk and interviewing Walt Pitowski about some two-bit rednecks that dealt drugs from their shack in the swamp. Amberson *tried* to be an honest cop, but on nights like this, it most certainly was *not* worth the effort. It was unreal. "*How about that shit that went down at the Deer Track?* You think that's going to hold up as a confession? Seriously? That's what you've got?"

"Yeah, that's their confession."

"In total?"

"In total. You'd have to understand the *context* of the conversation, Matt."

"The context?"

"Yeah, the context. The confession was sort of....*inferred.*"

"Pitowski, you are a fucking moron." This was *definitely* not worth the effort.

"That's a little unfair, Matt." Walt's feelings were hurt.

"Actually, it's not. It is *completely* fair." Final judgment was rendered. There was more head shaking accompanied by some cursing under his breath. Amberson *really* needed to get out of Rasmus, but good. The deputy stared at the ceiling tiles for a minute, trying to calm himself down before he did something he'd *truly* regret.

"Are we done?" If all the man was going to do was insult and scold him, Walt might as well go home. He hadn't signed up for this. It wasn't as if he was under arrest or anything. He was tired. His head hurt, not just inside, but on the outside, too. There was a knot the size of a quarter over his left eye, where his face had smacked the steering wheel earlier that evening. That seemed like a long time ago. His pants were still wet from sitting on the damp ground, and his back muscles were twitching with spasms from having spent too much time in the wet cold. The hard-backed metal chair in this interrogation room hadn't helped. He'd had just about enough. "We're done, right?"

"I sure hope so. Stay the hell away from my investigation. *Please.*"

"Well, alright, then." The deputy *had* asked nicely, after all.

Walt stepped outside the building and into the well-lit parking lot that hosted his borrowed van, Amberson's Police Interceptor, and little else. There were a couple of cars parked around the back side, probably belonging to whoever was working the midnight shift at dispatch and a janitor. He spotted a raccoon climbing a brown picket fence, a tiny cube meant to shield the building's dumpster from sight. The wee hours meant snack time for creatures of the night. Walt lit a cigarette, the last from the two packs he'd bought on his way to visit Pam. He needed to quit again.

In the distance a siren howled, wending its way down the expressway and continuing south of town. Whoever it was, their injuries required more help than little Rasmus Hospital could provide. The emergency vehicle was more than likely on its way to Saginaw. He leaned against the brick facade of the building, sucking warm nicotine deep inside his lungs. There was a new moon in the sky. As far as Walt was concerned, it ought to be called "no moon," because you couldn't see a damn thing. New moon, no moon, was there really a difference? It didn't help that a low-lying blanket of clouds covered the northern third of the state: no stars were visible, not a twinkle of light anywhere, except for what little seeped down from the street lamp above. He could feel the moisture in the air, feel the barometer plummeting by the minute. Those flurries they'd forecast for Monday were going to get here a lot sooner. A blue State Police cruiser rolled slowly through the blinking red stoplight at the end of the block, disappearing past the darkened theater marquee and up Michigan Avenue. Within seconds the cruiser was encapsulated by the lingering fog. The bell tower in the Episcopal Church chimed one as the ambulance siren faded into the night.

TWENTY-FOUR

The Watcher

For three days The Watcher had been hoping to catch a glimpse of the little blond girl, and for three days he'd come up empty handed. It wasn't his *only* focus, he did have a job after all, but he'd put forth the effort. On Wednesday he'd gotten moving quickly, trying to catch a glimpse of each and every kid at the middle school as they made their way into the building. He quickly realized that this was a lost cause. All of the school busses arrived more or less at the same time, and while there was probably *some* order to how those hundreds of kids made their way into that building, he'd be damned if he could understand it. Throw in the parents that dropped their kids off by car, of which there were many, and the stragglers that arrived by foot or bicycle, and there was no way he was going to spot her. You'd have better luck trying to locate a single buffalo in a thundering stampede.

So he'd changed tactics after this, doing drive-bys and stakeouts at places where the kids were likely to hang out after school. The pizza place, the city park, party stores: The Watcher quickly realized there were far too many locations for one man to cover. It was all hit-and-miss. Kids could be at any one of them, or none of the above. There was no rhyme or reason to their movements. Unless he got inside this particular kid's head, discovered who she was or who her friends were, he was groping in the dark.

On Thursday he tried more of the same and came up empty once again. By the end of the day the man had grown frustrated, knowing that sooner or later *someone* was going to talk. Was it the little girl, one of the Connelly brothers, or the woman from the bar that was going to do him in? It was getting harder to think clearly. Those little yellow pills he'd been taking had been great for numbing pain, but they also left him feeling groggy and anxious. The Watcher decided he'd limit himself to just four pills a day. Four pills a day was a reasonable amount and a test of his own willpower. Addicts required far more than four pills a day. He wasn't an addict, he was sure of that. He'd prove it. The downside to cutting back on consumption was the accompanying fatigue and nausea, but these symptoms he could override with the occasional amphetamine.

By Friday he knew that his stakeouts and drive-bys were a total waste of time. The Watcher didn't even bother. Instead, he set his sights on the Friday night football game. The Rasmus Helgrammites were hosting the mighty Red Devils of East Jordan. Rasmus' team was coming into the game undefeated, enjoying their best season in recent memory, while the visiting Red Devils were suffering through a winless year. Every kid in town should be at that game. Who wouldn't want to witness the slaughter? They'd all be seated in straight and orderly aluminum bleachers for the better part of two hours. If he was going to find the girl, this was probably his best chance. He'd have to remember to bring his binoculars. Unfortunately, it turned out he was wrong. *Nearly* every kid in town was at the game, but not *every* kid in town. The kid he was looking for wasn't there, or if indeed she was there, he didn't recognize her. It was a waste of time was what it was, so immediately after halftime he gave up, deciding instead to focus his attention on the Connelly brothers.

It was shortly after dark when he arrived, parking far to the east of their cabin on a neglected logging road. He hiked in on foot, bringing all the necessary tools in a lightweight day pack he wore across his back. He had a handheld GPS and a compass, not that he needed them. He wore a headlamp, and around his neck hung a set of night vision binoculars. He brought his sidearm and a throwaway gun tucked inside his boot as well. A roll of duct tape, just in case, and a few lengths of parachute cord were stashed inside the pack. The Watcher didn't think it would come to that. His goal was to kill the men, not to sit them down for tea. He'd make it look like a drug deal gone bad. You never really know, do you? The way things had gone wrong at the Deer Track, you just never know. Somebody might *need* to be tied up. He was feeling restless, amped up. He popped another yellow pill to calm himself down.

Unfortunately, once he got to that little cabin in the woods, he discovered that neither of the two brothers was around. Slip's truck, that big orange monstrosity he'd bought at a county surplus auction, wasn't in the drive. Billy's car, whatever five-hundred dollar beater he happened to be driving *this time*, well, there was nothing to suggest that he was here, either. All the man could do was wait and watch, two things he was particularly good at doing. He found a seat on a stump, high and dry of the moist ground. He was feeling calmer, that pill had helped. The Connellys should come along sooner or later. It turned out to be later, but not much later.

One advantage of night vision binoculars, and there are many, is that they allow you to see things in the darkness long before these things can see you. When the brothers finally arrived, it was easy to spot Slip's truck pulling onto the property and the two noisily strolling into the family homestead. He didn't need binoculars for that. No, where the binoculars came in handy was with things you might not expect, with spotting animals and the like. In this case, they saved him from marching directly into a new set of problems.

He'd decided to let the brothers get settled in their little cabin, figuring he'd give them ten or fifteen minutes to get situated before he came in and polished them off. He'd catch them off guard. A simple plan, but simple plans are often the best. At first the two were banging around inside the shack, even opening a cabin window that allowed him to hear them better. God they were dumb. Once the fifteen minutes were up, Dirtbag One and Dirtbag Two could be seen seated at their aluminum dinette, getting comfortably sloshed. The end game was in sight. The Watcher took one more quick sweep with the binoculars, just to make sure that everything was in order. That's when he spotted that schmuck from the Geological Service sitting on the ground outside their window.

Two murders he'd planned on. Three murders changed the equation dramatically. Could he realistically throw Pitowski into the "drug deal gone bad" scenario and expect people to believe it? Probably not. Pitowski was known around town as a hothead, an asshole even. Occasionally he'd been spotted getting ripped at the bar. But as far as The Watcher knew, Walt had never been caught driving drunk, let alone anything bigger. He wasn't even a *recreational* drug user to anyone's knowledge. Could you make him look like a wife beater? Probably. Could you pin him with the deaths of two known scumbags, three when you included Rayford Brown Sr.? It would be a tough sell. There was no motive. All of this newfound stress was giving him a headache, and that Oxy he'd taken had brought him down more than he wanted. The Watcher considered taking another hit of speed, just to level things out, but decided to wait a while. You didn't want to get *too* hopped up.

He looked back through the fancy optics. *A good set of night vision binoculars is worth its weight in gold.* Pitowski was now getting to his feet and leaving. He was walking back to the west, sneaking through the trees.

There was Walt's van, tucked off the road a half mile further up the way. Walt was almost back to the vehicle. Once Pitowski was gone, maybe The Watcher would carry through with the original plan. Maybe in another twenty minutes he'd sneak inside and splatter Billy and Slip's brains across the walls. Should he or shouldn't he? There were pros and cons either way.

He was still weighing this conundrum when he realized there was yet another vehicle hidden off to the side of Silty Creek Road. He hadn't noticed this one come down the lane. Either it had been there all along, in which case his observation skills were slipping dramatically, or the vehicle had rolled in with both its engine and its lights off. What was this, some sort of surprise birthday party? Silty Creek Road rarely saw three vehicles in a week, let alone in a single night. He couldn't tell who this second driver was, but the car was definitely a Crown Victoria. Law enforcement. He ran through the mental checklist in his head of who was working and who wasn't, and decided the driver had to be Matt Amberson. That pretty well put an end to plan "A." There was no way he was going to do a double homicide with Matt and Pitowski both kicking around. The Watcher slipped through the woods and back to his car. Tomorrow was a new day.

TWENTY-FIVE

The Girl

That guy at the hatchery, she knew she'd seen him somewhere before. At first she figured he just looked familiar because, well, really, who didn't look familiar? It was a small town, too small. She'd probably passed right by him, like about A Million Times, and never even paid him Any Attention Whatsoever. It's not as if she was Checking Out Old Guys, for cripes sake. And he was an old guy in uniform, so yeah, sure, she'd probably walked past him at school or downtown or at one of the Stupid Parades that Rasmus had Every Stupid Holiday. When all those cops started walking toward her at the hatchery, tiny little Erin hiding in the thicket, well, it dawned on her that there was more to it than the possibility she'd seen this man at a parade or at the fireworks. She could tell by his *gait*, if that was even the right word. "Gait" was on a vocab list recently, but she hadn't done so well on that one. She'd been up too late the night before and wasn't fully awake when the teacher plopped the quiz down on everybody's desks. She could tell by *the way he walked* that he was that same man who had been sneaking around the hatchery last Friday night. This was not a good thing, so she followed her first instinct: she ran.

At first the girl thought about running toward the pep rally, but then she realized this was a stupid idea. What if the doors to the school were locked and they wouldn't let her in? What if the rally was almost over anyways? Then she'd be hanging around outside with every other kid in Rasmus. If you were a cop looking to catch some kid that might place you at the scene of a murder, wasn't that the first place you'd look? She'd be a Sitting Duck. She'd be a Dead Duck. So she decided to hide in the Last Place On Earth anyone would ever expect to find her: the library. She stayed until well after dark, and then went directly home.

Of course her mom and dad were Royally Pissed when she came home way after dinner was served and eaten and the table was already cleared. She was Officially Grounded, was what she was, and that was fine by her. Grounded for three days, just until the weekend. She could go to school and back and no stopping anywhere else, not even for a second, *not if you know what's good for you young lady*. They promised they'd re-evaluate the situation on Friday night. That's the word they'd used: "re-evaluate." She wasn't going to say anything, but the girl wouldn't have gone anywhere even if you paid her, No Way, No How. Being Officially Grounded was a good thing. It gave her an excuse.

Those three days went by about as quickly as they can for a girl that's *only thirteen*, a girl that believes a Renegade Cop might be looking to hurt her. "Renegade Cop" wasn't on any vocab list, but it sure had a neat ring to it. She'd have to bring that up when she was telling Angie all about it, have to remember to use those exact words when she got around to telling everybody what had happened. Maybe someday she'd be famous: they'd be quoting her on the local news and everything. "The Girl That Solved the Murder," that's what the headlines would say. She wasn't ready for that conversation, not yet, but someday she would be. By Friday night her dad informed her that she was officially un-grounded, effective Saturday morning, and now she had a plan.

The girl knew she couldn't stay home all day long, Every Single Day. That was too obvious. If she never left the house, sooner or later her parents or her sister would decide that she was crazy and depressed. If she never left the house, sooner or later they'd start sending her to a counselor or an insane asylum or something. After three days of being grounded, it would look Majorly Suspicious if the girl didn't go out and do *something* on Saturday. At the same time, the girl knew that she couldn't hang around in her usual spots, not until that cop got busted or moved out of town. Not until this was over. If she spent even *one day* hanging around her usual spots, Renegade Cop was bound to recognize her.

She looked out her bedroom window. Dawn was just beginning to break, the morning sky filling with that pretty crimson glow that most people think is *so beautiful*, but really just means that a storm is on its way. This was *not* something she'd learned at school, by the way. An old guy that was a friend of her Grandpa had told her all about it a long time ago. Sailors don't like to see a red sky in the morning: it means nasty things are coming soon. They are words worth remembering. The girl slipped on her flannel lined jeans, her wool socks, and her good hiking boots. She put on her bra, which was nowhere near as big as Angie's giant double-barreled slingshot, but at least it was a *real* bra and not some stupid *training* bra like some of her classmates were still wearing. Over this she wore a long-sleeve t-shirt and her favorite hoodie. She added the brown Carhartt jacket that she'd gotten for Christmas last year and a brown watchman's cap and gloves.

Down the hall, her sister and her parents were still sound asleep. The girl crept into the kitchen, grabbed a bunch of granola bars from the pantry, and slid them into her pocket. There was some hunter's sausage in the refrigerator, and even though her dad had told her she couldn't take any, that it was *all his* and was meant only for special occasions, she grasped a handful of the spicy meat sticks and placed them in her other pocket. She was almost ready.

For a minute she thought that somebody else was awake, rattling around in the hallway. There was a sudden noise, like somebody stumbling on their way to the bathroom. It would be hard to explain why she was heading out the door this early, especially when it looked as if it was about to sleet or snow outside. The girl was relieved when her sister's cat came bouncing into the kitchen. She got down a bowl from above the stove, splashing water in it for her feline friend, Hollow Kitty. *God, if that isn't the stupidest cat name on Earth.*

On her way through the living room the girl made one last stop at the coat closet, silently opening the bifold door and reaching *way* in the back, behind all the clutter and stuff that nobody really seemed to need. She found the tiny cardboard box on the floor behind the broken umbrella and those cowboy boots that her mom no longer wore because they no longer fit. They made her feet hurt but they cost "a small fortune" so she "couldn't just *give* them away." Parents were *completely* illogical sometimes. The girl grabbed a handful of .22 long rifle cartridges from the box and put them in her pants pocket. She slipped the gun out of its case and took that, too. The girl quietly closed the front door behind her, vanishing into the woods. That's where she knew she'd be safe.

TWENTY-SIX

Walt Pitowski

It was well past one a.m. and there wasn't another soul on the road. In another forty minutes the bars would be kicking out the last of their patrons, but right now, in the wee hours of the night, the streets of Rasmus were deserted. The fog was growing denser by the moment, smothering everything in a heavy blanket of mist. Walt took his time. He was in no hurry to get back to the house, get back to an empty shell that contained nothing but his dog Doofus, snoozing on the couch. God, did he miss Pam. He turned on the windshield wipers, slapping away the thick layer of condensation on the glass. It was difficult to see much past the hood of the Montana. Walt eased off the accelerator, crawling along at a modest thirty-five miles per hour. It was probably still too fast. A pair of eyes reflected in his headlights ahead and he slowed down even further. Blondin would probably kill him if he totaled this van.

Amberson had been a world-class prick back at the sheriff's office. Walt couldn't say why this surprised him: Amberson had always been a world-class prick. He was a cop, through and through. The deputy was the kind of guy that thought the law was some unbendable truth, when in fact it was what you made it out to be. Sure, there were regulations and codes or whatever you wanted to call them: the *laws* that society was expected to live by. In theory, we all played by the same set of rules and we all got the same treatment when we strayed from those codes. Justice is supposed to be blind, or so people like to think.

In actuality, Walt recognized that justice is anything *but* blind. Justice is arbitrary and capricious. One guy gets pulled over for speeding, and because he's got his wife and kids in the car, he is let go with a verbal warning. The next guy gets pulled over for speeding, and because he's got a previous record, or maybe just because he doesn't smile nicely and say "yes sir, no sir," kowtowing when the cop speaks to him, he gets a ticket. Walt could cite a million examples of how the whole system was rigged. We all like to think that life is orderly and fair, that there exists in society a broad set of rules that we are all expected to obey equally. Walt knew better.

For a while he thought maybe his problems with Matt Amberson were through. Back on the Sparrow River, the two men had been forced to work together to solve that homicide. Walt thought maybe they'd finally put their animosity to rest, at least to a degree. He figured they had developed some sort of mutual *respect,* if not necessarily a *friendship.* Pitowski wasn't foolish enough to think they were on their way to friendship. Tonight the sheriff's deputy was still the same guy he'd always been: a by-the-book cop who tried to apply the law exactly the way it was written. Somebody needed to tell Amberson that that stuff didn't fly around here. It wasn't the way the world worked.

He was right about the dog: Doofus was snoring on the end of the couch. He didn't even wake up when Walt entered the house. So much for the value in having a guard dog.

"Doof, get up."

The snoring grew lighter, but his companion was still unconscious. Walt tried again, a little louder this time.

"Doofus, get up, you lazy bastard."

The snoring stopped, coming to a halt after a few muffled snorts, but the dog still didn't open his eyes or raise his head.

"Doofus, come on, you worthless shit. Get up and go outside."

The dog raised his head warily, then painstakingly lifted the rest of his body. He slowly eased his torso off the sofa. First his front feet touched the floor, and then he stopped to stretch. It was a long stretch that involved arching his back and yawning, before he dragged his hind quarters slowly off the cushion. The dog took one more step forward, paused, stretched again, and stepped outside onto the wet deck. Doofus looked around into the fog, promptly walked over to the charcoal grill that sat beside the doorway, and relieved himself on its base.

"Come on Doofus, at least step off the deck if you're going to do that." Maybe by morning the fog would wash it away. Pitowski was beginning to wonder if any dog could truly be *that* lazy, or if Doofus did things like this merely to tick him off. Perhaps the dog took after Amberson. "Get in here, stupid." The dog complied and immediately settled back on the sofa.

The house was cold, no more than forty-five degrees inside, but he didn't feel like starting a fire. Walt realized he could use a drink and remembered there was still a bit of cheap bourbon in that bottle he'd been sipping last weekend. It was raw stuff, but it was all he had. *Possum Urine Bourbon, tastes better the second time around!* He poured two inches of the liquid into his coffee mug, pitching a few ice cubes in as an afterthought. This was pathetic, but he was in the mood for feeling pathetic. Sometimes a man just needs to *wallow.*

Walt clicked on the television, waiting for the ancient cathode ray tube to warm up while he sipped from his mug. Three minutes later a picture slowly began to develop in the center of the screen, then quickly raced toward the outer edges before filling the remainder of the glass. Kids today didn't know what they were missing with their giant sixty-inch plasma screens on electronic standby. They'd never experience the joy and anticipation of waiting five minutes for a piece-of-crap twenty-five-inch console television set to spring back to life so that they could eventually flip through five or six channels of low-quality programming. Yep, *this* was the life. Walt was definitely wallowing.

On a really good day, if the weather was perfect and the leaves were off the trees, that old Zenith would pick up seven or eight stations. With the fog holding tight and fall foliage still clinging to the branches, Walt was receiving four today. The first channel was hosting an infomercial for a Japanese knife set that, shockingly, was not the Amazing Ginsu knife of his youth, but rather the latest variation on hard-sell television marketing. He watched for a few minutes. These guys didn't even bother to slice a tomato and then, with the same knife, cut right through a tin can. They lacked style. They lacked ripe tomatoes and tin cans. Did they even make such a thing as a "tin" can anymore? He had to wonder. In any event, there wasn't enough bourbon in the world to convince him that he needed this particular knife set.

He switched to the next station, which was showing an old Andy Griffith episode. Walt passed right by this one. While it was hard to dislike Andy, or anybody in Mayberry for that matter, the last thing he needed was a half-hour romanticized vision of small-town America. People like to think all small town cops are like Andy and Barney. They are portrayed as friendly, kind-hearted, goofy neighbors with the lone intent of helping those in need. Walt

163

knew better. In reality, small town cops were jerks like Frederics and Amberson or pencil-pushing administrators like Brimley. They were bullies. And the town drunks weren't colorful versions of happy-go-lucky Otis, either. They were mean-spirited fighters, angry punks and sad losers, old men and frustrated kids that might just as well run you over on their way home from the bar. The only similarity he could find between here and there, Rasmus and fictional America, as he mulled it over, was that cute school teacher he'd met at the diner and Andy's sweetheart, Helen Crump. The rest of them? *Mayberry indeed.*

The third station was featuring something called the "Nine Bra Blowout," yet another infomercial which turned out to be a gross disappointment. Walt watched for ten minutes and not a single bra burst at the seams, let alone blew out completely. It turns out that the "Blowout" portion of the show had more to do with sale pricing and nothing whatsoever to do with catastrophic undergarment failure. Plus, just watching it reminded him of Pam. Pam was sitting all alone down in that hospital in Saginaw while he was here sipping cheap whiskey in the dark. If it weren't so late, he'd phone her right now.

His last hope was once again the classic film channel, but when he turned to the old movie station the screen filled with nothing but snow. That was something the kids today would never get to experience with their digital cable and high definition screens: snow. It wasn't really "snow," but that's what people called the fuzz on the screen caused by what is technically electronic noise or radiated electromagnetic interference. He pitied those poor kids of today. They'd never experience the joy of wiggling those rabbit ears on top of an old television set, wrapping the antenna in tinfoil, running a bare wire from the back of the box to the ceiling and out a window, or holding the antenna in one hand while hopping on one foot, all in a vain attempt to get marginally better reception. Walt poured himself another three fingers of bourbon, raised his glass in a toast to those who would never suffer "snow" on their screens, and slammed it back. After a while, this cheap hooch didn't taste half bad.

Walt got up, stuffed a few pieces of paper and some kindling into the wood stove, and opened the glass door to draw some air. After a few failed attempts he finally got the green wood to light, then added two smaller sticks and finally half of a pine log. The pine would burn fast, too fast, but at least it would get the fire going. Oak and hickory, woods that gave far more heat and had a much slower burn, they'd come later. Get the chamber hot, then throw on the hard stuff. He slid back into the kitchen, made himself another short pour, and sat back down on the couch. Suddenly he was too tired to move.

When he finally awakened, the TV was still on. The virtual snowstorm of last night had been replaced by a Saturday morning cartoon, some inane Japanese anime thing where the lips on the characters didn't move in time with the words they were supposed to be speaking. There was a rapping noise coming from somewhere, and for a minute he thought it might be a woodpecker tearing up the siding. For some reason woodpeckers found his home particularly inviting. The seams where the siding panels met looked like they'd been hit by machine gun fire. He rubbed the sleep from his eyes and looked over at the sliding door. Elvin was standing on the deck, tapping on the glass with his hand. Just beyond his friend, outside the protection of the overhanging eaves, a sheet of freezing rain cascaded down. Winter had decided to make an early appearance.

"Walt, you awake? It's nearly eleven o'clock."

Pitowski was still seeking his bearings. Eleven in the morning already. He didn't even remember falling asleep. It must have been about three in the morning when he nodded off. He dragged his aching body across the room and opened the door for his friend. Doofus squeezed through the door and between the two men. The dog went to the corner of the deck and quickly peed on the barbeque, then raced back to the couch. Walt shook his head and retreated to the kitchen while Elvin quietly stepped inside.

"Sorry it's chilly in here. You want some coffee?"

"No, thanks. I already had some." His buddy was being unusually quiet. Reserved, even. He looked so sad: you'd have thought a dog had urinated on the legs of *his* Weber grill.

"What's with you? Did D.J. throw you out or something?"

"You mind if I take a chair?" Elvin was already pulling up one of the stools to the kitchen counter, so the question was rhetorical. He gingerly sat down. "I need to talk to you about something. Christ, Walt, you really need to get some heat in this place. It's like a refrigerator in here."

"She did, didn't she? D.J. finally got around to kicking your sorry butt out of the house. Hey, sad to hear it, but you know you can always crash here."

"Thanks, but no, that's not what this is about. She didn't throw me out. D.J. and I are fine. Did anybody call you this morning?"

"If they did I didn't hear it. I got in late last night, been sleeping all morning. I haven't talked to anybody. Why, what's up?" Walt was pushing beans through the coffee grinder, twenty seconds of metal blades violently assaulting hard roasted beans. It sounded a bit like a dental drill. Once he finished grinding he dumped the beans into the coffee maker's wire basket. Now that the racket had finally subsided, he asked again. "What's going on?"

"It's about Pam. I didn't want you to hear it over breakfast somewhere. You know how people are. I learned about it at the counter of the donut shop. She took a turn for the worse, Walt." Elvin was visibly distressed. It wasn't like him. Usually he was a happy-go-lucky guy.

Pitowski took the other stool and sat down beside him. This was another setback, and he'd had no shortage of setbacks lately. He had *thought* Pam was close to coming back home. Sure, he'd been preoccupied with other business, but he figured once she was back in Rasmus he'd win her heart all over again. How long was he going to have to wait this time? Hell, it had been over a week since the beating. Maybe he needed to drive down to Saginaw right now, cheer her up. He could bring her flowers. He didn't have anything else he needed to do today. "How bad is she?"

His friend looked as grim as could be. "She didn't make it, Walt. She passed away last night. I'm sorry."

TWENTY-SEVEN

The sheet of freezing rain shifted briefly over to sleet, little pellets of ice that ricocheted off everything in sight, before gradually converting to a wet, slushy snowfall. Walt was soaked through and through. He'd been out in the yard splitting wood ever since his friend Elvin had left. That seemed like a lifetime ago. For four straight hours he'd split the largest of the logs from his woodpile, the big ones, twenty-four inches or more in diameter. He took each log and stood it on end, flush against the hard-packed ground. For four hours he'd raised the ten-pound splitting maul high over his head, each time driving it with all his might deep into the fiber of the wood. He split each of the large cylinders into eight manageable sections, then dug out another log, starting anew. It was hard, repetitive work. His arms and his back hurt and he did not care. He was almost finished with the woodpile and regretted not having hunted down another cord or two of the big logs back when the weather was warmer. Walt thought about nothing else, nothing but the wood and the maul and how empty his life had suddenly become. The woman he loved was gone.

He wished he could stay out there forever, lifting and splitting and stacking the ash and hickory and oak into tidy rectangular stacks. It was *orderly,* and he needed order in his life. It allowed him to sense that somewhere, if only in the realm of his growing firewood stockade, he had *some* control over what happened in life. The cold did not bother him. In fact, he welcomed the cold. It numbed his body and his mind. If he wasn't just about out of full logs, or if the head of his maul hadn't started to come just a wee bit loose, he probably would have kept at it through the night. As it was, he knew it was time to quit. He'd step inside, warm up a bit, and put a new handle on the maul come tomorrow. The snow was beginning to taper off. There was at most two or three inches on the ground, with a slick layer of ice beneath. It would make for treacherous driving for a day or so, but that was about it. October was way too early in the season for the white stuff to stick around, though it would be pretty while it lasted. *It looks like Christmas,* he mused.

The coffee was cold and the house smelled of wet dog. He stuffed the wood stove full with red oak, packing a tight fire that would burn well into the evening and halfway through the night. Walt warmed his coffee in the microwave. The smell of wood smoke mingled with the scent of Doofus to produce that pleasant aroma which could only be called "home." How had things gone so wrong? He thought back to the events of the last eight days: Pam being assaulted, finding the dead body at the hatchery, the suspicions of the police, and their total lack of belief when he'd tried to point them in the right direction. What could he have done differently? Where did his life go from here?

He knew he should have been a better boyfriend to Pam. Everybody has regrets, that's what they say. There were things he would change, ways he could have been a better man, were it possible. It was too late for that kind of thinking. *What's done is done.* He couldn't go back in time, couldn't change the course of what had happened, but he could at least try to make things right. "Right," now there's an interesting concept. Who's to say what is "right" in any given situation? Regardless of what people say, in the end you have to rely on yourself and count on your own moral compass for guidance. At this moment, Walt's moral compass was pointing directly to a swamp south of Silty Creek Road. It was telling him he needed to locate those bastards who had done this, find the scum that had taken Pam from this earth, and make them pay.

Once in the van it took Walt ten minutes to make it back out to the highway. When he finally hit pavement, the roads were far worse than expected. That first burst of sleet and rain, combined with the falling temperatures, had indeed coated the highway and everything else with a quarter inch of solid ice. Throw a couple of inches or so of wet, mushy snow on top of that and the world becomes a skating rink. The county had its salt trucks out in full force, but it would take a long while before they covered even the major thoroughfares. He gripped the steering wheel with both hands, chugging along at twenty miles per hour. In the first two miles he spotted three spin-outs in the ditch, though it didn't look like any of the drivers were still around. Walt was glad they were out of their cars and gone. He didn't have time to be a good samaritan.

At Shambarger Bridge Road Walt turned left and almost buried Pinky in the trees. The Pontiac fishtailed wildly on the slick ice, gliding across the intersection and hurtling off the far side of the pavement. He came within inches of taking out a pair of large white pines before the van's tires somehow found traction again. Digging his way through the brush, Walt nursed the minivan back onto the road, making a mental note to be more careful at the next turn.

He managed to cover the next few miles without incident, sliding to a stop just before North Down River Road. His moral compass was telling him to turn right at the stop sign. The car that skidded past him on its way toward town, a blue Plymouth Breeze with a red fender on the passenger side and two Connelly brothers in the front seat, was telling him otherwise. Walt turned left again, starting in low-speed pursuit.

For all its mismatched paint and ugliness, the Plymouth must have a good set of snow tires on it. The blue car disappeared in the distance. Walt knew he was struggling to keep up. Twenty-five was about as fast as the Montana could handle on this glassy pavement. Walt figured it was less than six miles back to town, but the Breeze was already well out of sight. At the very least he could *guess* where they were heading.

He passed another paved road leading to the south, but there were no tire tracks in the fresh snow. He passed an assortment of dirt paths that angled away from the concrete, but none of these had been travelled either. He saw a Ram pickup truck rolled over on its side, fifty yards off the road and facing in the wrong direction. One door on the cab was open, so the driver and passenger must have escaped relatively intact. The snow was picking up again, pelting the van in heavy, wet bursts that made visibility iffy at best. His windshield wipers were struggling to keep up. You'd have to be crazy to be driving around in this weather.

As he came upon the M.A.T.E.S. facility, Walt realized that he still didn't know what those initials meant. Across the street from the military complex was the parking lot, the one for that little patch of recreational land where he'd first spotted the two men. That sunny day seemed like ages ago. The Connellys apparently hadn't stopped here today, either. There were no tire tracks in the lot. He forged ahead. The snow was finally subsiding, but the wind was kicking up with even more ferocity. Pinky shuddered in the sharp gusts.

When he finally reached the big s-curve, Walt had to dial it back even further. He was barely doing fifteen miles per hour, and still the van ached to shoot off the road's surface and deep into the trees. Pinky yawed heavily to the right where the road bent left, tilting and straining with all her might to stay upright. By now he was pretty sure he'd lost track of the brothers. How was he going to catch up with anybody by "chasing" them at less than twenty miles per hour? What was he doing out here anyway? This temporary pause for reflection nearly cost him. As he pondered his fate, the back end of the vehicle finally gave in to centrifugal force, whipping around and passing the front wheels. For a moment everything was spinning. Walt watched the left side of the road go by in a blur, then the right side of the road, and the left side once more. Pinky circled completely around twice and halfway again before coming to rest smack dab in the center of the road. The van was facing the wrong way, but at least he was still alive.

Cautiously Walt edged the vehicle back toward Rasmus. He had one big curve and less than a mile to go before he'd be back in the city, that booming metropolis known as the land of curbside garbage pickup and city-only salt trucks. The roads would be better once he reached the city limits. His neck was already getting stiff from his ride on the tilt-a-whirl, but other than that he'd come out unscathed. He'd been lucky. Walt kept pressing on.

There was no Matt Amberson lurking in the grove of trees alongside that last big curve. Walt hadn't expected to see his friend manning the speed trap, not this time. There would be enough legitimate emergencies to keep the Shawano County Sheriff's Department busy for the rest of the night. What he did find, just beyond that last big curve, was proof that a Plymouth Breeze is just as subject to the laws of physics as any other vehicle. The blue car with the mismatched fender had veered well off the outside edge of the bend and was now buried deep in the brush forty yards from the road. Walt parked along the shoulder, leaving his van running as he hurried over to the beater. There was nobody inside, but the hood was still warm. What snow had fallen on the vehicle's windows was melting. Two sets of footprints in the slush led away from the car toward town. Walt knew they couldn't have gotten very far.

He inched along. A quarter mile further up, a very painstaking white-knuckled quarter mile of driving further up the road, Walt crossed the concrete bridge with four lanes of interstate whizzing below. The churned footprints continued along the road's shoulder, up and over the short concrete bridge traversing the big highway. He was almost to town. The Compactor squatted just ahead and to his right, silent in the early evening gloom. Walt looked at his dashboard clock: five-twenty and it was nearly dark outside. Sometimes it was amazing what a freak snow squall could do. Any other day and he'd have at least another two hours of solid daylight.

The road here was infinitely better than what he'd been driving upon. The city crews had been out and salted the living daylights out of it. The pavement was wet, but no longer slick. They'd even shoveled the sidewalk, which presented yet another problem: no snow, no footprints. The two men's trail ended at the city limits. Walt stopped at the sign, the one posting that city ordinance about no parking on the street during snow emergencies. *Assholes. Why'd they have to be in such a rush to clear the snow?* There was no sign of the men, no two lonely figures shuffling through the streets. Now what was he supposed to do?

Walt stared ahead at North Down River Road. In a couple of blocks it met up with the main drag, Michigan Avenue. *Where would I go if I were them?* Their car was buried off to the side of the road quite a ways back, so at some point they'd need a tow. That probably wouldn't be their first priority, though, not right away. Running hard off the road and trudging through that wicked wind and blowing snow, the first place they'd go, if he was any judge of character, was the nearest bar. They'd be looking for someplace warm and sheltered, a place where they could hunker down and wait for a friend with a tow strap and a four-wheel-drive truck, and they would drink. They would drink hard until help arrived.

The Red Eye Saloon would be a good bet, but that was another mile as the crow flies. It wasn't *too* far to walk, not for a couple of men used to living out in the swamp. Hell, that was probably a hop, skip, and a jump for them. And the going would be a whole lot easier here, now that they were in town with the fancy shoveled sidewalks and the plowed and salted roads. There really couldn't be any other answer. They'd be heading to the bar. Walt put Pinky in gear and was almost committed to finding them at the Red Eye, let the chips fall where they may, when another thought occurred to him.

When he'd first spotted those two losers, cruising along in that battered Plymouth, Walt's first instinct had been to pursue them. He'd been on his way out to their place anyhow, looking to rain down retribution for what they'd done to Pam. He wasn't sure what he was going to do once he got there, but he knew where he was going. When they passed Shambarger Bridge Road, heading straight for Rasmus, he'd followed. The two men driving into town like this, well, it was downright *prophetic*. He took it as yet another indicator that he was on a righteous path. The fact that he didn't have to drive out to the swamp to find them? It was a bonus. It saved gasoline.

Now, as he was about to finish what he'd first set out to do, Walt realized that the Connellys probably *wouldn't* be at the Red Eye. Sure, it was possible, but it wasn't likely. *Nobody* would drive all the way to town on these roads, all the way from the bumpy dirt path of Silty Creek, just for a drink. It was inconceivable that the promise of a cold beer would be enough motivation to go out on a day like this, not even for the dumbest of the dumb. No, they had to have been coming to town with a *purpose*. Walt realized there could be a lot of different reasons for those brothers to show up in Rasmus: a fresh delivery of goods, a drug sale, receipt of some kind of payment. Hell, maybe they were about to replace that junked Plymouth with a new car. The list went on and on. It was frustrating, the breadth of possibilities, and Walt was beginning to get the feeling he was in over his head. He wasn't a cop, after all, just a guy following his instincts. So far that had been enough, *instinct,* but how long can you survive on instinct alone? Walt realized he was nothing but a bird dog stuck on point, except now there was more than one bird, and somebody had shoveled their trail.

Walt peered up North Down River Road one more time before it dawned on him. There on his left, a little further up, was the root cause of it all. It might or might not have anything to do with Pam, that old man getting shot. For all Walt knew, that murder and what happened to Pam were two completely unrelated events. On the other hand, it seemed like more than mere coincidence. Those two brothers, Slip and Billy, were both known acquaintances of the deceased. They had pretty well confessed to what had happened at the Deer Track that Friday night. The logical conclusion was that they *had* to have shot old Wood Tick. How that led them to the Deer Track he couldn't quite say, but Walt was about to find out.

He drove to the next intersection, the spacious white ghost of the hatchery in the valley to his left. Where most people would turn south on Michigan Avenue, heading toward downtown and all that lay beyond, Walt turned north onto Julia Way. There were a handful of houses up this way, but he wasn't looking for any house. After another three-eighths of a mile Walt found what he *was* looking for, a small trail leading to a pumping station for the city sanitation services, nestled deep in the woods. He bounced the van carefully down the snow-covered lane. At the end of the path was a brick structure no more than fifteen feet by fifteen feet. It housed machinery, possibly a well head or some kind of relay station for the city sewage system. He'd never taken the time to find out which. No one came back here, not unless there was a problem with the city's water.

The van door slammed shut, its sound muffled by the new fallen snow. In the near distance Walt could hear the gentle purling of the Grand Limoneaux River's East Branch. There was fresh track on the ground, a cottontail rabbit making its way to the wet land along the river's edge. Walt followed the rabbit's path into the trees, meandering left and right before soon coming upon the babbling stream. He traipsed along the edge of the river in the rapidly failing light. At best, Walt estimated he had another half hour in which he'd be able to see a damn thing. In a few short minutes he spotted the road bed for North Down River. It was the same street he'd just abandoned. Driving on the road, he'd barely noticed the river. Here in the valley the road appeared to ride high above the water. The river funneled into a viaduct, really no more than a large, corrugated steel tube, and on through to the other side of the road. Walt hid in the shadows, hugging the wall of the chamber and creeping slowly through the darkness.

He reached the far side of the tunnel and still found not a soul in sight. There in front of him was the birthplace of this whole fiasco. Two tall columns supported the overhang above the formal front door, an entrance that was no long used. He was sure this building was the keeper of secrets, a vault of lies and cover-ups and the place where he was going to find Slip and Billy and the answers to all his questions. It was the place where he would find the truth, stand up for justice, and inflict some serious pain. Walt was pretty sure he had more than enough pain to go around, pain for everyone involved. All the misery, all the wild goose chases and unanswered theories, all the wrongs and mysteries that had befallen this little town in the last eight days, each and every moment was a waypoint that had led him to here and now, led to this particular place at this particular moment. It all pointed back to the hatchery.

TWENTY-EIGHT

The Watcher

He peered out from behind the curtain and there was Billy, strolling right on past. The Watcher figured this was where they'd be headed, Billy and Slip. He'd been sitting in the vehicle, tucked neatly away between a small stand of pines and a larger patch of scrub brush, halfway through the big s-curve just outside of town. The Watcher wasn't looking for speeders, he was just waiting things out. Sooner or later, he knew, Dirtbag One and Dirtbag Two would come to town. They pretty much *had* to come to town. This is where their stock in trade lay, where their clientele was based. The one detail which The Watcher didn't know was exactly *when* they'd arrive in Rasmus, so he'd been killing time hiding out amongst the trees. It made him feel secure.

When Billy's Plymouth came swerving through those curves, pitching side to side like some drunken rodeo clown trying to run a barrel race, The Watcher couldn't believe it. Here was a gift, no doubt. He witnessed the little car lose it halfway through the second curve, pirouetting off the road and deep into the brush. It must have spun in circles four or five times before it came to a stop. Maybe he wouldn't have to kill them after all. It was entirely possible they'd already taken themselves out.

The man was disappointed to see them both emerge from the car none the worse for wear. They looked around, making sure that no one was present to witness their ineptitude. The Watcher could easily see both Connelly brothers, but they couldn't see him. *They aren't the sharpest tools in the shed, are they?* Billy and Slip started marching lockstep through the slush, up to the road's shoulder and on towards town. The man knew where they'd be going.

He'd have to pass them on the road to the hatchery. The Watcher didn't want to, but there was really no other way: one road in, one road out. His only other option would have been to drive the four miles out of town, head south, and double back in on the main highway. By then it would be too late. In this weather, on these roads? They'd be almost to Timbuktu before he ever made it back to Rasmus. The best he could do was to drive right past, keep his head down, and hope for the best.

The Watcher still found it hard to believe that they hadn't noticed his car. How could you *not* notice a Crown Victoria with all the markings and everything? Men like those two should have *radar* for this sort of thing. They were criminals after all: it was their *job* to notice something like that. He considered this, whether they were aware of his presence or not. If they knew, they were playing it cool. Maybe they didn't care. After a few moments he decided that maybe they *had* recognized the car, but they hadn't recognized *him*. The Connellys *might* have thought that he was Amberson. In any event, the two men didn't try to flag him down or otherwise call attention to themselves when he'd passed. He was in the clear. They *must* have thought he was Amberson.

He left the Crown Vic in a parking lot behind the hospital, high atop the hill. No one would notice it parked there, and if they did, so what? Wasn't that considered part of his job, part of being an active member of the community: attending to the sick or investigating accidents, something along those lines? The vehicle was hidden in plain sight, that's what it was. He'd be fine, just as long as no one noticed him slinking along the back side of the hospital and down towards the hatchery. The blowing snow and pounding wind would only help mask his identity.

There was no time for all the stealth and secrecy he'd used that last time. Sure, he had to keep his wits about him, but if he didn't get inside the hatchery quickly he'd lose any element of surprise. The Watcher had already proven to himself, with old Wood Tick taking a bullet in the skull, how valuable a commodity surprise could be. He'd need to cut a few corners. There was no time for slinking down the hillside, through the trees, and back up again. He made a beeline for the door and prayed that no one spotted him. The snow would be his protector.

Inside the hatchery he quickly picked his spot. The gun was loaded and ready, its safety set to "fire." There would be two this time, not one, and although the brothers weren't necessarily the smartest, it didn't mean that they weren't wary. Snakes weren't all that smart, but they were still wary. The Watcher needed to be ready, and he needed to be fast. He chose a position on the upper floor at the far end of the long hallway. If they came in the way he expected them to, the same way that their dead buddy had chosen, they'd be sitting ducks from the moment they stepped inside. Should they choose to enter somewhere on the lower level, he'd still have the advantage of higher ground.

He pulled back the curtain, peeping through the glass, and there was Billy, right on schedule. Billy was rounding the corner of the building and heading to that makeshift foyer, the plywood overhang with its big "KEEP OUT" sign. He'd guessed right. Billy was following right in Wood Tick's footsteps, but where was Slip Connelly? It wouldn't do to take down one and not the other. If anything, that might just make matters worse. He couldn't guess *what* Slip might do, if he knew his brother were dead. He'd run for sure, and he might possibly run his mouth, as well. The Watcher waited anxiously. Another one of those yellow pills might not have been such a good thing. The amphetamine rush was almost too much, and he wished he had something to calm himself down.

He could hear a key rattling in the door's lock, accompanied by a quick stream of veiled cursing. He lifted the curtain again and there was Slip, mere steps behind his brother. The Watcher heard more quiet discussion on the far side of the door. The words weren't very clear, but both dirtbags were standing right outside. Then the lock cylinder turned and two men stepped into the darkness. This was going to be easier than he'd thought.

TWENTY-NINE

Walt Pitowski

He saw them walking toward the hatchery, first Billy and then Slip. Pitowski's hunch was paying off. He couldn't say where the two men had been in the few minutes before this: maybe they'd walked over to the Clark station and phoned a tow truck. Maybe they'd slipped off into the woods to take a leak. He had *no* idea where they'd been for the last fifteen or twenty minutes, but whatever detour they'd taken, whatever temporary delay had drawn them away from the hatchery, it turned out that Walt had been right. Sure as shit, here they were.

Walt saw Billy first, appearing over the top of the bluff and striding straight for the hatchery. He lost sight of the man for a few minutes as Billy rounded the eastern face of the building. Three minutes later Slip followed right in his footsteps. *Theoretically* the two brothers could be going anywhere *but* the hatchery. This might be nothing but a coincidence. The pair *could* be on their way to the hospital, the Red Eye, or the pizza parlor. They *might* even be on their way to *church* for that matter. Walt knew better. Pitowski had no doubt where the Connellys were heading. They were coming around the top side of the building and they'd be going inside any minute.

He took a moment to assess the situation. He was at the bottom of a river valley, hidden inside the lip of the viaduct and still eighty yards from the hatchery. The building itself wasn't that far away, but his path between here and there offered nothing but open meadow. He could race to the hillside and try ducking through the bushes and trees, but Walt knew that would eat up valuable time. Daylight was fading quickly. By then they'd have come and gone. He'd have to take his chances. In many ways, the dying light worked in his favor. It made it less likely the two men would see him as he sprinted across the lea. They were on the far side of the structure, probably trying to jimmy that door at the top of the hill, while he was here doing absolutely nothing. The only logical move was to make a run for it and hope that nobody spotted him.

Count it down, measure the space, and count it down again in your head. It looked like eighty yards, more or less. Eighty yards and eighty strides for a man running at full tilt. Walt counted backwards from five before taking off at a full sprint. *Five, four, three, two, one.....* Only three steps in and he was up to full speed, head down and running like a bull. He was practically *flying.* His legs reached out, instantly finding a rhythm that pounded the ground with mechanical precision. Sixty yards remained, then fifty. Forty strides to go and Walt was halfway there. He looked up briefly to check the distance. Twenty yards remained and he was still flying. *Keep a steady pace and remember to breathe.* Ten more strides and he'd be flush with the western wall of the hatchery. Seven strides remained and he wasn't even *beginning* to get winded. Being an athlete, being a *Marathon Paddler,* (more than just an athlete) definitely had its benefits. Most men his age wouldn't have covered *half* that ground in the same amount time, not without puking their guts up. He was feeling a sense of pride. He was *a machine, a piston in a fine-tuned engine.* Four strides to go, he was almost there.

With three strides remaining, Walt realized that he hadn't gotten around to making a plan for what he was going to do once he finally got there. He could feel the blood pounding through his temples. Two strides remaining and a wall of white siding was about to smack him in the face. *Make up your mind, now or never, those two losers are going to be waiting for you inside.* One stride to go and it was time for action. Walt lifted his head again just in time to spot that window with the broken board, the one he'd first peered through and discovered Wood Tick's remains, an old man lying in a pool of dried blood. Pitowski was hoping like hell that the cops hadn't gotten around to reinforcing an inferior repair job. He launched his body through the air, two-hundred and thirty pounds of muscle in motion, and hurled himself at the darkened window frame. His inner voice was screaming for him to stop, but it was far too late for that: he'd already committed. Walt curled into a ball, exploding through that rotten wooden rectangle and onto the floor of the building's moldy basement.

Many things occurred to Walt as he came crashing to the concrete floor. These revelations came to him in a flood of thoughts and sensations, a wave of realization like he'd never before experienced. The first revelation, a thought he'd never contemplated to any serious degree, was that concrete was *hard.* Concrete was *really hard,* particularly if you came tumbling through the air and landed directly on your tailbone. People tended to underestimate how hard it could be, but he'd never make that mistake again. For a moment Walt wondered if he'd ever walk again, but the pain rapidly ebbed back to a lesser degree, a level of suffering most people would describe as "excruciating." When measured on a sliding scale, "excruciating" beat "dying" any day. Pitowski lay there in the darkness, still working on his plan.

A second revelation, and this was a big one, involved the fact that somewhere in this building were two men, the Connelly brothers. Those two men had killed Rayford Jefferson Brown Sr. and they'd killed the most recent love of his life, Pam Sharpe. They were ruthless murderers and they were somewhere close by. They may or may not know that Walt was lying here on the floor, as helpless as a newborn child. The brothers were also more than likely armed. Up until this point, it had never occurred to Walt that it *might* be a good idea for him to bring a weapon. It's not as if he didn't *own* a pistol: he owned a couple of them, as a matter of fact. He liked hunting, liked shooting sports. He owned a .22 semi-automatic pistol, a gun that he used for varmint hunting, and a .357 magnum that he used for blowing large holes in small targets at the shooting range. He didn't carry, though. Walt had never seen a point to it. Firearms were for hunting food and sport, not for shooting people. It was time to rethink that philosophy. Right now, either one of those guns could bring great comfort to Walt, and they were both locked inside his gun safe back at the house. A damn lot of good they were doing him.

Walt needed to move. *Get up, buddy, time to get moving.* He rose slowly, as an electrifying jolt of torment shot through his entire body. He grimaced in pain, stifling the scream that wanted to burst from his mouth. After a few seconds he managed to tamp down some of the misery. The epicenter of the pain throbbed a few inches below his belt line. It was in the bone, and it felt a lot worse than any bruise he'd ever had. As best he could tell, Walt was pretty certain he'd busted his ass.

His eyes were beginning to adjust to the dim light, and he surveyed the vast room. It appeared to be some kind of laboratory, an abandoned rearing facility that still reeked of fish. Walt began scrounging around for anything he could use to defend himself. There were glass beakers and miscellaneous instruments on a bench, but nothing with enough size or weight to do any real damage. A chair was pushed against a metal desk in one corner, of no use at all. The floor was littered with paper and mouse droppings. He couldn't imagine a scenario where tossing a handful of mouse turds was going to help him. Walt began rummaging through a pile of rubble crammed beneath a mildewed workbench. Eventually his hand landed on a broken table leg, a wooden baton about twenty-eight inches in length and two inches in diameter. From the top protruded two rusty nails, the wood soft and spongy where it had broken away from the tabletop. He hefted the stick in his hands and seemed satisfied: the very tip of this dowel may be rotten, but the rest of the wood was solid maple. It would have to do.

Again Walt rose from his knees, and again a flash of pain electrified his body. How was he going to fight anyone in this condition? A man can go a long ways on the strength of conviction, but even Walt had to admit the odds were against him. There were two of them, and at the moment they were in far better physical condition than Walt. He could hear noises coming from the upper story, scratching and rattling. This building was so big that it was hard to determine what or who was creating the sounds. This place functioned as one giant echo chamber. Were these the sounds of the brothers, and if so, what were they doing? The commotion was originating upstairs somewhere, but that was about as much as he could tell. He'd just have to find out for himself.

Pitowski limped across the room, aiming for the stairway while using the table leg as a cane for support. It helped some. At the bottom of the steps he paused to rest and realized that the scratching noises had stopped. Had they just now stopped or had they stopped a while ago, when he'd first started dragging himself across the room? There was no way of knowing. Walt sucked in a deep breath, mentally preparing to climb the steps. He knew the effort was only going to make his pain worse. God knows what he was going to find once he reached the top landing. Maybe if he used the same method he'd used to prepare for that sprint across the meadow it would help. Walt began the countdown in his head: *five, four, three, two....* He never made it to "one." Three gunshots rang out in rapid succession. Like any well-trained athlete, Walt bolted out of the starter's block and up the steps.

It was amazing how much ground he could cover once the adrenaline started flowing. He'd been right: racing up those steps only made the pain worse, *way* worse. Yet none of that seemed to matter. Walt's body had kicked into overdrive, that same mythical "extra gear" which allows a person to keep paddling down a river hours and hours after any sane person should have quit. Walt hit the landing atop the stairs in full stride. He rounded the corner ready to take on Billy and Slip, ready to take on all comers, but it was no longer necessary. Halfway down the narrow hall lay the two brothers, shot dead. Over them knelt a man he knew well. It was a man dressed in his nicely fitted, official uniform, with neatly creased pants and a properly starched formal shirt. Conservation Officer Lewis Carter was still holding his gun in hand.

"Carter? Holy shit. Thank God it's you." Walt leaned over and rested his hands on his thighs, trying desperately to catch his breath. The table leg leaned gently against the door frame. His pain was coming back, and it was coming back with a vengeance. Pitowski wanted to vomit. He was doing everything he could to avoid hurling all over the floor. If he did, Carter would never let him live it down. The last thing Walt needed in the town of Rasmus was another nickname. He gulped down a few gasps of the hatchery's stale air. He was feeling slightly better, beginning to think he *might* be able to hold it inside after all. Achingly Walt stood upright, preparing to explain the situation. "I was following these two idiots. I'm pretty sure they killed Pam."

The fish cop answered back. He answered with two shots from a nine millimeter pistol. Both bullets bit deep into the thick molding around the doorway, and Walt was instantly grateful that Lewis Carter was no marksman.

What in the hell is this about? Just taking two steps back around the corner hurt, pained Walt nearly more than he could bear. He crouched down on the small landing, out of the fish cop's sight line for the moment. Here he thought he'd been chasing the Connellys. Walt assumed that law enforcement would be on his side. *What does Carter have to do with any of this?* There wasn't much time to think. Lewis Carter was no more than seven or eight steps away. *Why is he shooting at me?* Walt made a mental note that if he ever again decided to go after a murderer, he really *would* bring a handgun.

He reached out tentatively to grab the table leg, currently resting against the door frame. Another shot rang out and a bullet tore through the fleshy part of Walt's right hand, directly below the thumb and out the other side. The table leg rattled to the floor, barely within reach. Blood was seeping from his wound, but he didn't think it was serious. It didn't appear as if the shot caught any bone, but that was small comfort. *Don't let anyone ever tell you that a surface wound doesn't hurt.*

"Shit, Carter, what are you trying to do, kill me?" He held the hand tight to his chest. Maybe if he put enough pressure on it the bleeding would stop. All the blood was ruining a perfectly good shirt, he was sure of that. The only good thing about the pain in his hand was that it took Walt's mind off the pain in the rest of his body.

It was the other man's turn to speak. "Come on out, Pitowski, and I'll make it quick and easy. I promise you won't feel a thing. There's really no other way."

"What are you talking about, Carter? Those guys were drug dealers. I'm on your side here. Ask anybody. Ask Amberson if you want. In fact, that's a great idea. Why don't you call Amberson? He'll back me up." This guy must be off his nut or something. Couldn't he see they were both good guys here? He heard one provisional footstep in the hallway, then what sounded like Lewis Carter bracing himself against a wall. *Jesus, the man is taking a shooter's position.*

"Come on, Pitowski, you really don't have anywhere to run. Make it easy on yourself."

Walt wrapped his left hand, his good hand, tight around the table leg. It wasn't a gun, but it was all he had. Table leg versus gun didn't seem like a fair battle. He was thinking it would have been a wonderful thing to have a little more firepower. Walt would even settle for a pocket full of mouse turds at this point: at least he could fling them in the other man's eyes. Why was this happening to *him?* Walt was on the side of virtue and justice and here he was, about to get gunned down in the darkness. It wasn't *right.* How long would it be before someone discovered *his* body?

"Look, Carter, I don't know what your beef is, but I'm sure we can work this thing out." It was a lie. He was beginning to suspect that they *weren't* going to work things out. Walt waived the table leg gently in the doorway as another shot rang out, ripping the stick from his hand. Diplomacy didn't appear to work. *If that's the way it's going to be, then that's the way it's going to be. How many bullets does that thing hold, anyway?* How long would it be before Carter realized that all he had to do was take seven steps down the hall, round the corner, and splatter Walt's brains all over the walls? Not long. Pitowski needed a backup plan, and he needed it fast.

He looked behind him at the stairwell. Down was his only option. How fast could he move, and how soon would Carter be upon him? It didn't appear as if he had much choice. He needed to try, even if it didn't work. Walt stood up without making a sound. He knew he'd have one chance, one chance and one chance only. If he was able to distract the fish cop, even for a few seconds, maybe he could steal enough time to get down into the basement. A few extra seconds might make all the difference in the world. Talk was one weapon he still had in his arsenal.

"Alright, I guess it's over. Fine, Carter, you win, okay? I don't know what I ever did to you, but I'm giving up, just don't shoot me, alright? Seriously. I'm on your side. I'm coming out on the count of five. I quit, you win. Story over. On the count of five. You can count it down."

Lewis Carter didn't get to be a Conservation Officer by being stupid. He was law enforcement, after all. He'd experienced much of the same training as any other member of law enforcement, and he'd dealt with more than his share of lying riffraff and lowlifes in the north woods. He'd heard the jokes: other officers deriding him as "fish cop" and "moose officer" and even "beaver patrol" behind his back. That didn't mean he lacked a cop's instincts. He could sense that something about Pitowski's offer wasn't right. It all sounded a tad too easy. Pitowski wasn't the kind of guy to just give up, hand over his pointy stick and surrender in the face of danger. For sure it didn't feel quite right. On the other hand, what was another five seconds going to hurt? He decided to go with it. What was the worst that could happen?

"Good, Pitowski, I'm glad you're beginning to see the light. Leave your big bad stick on the floor, and on the count of five come around the corner with your hands in the air. I'm not going to hurt you. I promise. Ready? On the count of five. Here we go. Take your time, slow and easy. One...two...three..."

The man never got past three. Before he reached the count of four, Lewis Carter heard a big "whumping" noise halfway down the staircase. This was followed by another dull thud as Walt leapt to the bottom. There came a loud groan from the basement, the groan of a wounded animal. Lewis Carter wasn't sure what had just happened. Had Pitowski fallen down the stairs? The Oxy must be slowing his judgment. This silence lasted a few seconds, but seemed far longer. Carter was trying to comprehend, trying to get a grasp of the situation. Should he move or should he wait? A few seconds more and the void was broken by the sound of footsteps on concrete. Carter now recognized the fact of the matter: Walt Pitowski was running for his life.

THIRTY

It turned out that jumping wasn't so bad: it was the *landing* part that hurt. The first jump went off without a hitch, six steps behind him followed by a flawless arrival in the middle of the staircase. It was downright *elegant*. The second leap he misjudged ever so slightly. Walt thought he'd gotten enough air under him, but he came up short. As his flight approached its less-than-spectacular ending, he could see that he wasn't going to make it. He stretched his body, but it still wasn't enough. Walt's right foot caught the bottom step, sending him head first into the wall at the bottom of the stairs. There were stars in his eyes. His skull hurt. His shoulder hit the corner hard, and he was thinking it might be dislocated. Every part of him was in pain, but Walt knew he didn't have time to lie around feeling sorry for himself. He rolled to one side, away from the landing and out of view from the top of the staircase. All of his ribs were on fire. He forced himself back to his feet, howling in misery. Then he ran.

He needed to make it across the big room without incident. One miscue and Carter would be upon him. He could see the window through which he'd first entered and the last few glimmers of daylight beckoning from that open box. Walt ran as fast as he could, knowing that Lewis Carter couldn't be more than a few steps behind. Six strides to the window. He heard no noise behind him, no movement on the stairs. That was a good thing. Maybe he'd be lucky. Walt was praying he'd managed to gain enough of a head start. Three more strides and he'd be out the window. He heard a rumbling on the stairs behind him: Carter had finally figured it out. Walt was dreading how much this was going to hurt, but there was no other way. One more stride. He stretched his arms out ahead of him, doing his best Superman impersonation as he sailed through the little rectangle.

The ground outside was cold and frozen, so frozen that Walt slid when he landed in the grass. The big belly flop carried him five feet before his body ground to a stop in the thick weeds. At least one of his ribs was broken, he was sure of that. All the parts of him that hadn't hurt prior to now would be hurting for sure. He got up, staggered, slipped, and fell anew. Pitowski struggled to catch his breath. Once again Walt got up and attempted to run.

He was trying to remember what had brought him here in the first place. How did he get into this mess? Whatever his original motive, it was no longer worth it.

He could hear Carter cursing in the basement, mere steps behind him. Pitowski turned to look over his shoulder, trying to estimate how much of a lead he truly had on the man. His feet lost traction again, and for a second time he fell face first into the slush. He was freezing cold, and ice stung his wounded hand. Carter was in the window now, attempting to cross the threshold. The man's shirt had become caught on a nail or a loose board and it was slowing him down. Thank God for small miracles. Walt might have forty feet between himself and the Conservation Officer, but that wasn't likely to be enough.

If he ran to his left he could follow a smoothly-paved walkway that would take him on a straight path across the grounds before fanning out into the lower parking lot. It was a hundred yards or more, and on any other day that would be the route he'd have chosen. It was the tourist route. But his jump on Lewis Carter was only about eighty feet, if that, and the fish cop was finally free of the window sill. *Luck never lasts.* Walt knew better than to try and outrun a healthy man with a gun, especially the way his body was failing. He was injured, badly injured. Trying to ditch Carter on a straight path with no obstacles would equate to certain death.

Instead Pitowski feinted left and broke to the right, racing across the "temporary" steel bridge that had been laid during one construction project or another and still remained years later. He zigzagged around the narrow raceways, cement ditches six feet wide and a hundred feet long. Each trough held three feet of icy water and not much else. Ornamental trees, planted to shade the water and protect trout in the summer, provided minimal protection from his pursuer. They were better than nothing, and Pitowski used them to his advantage. His plan was to play a high-speed game of hide and seek. Walt was giving it all he had, but he was hobbled and he knew it. Another look over his shoulder told him that Carter was closing the gap and was now only thirty-five feet behind: easily within shooting distance.

Walt desperately needed to add another variable to this equation or he'd be toast. He took a chance, abandoning his zigzag strategy. He went airborne, leaping across first one raceway and then a second. Pitowski yelped in pain with each landing, but it was still better than getting shot. Hurdling raceways was a gamble, but it worked. Either Lewis Carter wasn't much of a jumper or the man carried an unreasonable fear of water. He hesitated. He stopped running, stood at the edge, and lost momentum. The officer hemmed and hawed, pacing at the crumbling edge of the first raceway. Then he started to run around to the far end of the pit, taking three long strides before realizing it was a sucker bet. He turned back. Walt was pulling away. Carter finally screwed up enough courage, leaped across one chasm and then the next, and continued to give chase.

In the meantime, Pitowski had widened the distance between them to sixty feet. He was proud of himself for having stuck it out this long. *Not bad for a gimp on the run.* Another forty yards and he'd reach the far side of the grounds. Behind the big green utility shed, the one where they kept the tractor and other equipment, Walt knew there was a gap in the chain link fence. Beyond the gap was nothing but thick woods. If he could just clear this final forty yards, he'd stand a fighting chance. He could scarcely breathe, and still Walt kept on running.

He was fast approaching another raceway, and Walt prepared to launch his body yet again. Thirty yards to the green shed. He was getting the hang of this. It was a lot like paddling: everything comes down to *technique.* As long as he managed to keep the pain at bay he'd be fine. Walt hit the edge of the raceway in full stride, springing high into the air. He was almost free and clear. Pitowski was so close he could *smell it.* Thirty yards to the shed, the woods, and the chance to live another day. It was then that he heard the crack of gunfire, and then that he felt his right leg explode beneath him. Gliding in midair, Walt had an instant to consider his suddenly-shattered tibia. It was astonishing: *who knew that Carter was such an accurate shot?* A second round from the chamber echoed throughout the valley. Walt's world went wet, and then it turned black.

THIRTY-ONE

The Girl

"Let's try this a different way. Can I get you something to drink? A soda or something?" The girl had been in the room for over forty minutes, ever since her parents had arrived and taken their seats on the other side of the one-way glass. So far he'd failed to get a peep out of her. Matt Amberson was growing frustrated. He'd asked the girl's parents for patience, and thus far they'd acquiesced. It was hard to tell how long they'd stay patient. Don Frederics was sitting in the other room with the parents right now, trying to keep them calm and letting them know that everything would be alright. Amberson knew better. There was no point in making promises you couldn't keep. No matter *what* happened from here on out, it was likely to be a long while before things were "alright" for this kid.

"I know what you're doing." She'd seen them do this on TV, on all the cop shows and even in some of the movies: they'd pretend like they were your friends so you'd open up and spill your guts. Except right now, she *for sure* felt like spilling her guts, only in the *literal* way. The girl felt like spilling her guts *all over* the cop station floor. It was a good thing she'd only eaten some jerky and two granola bars or she'd have hurled by now. What she didn't feel like doing was *talking,* at least not to *this guy.*

"I'm offering you a soda, or a bottle of water if you prefer. Maybe some juice? What flavor would you like? Come on, you've got to be getting a little thirsty."

She *was* getting thirsty, or did she only *think* she was getting thirsty? Maybe this was some kind of a trick. Maybe she wasn't thirsty at all, and Deputy Amberson was putting ideas in her head that weren't even hers. Was this how it worked? She didn't know anymore; so much had happened. What the girl *did know* was that she was both tired and cold. It was warm in here, especially after spending most of the day in the woods, but she was still chilled inside. The girl was shivering. The deputy was standing over by the window, the one that they don't want you to know has a room on the other side but Everybody On The Whole Planet knows the window has a hidden room behind it, and whoever's in the room can see you but you can't see them. She wasn't *stupid.*

"Coffee." It was the first word she'd spoken since she got here.

He turned around to face her. "Excuse me?"

"I said I'll have a coffee. With one cream and two sugars." The girl looked him dead in the eye. "Please."

Well, at least the kid can speak. "Coffee" wasn't the answer he was expecting, but it was progress. "One coffee, coming right up. With cream and sugar."

"Two," she corrected.

"With cream and *two* sugars. You've got it. I'll be back in a jiffy." Amberson let himself out of the room and hurried off down the hall.

The girl snorted. "Jiffy." Who *uses* that word anymore? Good grief, this guy could be *so corny* it was hysterical. "Jiffy." He must have picked up his interrogation skills from a civil war handbook. The girl's parents didn't usually let her drink coffee, something about stunting your growth, but she didn't care. She was cold, she'd been through a lot, and she was thirteen years old. She was *practically an adult.* Plus, at this point, how much more trouble could she really get into? She was in a *police station* already. This was about as serious as it gets. There was only one good thing about this whole mess: Angie would be *so jealous.*

"Here you go: one coffee with one cream and *two* sugars." He placed the cup in front of her, one of those paper jobs with a little cardboard ring around the middle of it so you don't burn your hands. Amberson gripped a matching cup in his own fist. The deputy took a long sip, set his drink down, and leaned back in his chair. So far the direct route hadn't gotten him anywhere. Maybe he needed to let the girl find her own pace. They sat like this, staring across the table with neither one saying a word, for a good five minutes.

"Thanks for the coffee." She'd been taught to *always be polite*, even if you didn't mean it.

"You're welcome."

"I don't usually drink coffee." That was for the benefit of her parents on the other side of the glass.

"You don't say."

"I'm just cold, is all."

Amberson nodded in agreement, taking another sip from his paper cup. *Let her find her own pace.* There was another few minutes of peace before the girl spoke up again.

"I meant to do it, you know."

"Yeah?"

"I'm a pretty good shot."

"I think you proved that." Amberson took another hit of his coffee. "Do you want to tell me why you were there in the first place?"

"Not particularly." This coffee sure tasted good. Maybe a little *too* sweet, but still good. Her chills were going away and she no longer felt as if she was going to puke. If anything, she was starting to get a little hungry.

"Alright then. No hurry."

"Alright then," she agreed.

He waited. "But you will have to tell somebody, sooner or later, you know. No hurry." He took another drink.

"No hurry," the girl nodded. Her cup was almost empty. Sooner or later: those were her choices. This cop was probably right. They weren't going to let it rest, not with a man dead and all. She was going to have to explain what had happened, sooner or later. They'd want to know what she was doing in that shed and why she did what she did.

"Get you another cup of coffee?"

"No thanks, I'm good." This was another thing she'd learned from the movies: don't let them think they're your friend. The deputy crumpled the paper cup in his fist, lofting it high against the wall for an arcing bank shot. The paper smacked paint somewhere about shoulder height before rattling gracefully into the trash can below. The girl replicated his shot with her own cup. The score was officially tied. She smiled ever so slightly. "I suppose this doesn't look so good," she mumbled.

"I don't suppose it does." At least the kid was starting to open up. It wasn't much, but it was progress.

"Sooner or later?" The girl posed it as a question, not a statement.

"Yep. But no hurry. It doesn't have to be *me* you talk to: you can talk to officer Frederics in there or to the Sheriff himself. Any one of us, if you're more comfortable. It doesn't even have to be *tonight*. But sooner or later, we're going to need to hear about what happened at that hatchery."

She thought about this for a minute. For a cop, he didn't seem *all* bad. At least he was honest. "Can I get that second coffee after all?"

"Sure thing. Two sugars, right?"

"Two," she confirmed.

"And one cream," the deputy added. He'd been paying attention. Matt Amberson trotted off down the hall. When he arrived back with her beverage, the girl slowly began telling him everything.

The girl told him about last Friday night, and about how the movie had sucked so she didn't want to go to the show with all of her friends. She even used the word "sucked" despite the fact that her parents were sitting right there, on the other side of the one-way glass in the secret room that wasn't really a secret. She told him about hanging out behind that old shack at the top of the bluff and about how the older man went into the hatchery, but he never came out. The girl described hiding in the trees, the younger guy following the older man into the building, a loud noise and then the younger man slinking away in the night. She sipped her second cup of coffee with one cream and two sugars, spoke methodically, and told the deputy every last detail.

She glossed over the story of her Sunday squirrel hunt because it didn't have much to do with what happened that Friday. "I needed to get out of the house, so I went hiking in the woods all day." That was how she put it. Then the weekend was over. By Monday there were rumors all over the school. Everybody had heard about the murder. The girl recognized that she was the only one who *truly* knew what had happened. No, she hadn't gone out or discussed it with any of her friends: she worried that the killer might recognize her. She'd gone to school and then stayed home in the afternoon.

It was Tuesday that things really got complicated. She told him how the school was nutso with Helgrammite Fever Forever, but he knew about that already. That afternoon the girl had been at the hatchery again and the police were there, too. The Sheriff had been there, with that other deputy, the one whose name she didn't know, even though he always did the Don't Do Drugs stuff at the school and Moron Traffic Duty. There was a State Cop and a Conservation Officer, too. She described hiding in the bushes at the head of the staircase and overhearing some of what they were saying with the door to the basement wide open. Then she'd seen them walking outside. It took a minute, but she recognized him: "him" meaning the guy in the green uniform, that Conservation Officer. *He* was the guy that'd followed the old man into the hatchery that Friday. She was frightened. She had no doubt it was the same man. What if he recognized *her*? The girl didn't know what else to do, so she ran.

It took almost two hours, this telling, and she still hadn't even gotten to the good part. The girl wanted another cup of coffee, but figured that would be pressing her luck. Her parents were right there, on the other side of the mirror; and so instead she asked for a bottle of water and a bag of potato chips. She asked to use the bathroom, too, and the deputy showed her to a little room down the hall. When she was done she came back and sat down. The girl was getting tired, but she needed to get it all out.

The story jumped ahead to this morning, Saturday, and how she'd snuck out of the house with a pocket full of snacks and a twenty-two rifle in her hands. The girl's plan was to go squirrel hunting, maybe even grouse hunting. Grouse were a lot harder to hit, so mostly she concentrated on finding squirrel. She needed to stay outside for a while before her parents decided to give her The Third Degree. She was stalking through the woods just east and north of town. There was some pretty good hunting there if you knew where to look. Then the weather had turned bad.

It had started with freezing rain, then sleet, then snow. When the freezing rain started falling the girl realized she needed to get indoors *quick*, but she didn't want to walk all the way home. Plus, her dad would *kill her* if she brought his rifle home all wet and rusty: she wasn't even supposed to *touch* it. The girl remembered that green utility shed at the hatchery and how the kids at school claimed some homeless guy had been caught living in it years ago. The girl knew where there was a gap in the perimeter fence, so she went to check it out. It wasn't that hard to sneak into the shed: somebody forgot to lock the back door. She'd been in there since one that afternoon trying to stay warm, dry, and hidden. She found an old blanket. She'd eaten some jerky. The girl had fallen asleep, right there in the shed.

When she woke up, she heard yelling. It was coming from outside, way over on the far side near the big white building. The girl looked out the side window and it was nearly dark. She opened the window a crack. There was more snow on the ground than she'd remembered. Coming toward her were two men running some kind of crazy route around the trees and raceways. The snow was still falling, and it was getting harder to see what was going on out there. As they got closer to the shed, she realized that the guy in front was trying to get away from the other guy. Then she realized that the guy giving chase was that same Conservation Officer from Tuesday afternoon, and from Friday night. He was the younger guy that killed the old man in the hatchery. On top of that, he had a gun in his hand.

"Can I have another cup of coffee, please?"

"Are you sure? You're almost to the end of your story." Amberson hated for her to lose momentum, not when they were this close.

"I'm getting a little tired, and it will help wake me up. Plus, I really want to make sure that I tell this next part right."

What the hell, she's already explained most of it, Amberson decided. "Absolutely. I'm with you on that. I'll be right back." He stopped at the observation room and made sure that her parents were doing okay. So far they'd been content to let their daughter talk, hadn't decided to "lawyer up" or pull rank on the deputy. In all the times he'd interviewed minors, this was a first. *If only they were all this cooperative.* Five minutes later he was seated at the table, sipping his third cup of brew.

"I'm ready when you are." The girl had been sitting quietly for a few minutes since his return. He was beginning to wonder if she'd decided she was through talking. If so, it was a shame. She was almost there. "Is everything alright?"

"Yeah. I was just thinking, was all. This is a lot to deal with for a kid my age. I'm *only thirteen,* you know.*"*

*"You're right. It *is* a lot to deal with, especially for a kid your age. You're doing great. Don't worry about being only thirteen. You're practically an adult. Keep going."*

She kind-of liked this guy. He was alright: *for a cop,* anyways. "Well, I saw the guy in the front and he was running all crazy-like. I think he was hurt. He wasn't moving that fast, not really. He might have *thought* he was moving fast, but trust me, he was *slow*. He was weaving in and out. You could tell that the bad guy, what did you say his name was?"

"Carter."

"Yeah, Carter. You could tell that the bad guy, Carter, was gaining on him *big time.* There was no way the guy in the front was going to make it to the shed, or the woods, or wherever he thought he was going. Carter was gaining on him big time, and he had his gun out. He was going to shoot. I knew he killed that old man in the hatchery. I don't know why he did it, but I know he killed him. That's not right, killing somebody. I don't care what your reasons are."

"Again, pretty mature thinking for a girl your age."

"Don't try to butter me up. I watch television, you know. I've seen all the tricks."

"No offense intended. I apologize."

"That's what *you* say. You interrupted me and it was rude." She looked at him menacingly and then decided to continue. It was her show at this point. "Now where was I?"

"Carter was about to shoot the man he was chasing..."

"Right. So I thought maybe I'd, you know, *help things out. Somebody* had to. And I had the twenty-two right there. So I slipped the barrel out that window and I took close aim. But it was getting dark, and it was snowing, and they were running all crazy-like, not in a straight line. I didn't have a particularly clean shot." She stopped for a moment, looking sad and taking another sip of her beverage. "He's dead, isn't he? The man in the front who was trying to get away? The one I accidentally shot?"

"He's not dead; he's just in the hospital.   Keep going and I'll answer anything I *can* answer, once you're through."

"Well, the guy in the front, he decides to jump over the raceways, which was like, *a really smart move*. Because Carter acted like he'd never seen water before. He just stopped running for a minute and got all confused. I thought this was the best time to take my shot. So I lined him up really good, except that it was getting dark and it was snowing, and they were both still moving around. I thought the first guy was out of my way. And then I pulled the trigger. But he wasn't out of the way, and instead I shot him in the leg. Is he going to live?"

"Unfortunately, yes."

"But the other guy shot him too."

"The other guy shot him too, right after you did. Through the shoulder. He's still going to live. Don't worry about that, it's not your fault."

"You're sure? You're not just *playing me*, are you?" It was a phrase she'd heard Angie use, *like about a million times*. Boys were always *playing* Angie, at least that's what she claimed.

"I'm not just playing you. Walt Pitowski is going to be just fine. Go ahead. Tell me what happened after that." Amberson didn't want her to lose the thread.

"I saw the first guy, this Spitowski guy, fall into the water. I thought for sure he was dead. I thought it might be mostly my fault. I was the one that shot him, after all, but only because of the other one. And that meant two people were dead, all because of this Carter. He was still pointing his gun in my direction. So I aimed again. My second shot was *way better*. I put him down with one bullet."

"You shot him right through the heart."

"I told you I was a good shot."

"Indeed you are. And then...?"

"And then I set the rifle on the seat of the tractor. I walked straight over to the pizza place and I called nine-one-one. That's where you guys came and got me."

Amberson was betting this girl's troubles were only beginning. She'd be having nightmares for years. She'd probably require extensive counseling. On the other hand, it amazed him how much composure the kid had. This wasn't your average thirteen-year-old. Maybe she'd pull through. "You did good."

"It doesn't feel like it."

"Trust me, you did good." What else was he going to say? *Let her believe it.*

"And Carter's really dead?"

"Carter's really dead. Straight through the heart."

"Am I going to jail now?" She sipped the last of her coffee. The girl didn't seem flustered despite the magnitude of this question.

"I think your parents are going to take you home now."

She flashed him a pretty smile. Amberson could tell she was going to be a heartbreaker someday very soon. If she ever got past this, recovered from the inevitable grief that comes with having taken a human life, she'd be a holy terror: pretty, smart, *and* fearless. The boys in this town wouldn't stand a chance. He opened the door and her parents were waiting for her in the hall. The kid got up, took a few steps toward the door, and then turned back to look at the room one final time.

"You know, you're alright. *For a cop.*"

THIRTY-TWO

Walt Pitowski

Pitowski awakened to a continuous beeping noise, and it took him a while to figure out that he was in the hospital. He had an IV drip stuck in his arm and electronic sounds were emanating from a heart monitor mounted on the wall at the head of his bed. The monitor had wires coming out of it, wires that ran all the way down to little sensors that were glued to his chest. His shoulder was heavily bandaged. It hurt. His leg was in a cast. It hurt. His right hand was bandaged. He didn't see any other visible wounds, but the rest of him hurt just as much. He was somewhere on the second floor of Rasmus Hospital, and that was a good thing. It meant he was still alive and he'd probably be staying that way. Had his wounds been truly life threatening, he'd have been airlifted to a trauma unit in a larger city. Walt remembered everything right up until his leg had exploded beneath him. After that it was wet, cold, and dark. He could make sense of none of it.

He'd been certain that the Connelly brothers had killed Pam. He'd been certain of that "fact" right up until the point that he reached the top of those stairs in the hatchery. Now, Walt didn't know what to think. The Conservation Officer, wasn't he supposed to be one of the good guys? That's what he'd assumed until Carter tried to kill him. Walt should know better than to trust a fish cop. Carter had been kneeling there in the middle of the long hall. Two men were dead on the floor at the other end of the corridor and Walt had almost joined them. He scrunched his eyes tight, fighting back tears as he remembered Pam. All of this carnage, and for what?

A nurse stopped by the room and gave him a little cup with pain meds mashed into applesauce. Pitowski didn't ask what they were, he just took them and swallowed. The nurse opened his window blinds before she left. Autumn had returned, if only for a short while. The sun was shining brightly, the snow gone from the tops of the trees. It was a gorgeous day. Much had changed in the last eighteen hours. He closed his eyes again, starting to doze.

"You awake?"

He heard the voice, followed by a quick knocking on the door frame. He blinked his eyes open. Walt was in no mood for company. He rolled his head to one side, attempting to identify the visitor. It was Matt Amberson, probably come to rub salt in his wounds. "Barely."

"Well, you're alive, anyway. How are you doing?"

"How do I *look* like I'm doing?"

Amberson laughed. It was the same old Pitowski. "You *look* like you might have been better off if you'd kept your nose out of a police investigation: not so hot. It could be worse. At least you're alive."

"Yep. I've still got that."

"You're a lucky man."

"I'm not so sure about that." Walt thought about what the deputy said. "Lucky." He sure wasn't feeling "lucky." Amberson pulled up a chair and sat at his bedside. Walt had too many questions in his head. "What happened to Carter? Did he get away?"

"He's dead."

"Of what? High cholesterol? He shot *me*. I assumed he's long gone by now."

"Nope. Shot dead by a junior marksman." Amberson proceeded to tell him all that they had learned. The Sheriff's Department and the State Police were still piecing together a case, but it looked like Lewis Carter had a rather significant drug addiction and he'd been purchasing his supplies from Rayford Jefferson Brown Senior. It was more than likely that Carter had killed old Wood Tick. The motive was as yet unknown. Slip and Billy Connelly were friends of Wood Tick and appeared to have inherited Rayford's customer base. It was logical to conclude that the brothers were blackmailing Carter, either that or they screwed him on a deal. That might be why Carter killed them. It was all conjecture at this point. Preliminaries suggested that the same gun used on the Connelly brothers was used to kill Rayford Brown. They'd learn more after the autopsies and after the troopers had a chance to comb through the property of all the parties involved.

Forensics on the bullets would take a while longer. In any event, Lewis Carter, the Connelly brothers, Pamela Sharpe, and Rayford Brown were all dead. That was about twenty years' worth of killing for Shawono County. He was hoping they'd filled their quota for a while.

The man in the bed listened intently and didn't interrupt even once. There was so much he hadn't known, running on instinct alone. Walt was most surprised to learn that it *wasn't* Carter that shot him, or at least that it wasn't Carter that shot him *first*. Amberson recounted the girl's tale from last night, condensing the story slightly because he could see that the patient was weary. They still weren't sure what had happened at the Deer Track Inn that Friday, but they were looking at Carter as a likely candidate for that one, too. It fit a pattern of escalating violence, a man spiraling out of control. It would take some time, but Amberson promised he'd get to the bottom of it. It was a promise the deputy believed he could keep.

"I can see you're fading fast, Pitowski. I'll let you get some sleep. We're going to need a formal statement from you, but we can do that sometime tomorrow. I can send Frederics if you'd rather."

"That's alright. You can do it."

Amberson smiled. It was hard to tell if he and Walt were fast becoming friends, or if the man merely hated Frederics *that much*. Either way, he'd take it as a compliment, his second in as many days.

"See you tomorrow, then."

Pitowski gave the deputy an anemic wave as he stepped out of the room. It was work just to keep his eyes open. Walt knew he should be angry. He was *good* at it, *being angry*. He'd practically made a career out of it. In this instance there would be no shortage of people at which he could direct that anger: Lewis Carter, the two brothers, or their drug dealing friend that started this whole mess. Hell, even that little girl, whoever she was, the one that shot him in the leg: *there* was someone he should be angry with. On the other hand, that girl had also saved his life. When he looked at it like that, his leg wasn't such a big deal. It would heal. Walt decided he was too tired for anger. Maybe it was time he tried something else.

He was dozing on and off, letting the pain medications do their work and wishing the doctors would up the ante a bit. Everything still hurt, just not as much. Whatever that nurse had given him was barely enough to make the pain blurry around the edges. Later that afternoon Marcus Washington and Tom Dewers stopped by to visit. Walt pretended to be asleep, and they finally went away. He was in no mood for small talk. It was nearly five o'clock when he heard another rapping at the door. Walt figured it was one of his doctors, coming to check on his injuries. He was pleasantly surprised to see the face of that pretty school teacher from the diner instead.

"Hey, how are you?" She was wearing a Spartan sweatshirt and jeans, looking like a million bucks standing next to him. Her curly brown hair was pulled back with one of those scrunchy things and she wore a big, genuine smile on her face.

Pitowski's spirits picked up dramatically. He knew he wasn't looking his best, but what was a man to do? *Give it your best shot, buddy.* "I'm holding up okay." It was a lie. It was a big fat lie.

She shyly took one step closer to the bed. "A friend of mine is a patient just down the hall. I was visiting her and I heard one of the nurses mention your name. I thought I'd pop my head in and wish you a speedy recovery."

"Thanks. I appreciate it." He smiled back. Even smiling hurt.

"I'm not going to ask what happened to you. You look pretty beat up. Are you going to be alright?"

"Yep. I'll be fine. I'm indestructible. What's your friend in for?" He changed the topic.

"Oh, you know, *lady problems,*" she whispered. They both laughed nervously.

"Most of my life I've had lady problems," Walt joked. "I hope she recovers quickly, too."

"Thanks." They both fell silent for a minute. "Well look, I don't want to keep you, but get better, okay?"

"Will do," he answered back, managing another weak wave of his hand. The woman rounded the corner and stepped into the hall, disappearing from sight. A faint aroma of lilacs lingered in her wake. Some people seem to spread sunshine wherever they go. Pitowski wished he could be more like the school teacher, a harbinger of good things to come. He wasn't sure how you acquired that technique, if that's what you called it, but more than likely it came down to choices. A person decides what he's going to hang onto, and what he's going to release. Sooner or later you become an amalgam of all the events and reactions to events that preceded the moment. Walt didn't know if these effects were cumulative or if the process could be reversed through a single action.

Like right now: he could choose anger, or he could choose forgiveness. That's what you'd think. But maybe, just possibly, there was a third way: neither anger nor forgiveness. He would refuse to pick and choose, anger or forgiveness. Instead he'd leave the past behind: not bury it, necessarily, but not let it act as an anchor, either. The bad memories and the emotions that accompanied them could stay with their own kind, safely partitioned from what was still to come. What Walt needed was a fresh start, a new path as yet unseen. It was out there, *somewhere*, awaiting him. He just hadn't found it yet. Pitowski closed his eyes, letting the pain meds wash over him as he drifted off to sleep. The scent of lilacs wafted through the room. He didn't need anyone's permission. Walt allowed himself to dream.

EPILOGUE

It had been a long winter. He'd been in the hospital for ten days, which Walt believed was ten days too many. There was a temporary complication involving a blood clot in his leg, along with a concern about the possibility of osteomyelitis. "Osteomyelitis" was a big fancy Greek word for "infection of the bone." The doctors loved to use big words. It turned out there was no infection, but he'd given them a scare. As a result, the hospital chose to hold him hostage a few days longer, placing him on a course of general antibiotics. His shoulder was fine. Lewis Carter's bullet had passed in and out without hitting anything other than soft tissue. It was painful, but it would heal. The wound in his hand required fourteen stitches to close. Once again he'd been lucky: no broken bones there. Pitowski *did* have three fractured ribs, none of which was displaced. They hurt like hell, but they'd be fine too.

He'd come home to a cold house. Walt stoked the fire box and prayed that his water pipes hadn't frozen. It was still too early in the season for that to be a serious threat, but you never knew. Rasmus nights could get awfully cold, and it was already late October. It turned out he needn't have worried. It took less than half a day with a roaring wood stove to drive the chill from his house. Doofus was there waiting, finally home after being temporarily fostered by Elvin and his wife. The dog seemed genuinely glad to see him. He even seemed respectful that Walt was far from one-hundred percent. Pitowski would walk with a cane, at least for the first few weeks. He'd be avoiding the stairs, limiting his roaming to the living room and kitchen. He read vociferously, occasionally watched television, and ate when he remembered to eat. At night Walt slept restlessly on the couch.

Walt was plagued by nightmares, some of which made sense and some of which he couldn't understand in the least. Lewis Carter appeared in a few of these visions, and others featured Pam in the starring role. Those horror shows didn't bother him so much: he'd expected repercussions from what had happened at the hatchery, and getting shot in his sleep, night after night, seemed like a nominal price to pay. No, the ones that upset Walt the most, and were his most *frequent* sleepy-time torments, involved that little girl, the one he'd yet to meet. In each of these nocturnal picture shows the girl was in some type of trouble: lost in the woods, stranded in quicksand, under attack by a pack of wolves. Somehow Walt knew it was his responsibility to rescue her, and each and every time he came up short. After a few weeks of these tragic scenarios, each ending with the death of that child he'd never laid eyes upon, Pitowski was afraid to fall asleep. He drank coffee night and day in an effort to avoid dozing off, and he rarely left the house. Doofus seemed to sense that his master was hurting, and was particularly gentle and friendly. For a bit Walt questioned whether someone had replaced his dog with a better-behaved and same-colored golden retriever.

One day, almost a month after he'd been released from the hospital, a metallic gray 2003 Ford F-150 appeared in his driveway. The truck was empty and the keys were in its ignition. He hadn't seen Elvin come or go, but he knew damn well where the truck came from. For two days he refused to step beyond the porch. On the third day he finally limped out to the vehicle, cautiously opening the hood and starting her up. It ran like a dream, the good kind of dream. It was the kind of dream he hadn't had in a while. Walt promptly dropped a check in the mail to Elvin's father-in-law for fifty-six hundred dollars. It was every penny he had. He'd make up the shortfall later.

On the first of the year Pitowski returned to work. He'd dropped thirty pounds, most of it muscle mass. Walt appeared ashen and gaunt, almost unrecognizable. His coworkers hardly knew what to say, so instead they said nothing. It was different, their old wariness and fear of his explosive temper having been replaced by a new wariness and fear of the unknown. Walt was quiet, almost introspective. People no longer knew who he was or what to expect of him. Marcus Washington recommended that he might want to seek counseling, but Walt respectfully declined. Washington let the issue drop. Walt Pitowski knew exactly who he was, and he knew where he was going. He got to work early each day, did his job with quiet efficiency, and went home every evening to his wood stove and his dog.

The nightmares were becoming fewer and far between, and Pitowski slowly regained most of the weight he'd lost in the weeks following the incident. His diet improved. Walt still wasn't completely recovered: he tired easily, and when the weather was about to change he could feel an aching in his leg. He was gaining back much of his strength, but was a far cry from the man that had placed forty-sixth in the Grand Limoneaux Canoe Marathon last

July. There were days he wondered if he could ever be that man again, though his stamina was improving.

Walt was grateful for this day, this second day of March. He'd been waiting a long time, and he was glad to be alive. It turned out that the F-150 was better than advertised. The truck drove straight and true down the road, pulling a five-foot by eight-foot trailer loaded with household goods like there was nothing there. He had to hand it to Elvin: this truck was probably the best vehicle he'd ever owned. He'd dropped a check in the mail just yesterday afternoon, the final four-hundred dollars that he owed to Elvin's father-in-law. The sun was out; it was the first time that big ball of gas had made an appearance in well over six weeks. The pavement of North Down River Road was bone dry, though there were still piles of plowed snow lining both sides of the highway. Dirt two-tracks that he'd explored in the summer months were temporarily inaccessible, completely barricaded by dirty mounds of snow, ice, and sand. Those waist-high reminders of winter wouldn't melt for another month or more.

He passed the M.A.T.E.S. facility to his right and the parking lot for that parcel of recreational land to his left. Walt drove through the s-curves, tapping the brakes and making sure that he didn't exceed the posted speed limit. He needn't have worried: there was no Matt Amberson or Don Frederics lying in wait this day. He eased the truck across the highway overpass, coasting in through the open gates to the Compactor a little further beyond the bridge. There was no traffic backup this Saturday morning. The old folks and downstate cabin lovers had come and gone over an hour ago. Besides, it was the beginning of the slow season around Rasmus: that stretch where it was too cold to fish and too warm to ski. The F-150 rolled to a stop at the top of the incline and Walt shut the engine off before stepping down from the cab. He had but one small bag of trash, the last of the odds and ends from when he'd cleaned the kitchen late last night.

"Pitowski, what's with the U-Haul? And where'd you get the truck?" It was Delaney, calling to him from inside the control booth.

Pitowski walked over to the sliding window and stuck his head inside the shack. "What, no Wally today?" Walt hadn't been to the Compactor in a while; his last few loads of refuse he'd taken straight to the landfill.

"Wally retired. I thought you knew. I'm the big kahuna of Shawono County trash nowadays. What's with the trailer?"

"I'm loading up the truck and moving on, as they say. I put the house up for sale with Fishman just last week. Yesterday was my last day on the job."

"Well, I'll be sorry to see you go. The town's losing people left and right. Did Fishman think he could move the house for you?"

"Probably not. It's so far underwater he's probably listing it as an in-ground swimming pool. There are a ton of places on the market around here, but you never know until you try. I told him if it doesn't sell in a couple of months I'd consider leasing the place."

"Good luck with that. You know what kind of renters you'll get around here."

"Yeah, I know." Walt kicked at a piece of ice that was stubbornly hanging onto the edge of the pit. Leasing the place wouldn't be his first choice, but you do what you have to do. He wasn't going to worry about it.

"Say, where're you heading?"

"Escanaba."

"The Upper Peninsula? What, we don't have enough snow for you? You might as well be moving to the North Pole if you're moving to Escanaba. What the hell you gonna do there?"

"I hear it's not so bad. Besides, the USGS has a field office in Escanaba and I'm moving up a pay grade. Maybe I'll become a Packers fan. Plus, I hear the fishing's good."

"I hear the fishing's good everywhere but here. Everyone always says it's better someplace else; it's best wherever you ain't. As for Packers fans, they've got enough of 'em. The whole damn U.P. is for the Packers. The Lions need every living body they can get."

"Well then maybe I'll become a Bears fan instead. Make sure you say goodbye to Wally for me. He's a good guy."

"Alright. Stop in and say 'hello' next time you're in town."

"I'll be sure and do that." They both knew he wouldn't be likely to swing by the garbage transfer station on his next vacation. Walt pitched his kitchen trash bag into the pit, got back into his truck, and started on his way. He pulled around the little shack at the top of the hill, making sure to swing wide so that the trailer behind him didn't clip the corner of the building as he went by. He eased the truck down the incline, past the big dumpster to the right and the recycling center on his left. At the end of the drive he stopped, waiting for traffic to clear before pulling onto the roadway. Doofus was nestled quietly in the back seat, sound asleep. Everything Walt owned in this world was squeezed into a five-by-eight trailer directly behind him.

To Walt's left was the expressway, not a hundred yards away. He could pull onto North Down River, cross over the bridge, and slide onto the entrance ramp for the big road. From there it was a straight shot, ninety miles of uninterrupted four-lane interstate, due north, until the Mackinac Bridge. The bridge itself was five miles long, a total of 26,371 feet of twin-suspension magnificence straddling the Straits of Mackinac two-hundred feet below. Once he reached the far side Walt would stop at the toll booth, pay a small fee, and continue on his way. Then it was one-hundred and forty-two miles, roughly two-and-a-half hours of non-stop driving due west on Highway Two, before he'd reach Escanaba.

He sat behind the wheel of the Ford, its engine idling quietly at the gate. Three blocks to his right lay the hatchery and just beyond that lay Michigan Avenue and downtown Rasmus. It was tempting to take one last swing down Main Street for old time's sake. Pitowski thought about it. He was *part* of this town, had poured his love and sweat and heart into this town. He'd nearly seen a man *die* in this town, or at least *would have* seen him die, if only Walt hadn't been so busy nearly dying himself. He'd paddled the Canoe Marathon and finished forty-sixth in this town, no easy task and a feat which should pretty well make him royalty to these folks. He had a job here, owned a home here. He had *friends* here, for God's sake. Walt sat there for a minute, thinking about what it all meant.

A nineteen-fifty-something International Travelall crossed the overpass to his left, passing directly in front of him as it made its way toward town. He recognized his pal Red Blondin, the collector of all things archaic and motorized, behind the wheel. The International traversed those three blocks past the hatchery and turned left onto Michigan Avenue, disappearing around the bend. Walt thought he might catch up to the man, express his gratitude for all that Blondin had done for him in the past. It was the least he could do.

He slipped his foot off the brake, carefully looking both ways, left and then right, then left once more, to make sure that traffic was clear. He eased the truck forward, foot on the accelerator, both hands on the wheel. It was one of those small choices a person had to make: left or right. Could your fortunes be made or broken as a result of one single action? Pitowski still wasn't sure. Anger and forgiveness, love and hate, all those things were so tightly intertwined that it became hard to tell one from the other. Left or right, you might as well flip a coin; let the quarter spiral through the air before deciding your fate. Walt brought his truck wide onto the road's surface, making sure that the trailer didn't clip a fence post on its way past. Doofus awoke from his nap, raising his head in the back seat.

"You're okay, boy. Go back to sleep. We're almost home."

The road was clear ahead. Walt turned left, leaving Rasmus behind him.

AUTHOR'S NOTES

For those of you not from Michigan, you might be surprised to learn that the template for the fictional town of "Rasmus" is based (not all that loosely) on my former hometown of Grayling. If you are from northern Michigan, you've probably already figured that out. That isn't to say that Grayling and Rasmus are one and the same: layouts of the streets are similar, even where the names of roads have been modified or disguised. A few of the buildings described in this book indeed have a corresponding real-life twin. In most cases, though, I took the liberty of changing locations and names of specific structures if I believed it would help make for a more interesting tale. Wherever possible, I generated names that contained some historical significance to the area. One example: Shawono County was the original moniker given to the area in 1840, before it was renamed Crawford County in 1843.

Most of the key locations in this novel contain elements from some local establishment, but more often than not they contain elements from various local establishments. These places are to degrees amalgams, whereas others are outright fabrications. For instance, there exists a block on Michigan Avenue with one brown house, one yellow house, and one pink house: that which I refer to in the book as "the one block that reminded him of Neapolitan ice cream." The hatchery building in this story is a fairly reasonable replication of the Grayling Fish Hatchery, as it sat vacant years ago. Is the floor plan true to life? While it isn't precise, I'd say it's relatively close. Those two examples linger somewhere close to reality. Yet there is no Red Eye Saloon, nor is there a Deer Track Inn. Although these two places do have similarities to many bars I've set foot in, they definitely fall under the heading of amalgams/fabrication. I've been asked why I didn't just stage the story in Grayling, describe everything exactly as the town currently exists, and be done with it. I have only one answer: I chose not to be married to the truth because The Hatchery is, in the end, fiction. Strict adherence to reality can handicap a perfectly good story.

That brings me to the characters in this book: again, there is no one character in this story that is based outright on any one individual. Most of the characters are totally imagined, while a couple are composites of traits and personalities in people I've observed. Walt Pitowski is a rare example: while he was based extremely loosely on a good friend of mine, I amplified some of my friend's worst tendencies twentyfold. Then I added in my own flaws, flaws I'd observed elsewhere, and flaws I'd only imagined. In the end, Walt bears only a superficial resemblance to the good man that I know and love, and I'm grateful that he has a sense of humor. If you see yourself in some facet of any of these characters, I'll take that as a compliment.

I need to thank my editor, Paula Leshkevich (The Comma Assassin). Every author needs someone to point out bad habits. Paula's offices in Michigan and Rwanda were integral to making this a better book, and should the reader discover any flaws herein, it is most likely an example of my failure to follow good advice.

Lastly, I'd like to thank the good people of Grayling, a town I still consider "home" even though I didn't grow up there and haven't resided in that city since 2010. It is an inspiring town full of good people where the word "community" still has meaning. To my friends Jane and Bambi at the Devereaux Memorial Library, Toby, Jessica, and Ed, as well as everyone else who encouraged me and still to this day treats me as one of their own, I can only say "thank you."

About the Author

Kevin J Garrity was born in 1964 in the city of Detroit, the eighth of nine children. Throughout his high school and college years, he performed as a musician of some local renown. After studies at Wayne State University, he moved to Traverse City, Seattle, back to Detroit, Chicago, and then to Grayling. Kevin currently resides in southeastern Michigan with his wife Deanna and two sons. He is an avid hunter and fisherman. His critically acclaimed first novel, Sparrow River, reflects his great love of the outdoors and all things wild. The Hatchery expands upon that narrative, successfully capturing the drama, tumult, and turmoil of rural northern life.

www.ingramcontent.com/pod-product-compliance
Lightning Source LLC
Chambersburg PA
CBHW031415250626
47155CB00004B/1495